JANE AND DAN AT THE END OF THE WORLD

TITLES BY COLLEEN OAKLEY

Jane and Dan at the End of the World
The Mostly True Story of Tanner & Louise
The Invisible Husband of Frick Island
You Were There Too
Close Enough to Touch
Before I Go

JANE AND DAN AT THE END OF THE WORLD

Colleen Oakley

BERKLEY
NEW YORK

BERKLEY
An imprint of Penguin Random House LLC
1745 Broadway, New York, NY 10019

BERKLEY and the BERKLEY & B colophon are
registered trademarks of Penguin Random House LLC.

Book design by Ashley Tucker

ISBN 9780593200827

Printed in the United States of America

For Todd Servick. I don't think you've
read one word of any of my books,
and this way I'll know for sure.

It is nearly always the most improbable things that really come to pass.

—E.T.A. Hoffmann

JANE AND DAN AT THE END OF THE WORLD

FOUR HOURS
AFTER THE END

PROLOGUE

"DO I NEED A LAWYER?"

Jane's voice trembles. She's never been interviewed by the police before. She's trying to remember the last time she even *spoke* to a police officer and thinks it must have been nineteen years ago when she was nine weeks pregnant with Sissy, driving (above the speed limit) home from her granddad's funeral where she had eaten too many ham biscuits, causing the top button of her jeans to pop off when she sat down in the driver's seat. When the policeman said "Do you know why I pulled you over?" she burst into tears, all the emotions of her granddad dying, and Dan not being able to be with her because he had to work, and the embarrassment of her pants being undone rushing to the surface at once. The man in uniform was so bewildered, he pretended he had a call on the radio and darted back to his car, shouting, "Slow down and be safe!" over his shoulder.

She's only asking because everyone who's ever seen a cop drama knows you're always supposed to ask for a lawyer.

This police officer—Kip, as he had introduced himself, and Jane thought that was a rather jaunty name for a cop. Informal. Missing the gravitas that someone who wore a pistol holster slung round his waist should inherently have—cocks his head to the right. Dirt mars his forehead and his hair is mussed. Jane thinks she sees a twig stuck in it, and she wonders for the first time what *she* must look like. He grins kindly.

"No, I don't think that will be necessary." He pauses. "Unless you're secretly one of the criminals."

A sound escapes Jane's throat—high-pitched and hyena-like. She's unsure if she's ever made a sound like it in her life. "I think they were more like . . . *activists*," she says.

"Activists," Kip repeats.

"Yes."

"With guns."

"Yes," Jane says again, her voice a bit weaker.

"OK." Kip clears his throat. "Let's move on. You've been through quite the ordeal and I'm sure you want to get home to your family. All I need is a witness statement from everyone involved. Can you tell me what brought you to the restaurant La Fin du Monde last night?"

Jane clears her throat. "It was, uh . . . my anniversary. *Our* anniversary. My husband, Dan, and I. Our nineteenth."

Kip checks his notes. "Huh. That's not what your husband said."

"You've talked to Dan?" Jane's heart squeezes, remembering the last time she saw her husband. And she wishes for the hundredth time they'd had a chance to get their stories straight.

"He said it was your twentieth."

Jane closes her eyes longer than a blink—out of both relief and annoyance. Of course he did.

"No matter," Kip says. "And can you tell me in your own words what happened? Starting with when the *activists*"—he looks at Jane pointedly—"came into the restaurant."

Jane suddenly finds it important to try to smooth her hunter green dress down, as if it's not ripped in two places and covered in soot. Having been awake for nearly twenty-four hours— and having just been through an *ordeal*—she thinks again of her appearance. The bags under her eyes are likely even more pronounced than usual. She reaches up to comb her fingers through her hair and finds it snarled—impossible to get through.

"Take your time," Kip says, but he looks weary, and he says it in a way that conveys he wishes she'd hurry the hell up so he could get home. She wonders if he has a family. A spouse. His ring finger is bare.

Jane opens her mouth to speak, but a knock on the door interrupts them.

"Zimmerman wants to see you."

"Now?"

"Now."

"Excuse me for a minute."

Kip leaves the tiny room and Jane is alone. Typically, she would use time by herself to observe. A writer, she always tries to log details for future work—especially unexpected specifics. Like the fact that instead of an empty cement block room with a long table and a two-way mirror like in every crime television show Jane's ever seen, she's in what appears to be a storage closet. Overflowing filing cabinets squeezed together, a mess of office detritus—staplers, folders, boxes of pens strewn about. "This is temporary," Kip said apologetically when he opened the door to it and gestured her in. "We're building a new precinct. Much bigger. State-of-the-art!"

But her mind isn't on her surroundings as much as what she's going to say when Kip comes back. Only seconds ago, she wished for time to get her thoughts together, but now it only ratchets up her panic. Is she going to *lie*? To a police officer? Given her actions of the past twelve or so hours, it wouldn't be the worst thing she's done, but still. She takes a deep breath and exhales, counting to five. He just needs a statement! He said it himself. And that's what she'll give him. She'll keep it short and simple, and stick to the truth as much as possible.

The door opens and Jane startles. Kip reenters, but this time is accompanied by another officer—this one older, his chin covered with white-gray stubble, his skin carved by time.

"You're Jane Brooks," the older cop says, peering at her.

"Yes."

"As in Jane Brooks, the author?"

Jane would normally be thrilled by this question. Before her one and only novel had been published six years ago, she dreamt of people coming up to her on streets, in airports, fawning over her, clutching dog-eared and worn copies of her book to their chests, able to recite passages from memory. *You're Jane Brooks! Would you mind terribly signing this?* And she wouldn't mind! She would be *honored*.

And yet, this was the second time in two days someone recognized her as the author Jane Brooks, and she was already quite content to never ever hear it again.

"You wrote this book." He holds up the familiar cover—the one that brought tears to her eyes when she first saw it on her computer screen so many years ago. Her name! On the cover of a book!

Now Jane's knees go weak at the sight of it. Her stomach flops like a fish on dry land. She nods. It wouldn't do to lie in this situation.

"This book that is about"—he glances at the back jacket copy, as if he's already read it but still can't quite believe what it says—"terrorists taking over a restaurant?"

Jane holds up a finger. "Technically, it was a tearoom? Not a restaurant."

The chief's nostrils flare, which Jane takes to mean he's not interested in the distinction.

"Do you know why this book—*your* book—was in the front seat of the van found at the crime scene?"

Jane knows. Oh, does she know.

"I don't know," she says. She finds that some situations warrant lying.

The second police officer's eyes look as though they may pop out of his head at any second—like buttons off the waistband of too-tight jeans when one is nine weeks pregnant and has eaten too many ham biscuits at a funeral. "That's awfully ironic, don't you think?" He's nearly shouting now, as if he and Jane are on an emotional seesaw and the more calmly she responds, the higher his agitation grows.

And even though her heart is thundering and she's dead panicked that she's likely going to find herself under arrest and behind bars for the rest of her life, she whispers: "I think you mean coincidental." She knows Dan finds it annoying, how she constantly corrects people's grammar, but she's positive there's not one person on earth who uses the term *ironic* accurately, and she can't help herself from pointing it out any more than she can keep the sun from rising each day.

"What?" he roars.

Instead of repeating herself, she looks at Kip. "I can explain."

This time his head cocks to the left instead of the right, as if appraising her from a new angle will give him some kind of perspective or insight he didn't have before. And then he says: "I think you'd better."

She clears her throat and opens her mouth. Closes it. She repeats this exercise—opening and closing her mouth like a glitching elevator door—six more times, until she realizes the problem: She can't explain. Not really. She opens her mouth one final time and says: "I think I need a lawyer."

THE BEGINNING
OF THE END

CHAPTER

1

"HAVE YOU SEEN MY WALLET?" DAN YELLS FROM another room in the house. Jane can't tell if he's in the kitchen or his office or the den. Not that it matters.

This is the last time.

This is the last time.

This is the last time.

As she repeats her mantra, Jane slicks a tube of bright red across her lips and stares at herself in the mirror. She never wears red lipstick. She never wears lipstick, actually. But a few days ago she saw this post on Instagram: *Change your lipstick, change your life!* It was written by one of those pseudo-serious influencers who fluctuate between penning deep, thoughtful, and slightly condescending captions about loving your cellulite or your crow's-feet because YOU ARE ENOUGH and making a six-figure income hawking clothing and cosmetics that will improve your life in some way because you're very obviously not enough. Of course, these women don't actually have all the answers but have somehow convinced their one hundred thousand desperate followers they do. Jane knows it's all bull-shit. Jane is also desperate.

"Babe?" Dan calls again.

She takes a deep breath. *This is the last time.*

"Have you looked on the table beside the door?" she says.

Where it always freaking is? she does not say.

"Beneath the mail," she says.

A few beats of silence follow. "Found it!"

Jane scrutinizes her reflection in the mirror. She raises her eyebrows and watches the horizontal lines deepen on her fore-head. She wonders, as she often does, what she'd look like with Botox, even as she knows she doesn't care enough to get it. Or maybe it's that she cares more what it would say about her if she did. She often fancies her anti-Botox stance as part of her long-fought battle against the patriarchy—yet she dyes her hair and applies mascara daily and she's not sure how to rec-oncile her hypocrisy, except to say that shooting poison into her face is a bridge too far. She wishes women would make a pact to just not get it (much like the Wait Until 8th campaign a group of parents spearheaded when Sissy was in middle school to not buy their kids cell phones until the eighth grade), not because of the patriarchy as much as her selfish desire to not look so old and tired compared to her smooth-skinned friends. The irony isn't lost on her that the fact that she thinks this much about her aging appearance and Botox at all means the patriarchy has already won.

She plucks a tissue out of the box and wipes the slash of cherry red off her mouth, replacing it with her reliable unflavored lip balm, and thinks: *When we're divorced, Dan will never find his wallet again.*

Pinpricks of excitement tingle her neck, then shoot down her spine: the same feeling she's experienced every day since she decided she was going to finally do it. It doesn't bring her joy to think of Dan losing his wallet for good. There's no schadenfreude to be found in his inability to look under or behind things. She's genuinely concerned with how he'll get on when they're apart. And how she'll get on without him.

She hasn't had to take out the trash in nineteen years. Or iron a shirt. She doesn't even know where the ironing board is. Or whether everything needs starch or just some things.

But that's no reason to stay together, is it? Whenever someone asks the secret to making a marriage last, the answer is never, *He's the only one who knows where the ironing board is kept.*

"Mom, I can't find my charger and my phone's about to die and I was supposed to leave ten minutes ago!" Sissy comes rushing into the bathroom like her hair is on fire and not like she loses her charger four times a week, which she does.

"Mom!" Jane hears Josh's voice before he, too, appears in the bathroom. "Can you drop me at King's house on your way out?"

Jane turns to Sissy first. "That's the third charger I've bought you this year."

"I know," Sissy says, her voice laced with irritation, as though it's Jane's fault that Sissy keeps losing her chargers and Jane keeps replacing them. *It actually is my fault,* Jane thinks, knowing she's made it too easy, hasn't made Sissy feel the consequences of her actions.

"If you can't find this one, you're paying for the replacement."

"Fine! Whatever. But I need a charger *now*."

Jane takes a deep breath and tries to tamp down her own irritation, knowing it will do no good to match Sissy's anger with her own. "Use mine," she says.

"Really?"

"Yes." Jane never lets Sissy use her charger precisely because she is so prone to losing them, but she's about to ruin Sissy's life by divorcing her father, so she figures this one time it won't hurt. She turns her gaze to Josh.

"Are King's parents home?"

"I think so."

She cocks an eyebrow at him.

"I'll double-check." He darts out as quickly as he appeared, Sissy trailing in his wake.

"Wait! Sissy!"

She turns around.

"What are you ten minutes late for?" Jane can barely keep up with her own schedule, much less those of two busy teenagers.

"I'm going to Jazz's house to watch the final episode of *Yellowjackets*, remember?"

"Are *her* parents home?"

"Mom," she says, disgust overpowering the irritation. "I'm eighteen."

"I know you are," Jane says wistfully.

Sissy hesitates, her face softening. "Thanks for the charger," she says, and then she's gone.

Jane glances at the counter and considers swiping the makeup tubes and compacts out of the way with her arm so she can lay her head down on the cool surface of the quartz. It's not the parenting that's so exhausting as much as the performance of the same script day in and day out. Or maybe it's the trying to fix all the things for all the people in her family, when she can't even fix herself.

Or maybe it's the anticipatory grief she feels at Sissy leaving for college in four short months. There was a time—when her children turning eighteen seemed so far off it was another lifetime—that Jane fantasized about what those years would be like: the freedom of having her house, her time to herself again. But at some point, as the reality of Sissy's leaving drew nearer, it started to feel less like gaining freedom and more like a cavernous, overwhelming loss. Even though Stanford is on the same coast, it's still six hours away by car, and though Jane was overjoyed and so ridiculously proud when Sissy got in, she can't imagine not seeing her daughter every day, not knowing what she's doing, whom she's with—and more importantly, if she's safe, alive, and well. The thought of her leaving is a mix of anxiety and grief so encompassing, she doesn't understand how other mothers have survived it.

Jane sighs, taps the screen of her phone on the counter, and pulls up her email, scrolling past one from the publishing house of her first book announcing a *brand-new publicity team!* that Jane thinks is about six years too late, then opens the latest

15

editor's rejection she received from her agent that afternoon for her sophomore novel—a book she's been working on for the past six years that has been on submission for nearly five months. This was the seventh rejection.

She knows she shouldn't let it get to her. Rejection is part of being a writer. Harry Potter was rejected by twelve different publishers! But Jane thinks rejection—like most bad things—is probably an easier pill to swallow in hindsight, once you're a worldwide fiction-writing phenomenon, raking in millions of dollars and living in a country estate with an oak-paneled library to shelve all the international editions of your novels. And Jane doesn't even want millions of dollars! She's not greedy. She'd be happy with *minor* success. And OK, truth be told, she also has one tiny recurring daydream of being the author guest on *The Tonight Show* with Jimmy Fallon. She's even gone as far as to practice in the mirror looking very humble and grateful, yet composed and confident, while saying, *No! I had no idea my book would go on to sell hundreds of thousands of copies, Jimmy!! It's all been very surreal.* And then she always adds: *But I couldn't have done any of this without my husband, Dan.* It's not true, but it's what celebrities always do when accepting awards—deflect their accolades, shine a light on the support of their loved ones. It's easy to be self-effacing when you're feeling magnanimous about the state of things.

All that is to say, Jane has had exactly one book published, exactly six years ago, and it was nowhere near a bestseller and certainly nowhere near the radar of Jimmy Fallon—in fact, more books got returned to the publisher than actually got sold. It was devastating, yes, but she knows logically that it's ridiculous to care as much as she does; that as adversities go, not achieving her lifelong career dream to be a bestselling novelist is a first-world problem, at best. She has so much in her life to be grateful for—her kids, her health, a roof over her head. That's what those influencers she follows remind her of every day with their platitudes. *Never let the things you want make you forget the things you have.*

But they were dead wrong about the lipstick, so . . .

Dan appears at the open door of the bathroom, staring at his phone. "Did you hear that cryptocurrency Ottobyte just knocked off Bitcoin as the most valuable? It's worth thirty-eight thousand dollars per coin."

Both Dan and Sissy—who had more understanding of technology and economics by the time she reached middle school than Jane had ever possessed in her entire life—had tried to explain cryptocurrency to Jane on numerous occasions, once even going so far as getting potatoes out of their pantry as a visual aid. Jane still didn't understand it and thought it was absurd that people spent their real money on money that didn't actually exist.

"Huh," she says, because saying anything else would provoke Dan into yet another explanation she wouldn't understand.

"I knew I should have bought some," he mutters as he grabs the handheld mirror and angles it behind and slightly above his head to better study the thinning hair at its crown. It's a bald spot, to be honest, but Jane never calls it that, to spare Dan's feelings. Dan looks at it every day, as if closely monitoring the hairs like an unruly dog one is trying to train will make them stay. Satisfied, he puts the mirror down on the counter, then meets Jane's eyes. "You ready, babe? I don't want to be late."

She stares back at him, her husband. Dan's wearing a navy-blue-and-red-striped tie his mother bought him for Christmas a decade ago. It doesn't go with his gray suit jacket. The paisley lavender one would look infinitely better. Jane would say something, but Dan's going to have to pick out his own ties from now on, so, she figures, he may as well start now. She stands and smooths her dress, then moves to walk past him to the bedroom, where her purse is. He grabs her wrist gently.

"Hey," he says. "Happy anniversary."

She stops. Looks into his muted blue eyes. They're not ice blue or slate blue or pure blue or pale blue or piercing or sparkling or any of those clichéd adjectives people use to describe blue eyes. She remembers texting him once, years ago, when the wall color greige was all the rage for suburban women who watched too much *Fixer Upper*.

Greige-blue! she typed. That's your eye color.

She doesn't remember what he wrote back. Probably something benign and loving like: *You're a nut.* That was before. When things were good. When Jane couldn't even fathom divorcing Dan—aside from the normal, expected moments every wife fantasizes about leaving her spouse, like every time Jane sees Idris Elba strutting in a trench coat on-screen, or in the middle of the night when she would go to the bathroom in the dark, only for her bare ass to meet the *top* of the cold, hard toilet seat. While most men were prone to leaving the toilet seat up after relieving themselves, Dan put down the whole kit and caboodle and Jane found it maddening.

"Happy anniversary," she says.

This is the last time we'll celebrate it, she doesn't say.

"You should wear the lavender tie," she says.

CHAPTER

2

SOMEWHERE IN THE MIDDLE OF THE CALIFORNIA coast, a cliff grows out of the Pacific Ocean and climbs straight up, like a beanstalk in a children's fairy tale. So tall that if you tilt your head just right on some days, it looks as though the land wears the clouds like a bad toupee. Perched atop the cliff sits a restaurant, its western wall made entirely of glass so patrons can appreciate the stunning sight of the orange sun slipping back into the water every evening—a million-dollar view, if there ever was one. *Dinner and a show,* the three-Michelin-star-lauded head chef of La Fin du Monde, Lars Johansson, jokes nightly to the highest-earning clientele—the A-list celebrities, the tech tycoons, the media moguls—when they are afforded a private audience with him at the end of their meal.

But the view isn't even what gives the restaurant its renown. It's most known for its Guinness world record of having the most expensive, decadent dessert on a menu ever. The Semlor

Guld is a Swedish concoction consisting of a cardamom-flavored bun filled with almond paste and whipped cream, flaked with edible 24K gold, and served on a pure gold platter. The true expense comes from the Harry Winston 9.7-carat diamond bracelet delicately draped across the top of the pastry. (The dessert costs a whopping $8.4 million and has famously been ordered only once, by a New York Yankees player for his wife, the week after his sext messages with a Southwest flight attendant went viral.)

There is only one way into the restaurant and one way out—a two-lane road that snakes up through the dense slope of forest, back and forth like the thread in a weaver's loom.

After they've been on that winding road for thirteen minutes with no end in sight, Jane asks: "Are you sure this is the right way?"—even though they're following the portable GPS suction-cupped to the dash of Dan's Subaru Forester. The same Subaru Forester Dan's had since Jane first met him twenty years earlier, because Dan refuses to get rid of it, even though the air-conditioning no longer works and the back seat has a red stain the size of a throw pillow where Josh once threw up an entire cherry Icee after a peewee football game.

"Yes," Dan says, even though Jane knows he's not sure.

It's a road neither has ever been on before (and will ever be on again), as they aren't A-listers or tycoons or moguls, and while they know of La Fin du Monde, and it's only ninety minutes from their home, it feels like a faraway destination they've heard about but would never visit—like Lake Como or Saint-Tropez. A playground for the rich. Not for a podiatrist and a failed author in their midforties who, though they could afford it, still got a bit panicky when each of their children needed braces.

But it's their anniversary. And while they would typically enjoy a less expensive evening out to celebrate (like the Macaroni Grill, for instance, because Jane made the mistake of offhandedly saying she enjoyed their chicken scaloppine and Dan took that to mean it was Jane's favorite restaurant and booked it most years without consulting her, thinking it was a romantic gesture), Dan had apparently bought a twenty-dollar raffle ticket from a pharmaceutical sales rep who was selling them for her daughter—some fundraiser for the kid's ridiculously expensive private school. When Dan told Jane he won, he said proudly, "The dinner is on the same date as our anniversary. It's kismet," and Jane remembered thinking: *The tuition to this school is forty-five thousand dollars a year, why do they need to raise funds?*

It was Jane who pointed out, after Dan had already confirmed the booking, that the gift certificate was for the reservation only and did not actually cover the cost of dinner. "What?" Dan snatched the vellum paper from his wife's hand. He borrowed Jane's readers (Jane had offered to buy him a pair, but he swore he didn't need them), and the small print at the bottom became clear.

"I paid *twenty dollars* for a reservation I could get for free?"

"Well, you likely couldn't have gotten a reservation. It's notoriously booked out. I think a year or two ahead of time."

This didn't appear to make Dan feel better.

"We don't have to go," Jane said.

"It's our twentieth anniversary," Dan said. "We're going."

"It's our nineteenth."

"Is it?" he said. "Well. Still."

Now, to Jane's surprise, the road finally ends, the trees part, and they encounter a house that looks like something out of a movie set. Very Californian—all sharp lines and angles, softened by perfectly manicured desert-tolerant vines and shrubbery. Jane says "Is this it?" even though a dramatic iron sign announces LA FIN DU MONDE so they know they are in the right place. "Seems to be," Dan says, because after you've been married for so long, sometimes you state even the most obvious observations out loud. Perhaps it's a consequence of being parents—an old habit left over from the many years of pointing out things to your young children excitedly as they learn about the wonders of the world around them. *Look! A bus. Look! A butterfly. Look! A helicopter.* Or perhaps—and Jane thinks this is most likely—it's just to fill the air because you've run out of other things to say.

INSIDE, THE DECOR is sparse and light-filled, thanks not just to the wall of windows but the light oak floors and white tablecloths and white walls. Dan and Jane hover near the door along with ten other people, all waiting—for what, Jane isn't quite sure.

"I'm nervous," Jane whispers to Dan. She tries not to be awed by the view of both the expansive Pacific Ocean and the affluent fellow diners whose well-cut, high-end attire makes her favorite hunter green A-line Ann Taylor dress dim a bit in comparison.

"You are?"

"Yes." She's been harboring a sense of doom about the evening ever since she stepped into the shower that afternoon to get ready. She supposes, given the circumstances, it's probably normal, but she's never asked anyone for a divorce before, so how is she to know? To Dan she says: "It feels like in high school, that fear that someone is going to point out you don't belong."

"I'm nervous we're about to spend one thousand dollars on a meal and could still be hungry afterward," Dan says.

The couple standing closest to them chuckles. Jane, embarrassed to have been overheard, appraises them—a nicely suited man with a closely shaved head and a bushy mustache, and a woman who looks like she stepped out of the pages of *Essence* with her flawless makeup and a dress that hugs her body in all the right places. (Jane actually hates herself for thinking it as soon as she does. All the *right* places? Implying there are wrong parts of a woman's body, a belief she has tried to keep her children from being indoctrinated in.)

"Is this your first time here?" Dan asks the couple, as Jane knew he would. An introvert, Jane would nearly always prefer to keep to herself, while Dan finds it impossible not to engage strangers in small talk.

"It is," the woman with perfectly arched eyebrows says.

"Special occasion?"

"For work, really," she says.

"Oh! What is it that you do? I'm Dan, by the way."

"Ayanna, and this my husband, Rahul," she says. Rahul keeps his hands in his pockets, but smiles and nods, and Jane thinks he must be the more introverted of the pair. "I'm a food influencer."

Jane has to stop herself from visibly rolling her eyes. *Jesus Christ*, she thinks. *They're everywhere.*

"A what?" Dan doesn't have any form of social media and up until two years ago thought *meme* was pronounced *mi-mi* (and, gun to his head, couldn't exactly tell you what one was).

"A food influencer," the woman repeats, as if Dan is just hard of hearing (he is) and not like he lives under a rock and wouldn't have any clue what an influencer actually is. "Although I've heard they won't let us take any pictures of the food, which is going to make my job difficult."

A woman finally steps through the swinging door at the back of the restaurant, saving Dan from the impending embarrassment of repeating his query, and walks toward the group. "Welcome to La Fin du Monde," she says. "I'm Monica and I hope you're all ready for an incredible culinary adventure. We have just a few reminders before we get started."

"More rules?" Jane whispers. She recalls the email Dan forwarded to her confirming their reservation, bidding diners to not wear cologne or perfume as it could interfere with the *full gastronomic experience of both yourself and other diners.* And *guests running late for their reservation will be "caught up" only at the chef's discretion.*

Dan flashes an amused grin as Monica continues: "All dishes have been created by Chef to work in perfect harmony, and so no substitutions or changes will be granted. If you have food preferences or allergies that you have not already brought to our attention, please do so to your dinner captain—me or Javier—at the beginning of the meal. Chef also requests that there be no cell phone use at the table, and photography is prohibited." She smiles. The model-esque food influencer Ayanna frowns. "Now, I will be happy to escort you to your table, starting with the"—she checks the notepad she's holding—"Harris party of two?"

Jane wonders when they started calling waiters *captains* and if it was around the same time they started calling bartenders *mixologists*.

Jane and Dan's table is not by the window, but closer to the front of the restaurant, near the door to the kitchen. Dan mumbles that for twenty bucks—and with only five tables in the entire restaurant—they could have at least gotten one with an unobstructed view.

"Good evening," a bespectacled man in a black vest and white button-down greets them. "My name is Javier, and I am at your service this evening. Monica will be assisting me. Please let us know if there is anything we can do to make your experience more enjoyable. Is this your first time?"

"Yes," Dan says. "Be gentle."

Javier laughs as if he's genuinely never heard the joke before. Jane is impressed with his acting skills.

Javier claps his hands together. "Absolutely, sir. Are we celebrating anything special?"

"Nineteen years of marriage."

"Ah! The bronze anniversary."

"Is it?" Jane asks.

"Indeed," he says. "In which case, may I recommend one of our specialty cocktails? The House Negroni, a blend of gin, sweet vermouth, and Campari infused with the bronze fennel from our organic herb garden on the property."

"We'll take two," Jane says. Dan raises his eyebrows at her, and she knows it's because he knows she doesn't like fussy drinks *or* being upsold, and always orders a glass of wine, preferably pinot grigio, but she's tired of being predictable.

Javier takes their water preference (flat) and leaves them each with a menu and instructions. "Although it's a set nine-course dinner, you'll have a few choices to make between seafood and meat, as indicated on the menu, and whether you want to supplement any dishes with the chef's suggestions," he says. "I'll get your drinks for you and be back to answer any questions you may have."

When he leaves, Dan—wearing Jane's readers perched on the tip of his nose—leans over the table conspiratorially. "I have questions. What is matsutake mushroom foam and why does it cost two hundred dollars extra?" He glances back at the menu, and then: "Are the goose barnacles flown in from Galicia, Spain, made from actual geese?"

"I don't know, but it's pretty clear what a quarter suckling pig is," Jane says. "Who writes these things—they couldn't dress that up? That's why the word 'pork' was invented. Nobody wants to eat *Wilbur*."

Dan grins at her, and it's amazing to Jane how effortless their banter still comes. Or maybe what's amazing is how she used to find it so charming and delightful—a surefire sign of their fated connection (because isn't that what every couple wants? The proof that their union was ordained in some way, no matter what your beliefs?)—but now, like an ill-fitting shoe, it chafes. Because it's all an act, a role they've each played for so long it's become as rote as brushing one's teeth—and they *could* play it for years more, 'til death do them part. But Jane has gotten to the point where she thinks she might rather die.

"Javier," she says. "That's funny, isn't it?"

Dan blinks at her. "What's funny?"

"Remember? From my book? He's the tea sommelier."

"Oh. Right," Dan says. But Jane can tell he doesn't really remember and is just being agreeable. Jane's not entirely convinced Dan ever even *read* the one book that she's managed to get published—and is that really too much to ask?

Irritation grips her and suddenly she can't participate in their charade for one more second. She had planned to wait until they got home from dinner to share her decision. (Jane pictured them in their pajamas, perhaps when they were both facing the bathroom mirror, Dan flossing and Jane plucking her errant chin hairs, comfortable and at ease, disarmed.) But now she thinks, *Why?* What is she preserving? It suddenly feels like a belt that has become too tight after Thanksgiving dinner and she has to unbuckle it immediately. It would feel so good to breathe.

"So, the meat and seafood," Dan says. "What are you thinking?"

Jane takes a deep breath. "I think we should go our separate ways." She exhales and feels the belt loosen, the weight lift from her shoulders.

"OK, so you get the lobster galette and I'll get the charcoal-grilled Wagyu, maybe without the supplemental foam, so we can still send Sissy to college?"

"No," Jane says, slightly annoyed. "Well, yes. That sounds fine. I also think we should get a divorce."

He laughs, as if they're still engaged in witty repartee, but when he looks at Jane's face, he becomes serious. "What?"

"Here we are. A couple of House Negronis and water for the table." Javier sets two glass tumblers filled with bright orange liquid in front of them. "Do we have any questions, or have you made some decisions?"

Jane waits for Dan to speak, but he continues to stare at her, as if his brain has short-circuited. She takes a sip of the Negroni—it's bitter and the gin kicks her in the back of the throat, which she typically doesn't like, but right now it feels perfect.

Jane clears her throat. "He'll have the Wagyu and I'll do the lobster. And no supplements for us, please."

"Wonderful," Javier says, glancing at Dan once more. "I'll leave a menu at the table so you have a road map for your dinner, and we'll get started with the first course shortly."

He leaves, and when they're alone again Dan says one word: "No."

Jane sighs. What did she think? That he was just going to say yes and then they'd eat their nine courses and laugh and clink glasses, agreeing they'd had a good run and good on them?

Well, yes. She did, actually. She thought it would be a relief not only to her, but to him, too. That they'd been at this for so long. Pretending everything was fine. Good, even.

"Dan, yes," she says. With not exasperation but kindness.

She's feeling magnanimous now that it's out in the open. Now that the weight has been lifted from her chest.

"Why?" he says, and he seems genuinely shocked.

She tries to pinpoint, as she has for months, where it all went wrong. They did the therapy. Well, not with a trained therapist—Dan believed sharing anything deeper than polite chitchat with a stranger was unconscionable. But the books— oh! The books!—they read *The 5 Love Languages* (Dan: Acts of Service, Jane: a mix between Quality Time and Physical Touch) and took the Enneagram quiz (Dan: a Reformer/Peace-maker, Jane: an Achiever/Helper) and went on Eight Dates to a Better Marriage and even plugged halfway through a tantric sex workbook. Dan went along with all of it in his good-natured way (though he drew the line at licking honey off each other—*It's so sticky! The sheets will be a mess*—and Jane had to agree). Jane wasn't sure what she had been hoping for in performing all these exercises. A breakthrough of some kind? She didn't even know what that would look like, exactly. She just wanted . . . more.

It wasn't that she didn't love Dan. God, she loved him. And not in that juvenile I-love-him-but-I'm-not-IN-love-with-him way. What did that even mean? It's something said by children who still believe love is a feeling. She loved him the only way you can love someone who you've been with for nearly half your life. It's the same way you love your arm, she often thinks. Not your lungs, mind you. Your lungs are a necessity. But your arm. It's always there. It's part of you. You could live without it, but honestly it would be easier not to.

That was why Jane had been thinking about divorcing Dan

for more than a year now and had never pulled the trigger. Not until her hand was forced.

She doesn't want to have to say it. She doesn't want to reduce their relationship—everything they shared over the years, their *life*—to this. But she sees that he's going to leave her with no choice.

"I saw the text messages."

She scrutinizes his face as she says it, a part of her still hoping she's wrong, even as she knows she's not. Which makes it complicated at best, because she felt relief when she found them—a tangible excuse to leave. (It also explained that one time he'd come home without his wedding ring on and made that lame excuse that it had been causing him a rash. Oh! And his recent, unexpected interest in jogging. She'd nearly laughed at herself for having not one but *two* of the most clichéd red flags right in front of her and not seeing them.) She knows every single expression on his face, better than she knows her own. He's the one she's been looking at for nineteen years—longer, if you count the time they dated. And that's how she knows he's lying when he says: "It's not what you think."

This is what breaks Jane's heart. Not the affair, but the lie. That he couldn't even let her have this. The dignity of walking away, pride intact, instead of belittling her intelligence with such a tiresome, predictable denial.

AS JANE BATHES in her disappointment and gin at the top of the hill, at the bottom of the hill a large van makes the same right turn Jane and Dan made some twenty-five minutes earlier at the base of the winding road—the only road to and from the restaurant. From the outside, the white van looks like one that might transport a church youth group singing "Father Abraham" in unison or supplies for a home-renovation business, not six members of an underground extremist group on the FBI watch list. A second white van, driven by the seventh member, turns onto the road behind them, following at a close distance, its only job to turn perpendicular to the road halfway up, creating an effective blockade of sorts, so no other cars can come in.

Or get out.

CHAPTER

3

A HIGH-PITCHED SHRIEK FILLS THE AIR, STOPPING Jane's heart and stealing her attention from Dan.

"It's freezing!" screeches a brunette woman at the table by the window, who is half out of her seat but not fully standing, as if she isn't quite sure what to do. Jane does a double take, as the woman looks so recognizable, but Jane can't place her. Or maybe she just has one of those faces.

"I'm so sorry, madam," Javier says, reaching out with his hand towel to try and pat the arm of her white blouse, which Jane can see is wet. Javier must have accidentally knocked her water glass over.

"Don't touch me," the woman snarls. "This is mulberry silk!"

Jane has to suppress an eye roll. Mulberry silk? The shirt isn't purple, which leads Jane to believe mulberry silk is some special type of silk she's never heard of. A type of silk that only a woman like this, whose neck and limbs are dripping in jewelry, could afford.

The diamond on her finger alone has to be at least four carats. Jane's never been a jewelry person; she doesn't covet the ring for herself, she's just in awe of the size, of how much it likely cost, of how many people that money could house and feed. It isn't a fair judgment, she knows. Her own ring cost thirty-five hundred dollars, an amount somebody could easily argue could also be better spent feeding the homeless. She glances at the small diamond with the simple gold band on her left ring finger, remembering the day she and Dan picked it out. Jane thought they were just going to look, for Dan to get an idea of what she liked, but to Jane's surprise, he bought it right then and there. When the saleswoman gave him the box, he, in turn, handed it to Jane—no bended knee, no question asked. Dazed, Jane slipped the ring on her own finger and in the car on the way home said: "Are we engaged now?" to which Dan replied, "For the amount of money I just spent, I should hope so."

It wasn't a romantic story as far as proposals go, but over the years, Jane and Dan had turned it into a self-effacing funny anecdote, one they kept in their arsenal of couple stories and dusted off at cocktail parties to entertain and amuse—a smoothly practiced act, where they each knew their lines and when to pause for laughter.

Jane turns her attention back to the woman, who's in her seat and carefully dabbing at the sleeve of her blouse, and her dinner companion, a teenage girl around Josh's age. Likely her daughter.

"Jane," Dan says.

"Yes?" Jane looks at her husband.

"What are you staring at?"

34

"That woman," Jane murmurs. "She looks so familiar."

"Are you *serious* right now?"

"Yeah, look at her. What's she from?"

Jane knows she's seen her before; she just can't place her. Maybe she's an actress? Or one of those real housewives? As a forty-six-year-old woman, Jane's embarrassed by how excited she feels at a possible celebrity sighting, while simultaneously disappointed that it's not someone bigger like Sandra Bullock or hotter like Keanu Reeves.

"Remember *Speed*?" she says. "That was a good movie. Ooh! Do you think they'll order that crazy-expensive dessert? They look rich enough to afford it."

"Have you had a stroke?" Dan looks at her with a mix of astonishment and concern.

"What? They do."

"You've just asked me for a divorce," he whispers through gritted teeth. "And now you're . . . I don't even know what you're doing."

Jane sighs. "I'm just trying to have a nice time."

"A nice . . ." he sputters. "Do you even hear yourself?"

"Here we are," Javier says, sliding a small white plate in front of Jane and then Dan. Jane notices he said the same thing when he brought the Negronis, and she knows it's simply something waiters say—a statement that accompanies the presentation of the food—but for the first time the phrase strikes her differently. She looks at Dan and thinks: *Here we are.* In a place, both literally and figuratively, she never thought they'd be. Literally, at La Fin du Monde, about to dine on goose barnacles in a leek-sherry coulis with fiddleheads, celery, and wild greens, according to Javier. And figuratively, a middle-aged couple on the precipice of divorce, joining the ranks of the many—the majority of, if the studies are to be believed— couples before them. Divorce: an American pastime as traditional and commonplace and boring as baseball. She knows they both believed the lie that they were different—the exception to the rule. But when one gets married, divorce is nearly as inevitable as death is when one is born.

"These are terrifying," Jane says, taking in the two prehistoric dinosaur claws on her plate after Javier slips back into the kitchen.

"Jane," Dan says, still staring at her. He hasn't even glanced at his plate.

"Look, Dan! It's like they harvested them out of Sigourney Weaver's stomach."

"Jane!" He lightly pounds his fist on the table, rattling the silverware and glasses and drawing the attention of the diners at the nearest table.

Jane startles. Dan is so even-keeled, logical. Losing his temper is such a rare sight—like the aurora borealis or a white rhinoceros—all she can do is stare.

"I am not cheating on you," he says, enunciating each word. His eyes bore into hers as if he can will her to believe him, as though he's attempting some kind of marital Jedi mind trick.

She considers his declaration. Considers if she even wants to believe him, which honestly is more important than if she actually does believe him. She thinks of Sissy and Josh and how she and Dan had to carry on being Santa long into the kids' middle school years, not because the children actually believed anymore but because they wanted to. *Wanting* to believe something is the basis of most successful relationships, she thinks. Wanting to believe that the person you are with is good or decent or that they would never do anything too terribly immoral or heinous like double-dipping a chip at a party or murdering someone. But the truth is, wouldn't most humans do the terrible thing, given the right circumstances? If no one's looking, you likely would double-dip a chip. If your child was kidnapped, you'd murder the person who took them. Look at any apocalyptic movie or television show—you do what you have to do to survive. Morality isn't an absolute; it's situational.

And if she's really honest with herself, she can even understand why Dan would have an affair. How nice it must be to feel excitement about something—*anything*—again.

"I don't really care, Dan," she says, waving her hand.

He scoffs. "You don't *care* if I'm having an affair? Nice."

"It's not—" She stops. How can she explain? "It was just the last straw. I've been thinking we should get a divorce for a year, I think? Maybe more."

"A *year*?"

"Yes," she says, drawing out the word, trying to comprehend his apparent shock. She had assumed that while she had been thinking it, he had, too—and maybe that was why she wasn't surprised when she found the text messages. A spark of anger, sure. Betrayal. But then it was almost a relief that they were—ironically—on the same page. "You can't honestly tell me you haven't even thought about it. That you've been *happy*."

"Happy? Happy?" He half laughs. "Nobody's *happy*, Jane. This is marriage."

She blinks at him. And then picks up her fork and knife to signal she has nothing else to say on the matter and pierces the meat part of the alien claw. The fleshy toe. She tries not to let the disgust register on her face. *This* is fine dining? She manages to shave off a small sliver of spongy pulp with her fork and places it delicately on her tongue. "Oh!" she says, shocked at the pleasant surprise of a briny, tangy, and slightly sweet mix of flavors bursting in her mouth. "That's actually delightful."

Dan's plate remains untouched. "What do you want me to do?"

"Do?" she says, confused.

"Is there another book we can read? Date night? I'll go to therapy. Whatever you want. We're not getting divorced."

Jane lets out a puff of laughter. "Now you want to go to therapy," she says under her breath. She points her fork tines toward his plate. "Try yours. It's delicious." She cuts a larger sliver, gently pulls the morsel off the fork with her lips. Chewing, she closes her eyes, enjoying the spongy texture, the flavor. In fact, that's one of the things she's been working on this year: being present. She downloaded an app, even though she listened to only one fifteen-minute "sleep story" that absolutely did not help her go to sleep. She tries to meditate every morning, even if she's really just thinking about what she needs to buy at the grocery store and how much she doesn't want to go. She bought a gratitude journal online, and it sits untouched on her nightstand. Still, she practices being present with the goose barnacle now, savoring the mouthfeel, and then wonders if she remembered to turn off her curling iron. She thinks of her daughter at home, sprawled across her bed, engrossed in Tik-Tok or Snapchat. She thinks of the house catching on fire, Sissy perishing in the smoke and flames, all due to her own mother's negligence.

Jane reaches into her clutch, which is resting on the table, and fishes out her phone, scrolling to Sissy's name. She types: Can you check the curling iron in my bathroom? Think I left it on. She presses send and the blue bar at the top of the screen begins its journey from left to right, stopping about a quarter of the way. She holds the phone up, closer to the ceiling, then out to her right, willing the message to send, but the bar doesn't move.

"Huh." She glances at the bars in the upper-right corner of the screen and notices they're empty. "I don't have service. Let me see your phone."

Dan reaches into his sports jacket and digs his phone out of the interior breast pocket. "Here," he says. After entering his passcode, she notices his bars are empty as well.

Before she can say as much to Dan, Javier is back at her side.

"I'm so sorry, madam," he says in a soft, kind voice, so that he genuinely does sound sorry. "We do have a no-cell-phones-at-the-table policy here."

Jane feels a little embarrassed, as though she were a child getting chastised by a teacher at school, but that quickly morphs into indignation. She's a grown woman. And she's *paying* for this meal. "There's no service anyway."

"Correct," Javier says. "As I said, Chef prefers—"

"What if there's an emergency?" Jane cuts him off, finding his use of *Chef* as the king or dictator whom everyone should bow down to grating.

"There's a phone in the lounge for customer use."

What Jane wants to say: *What if I left my curling iron on and my house is on fire and Sissy is trying to call me but can't because my phone doesn't work? What if she* dies?

What Jane says: "What if someone were trying to get in touch with us?"

"Are you expecting a call? You're welcome to step into the lounge and give them that number. I'd be pleased to show you the way."

She's not sure if she should get up and call Sissy or if it's her anxiety talking. "No," she says. "I'm fine." If she did leave the curling iron on, it likely wouldn't burn down the house. That's what Dan would say if she asked. She knows it's what he'd say because he's said it before, the other fifty times she's worried she's left the curling iron or the oven or the coffee maker on.

The uneasiness she's been feeling since getting ready that afternoon intensifies. Is it her maternal instinct? Is her daughter in peril? Jane briefly wonders if this is what her sense of doom about the evening was foreboding—her house burning down while they're at dinner. Then again, she's always worried about her house burning down, or her children getting hit by cars, or a minor rash being the symptom of a rare but deadly illness—and whether or not she should do more to prevent these catastrophes, if she's done enough, if she's *doing* enough. Jane often thinks all of the difficulty with parenting can be summed up by one sentence: *Am I overreacting?* And how 99 percent of the time, the answer is yes, but how is one to know when it's the 1 percent of the time worrying is warranted? Frankly, it's exhausting.

Then, all at once, she remembers: Sissy isn't even home! She's at Jazz's house watching that show. And Josh is at King's. So if the house burns down, at least no one will be in it. Jane breathes a sigh of relief.

"How are the goose barnacles?" Javier asks, throwing a brief but concerned glance at Dan's untouched plate. Jane's grateful for one question she wholeheartedly knows the answer to.

"Absolutely incredible."

"I'm so glad." Javier cups his hands together and nods in deference. "Please let me know if there's anything else I can do."

"Dan, you really should eat," Jane says when they're alone once again. She knows he's going to push back, to fall once again into the divorce discussion, which Jane feels should center not on the questions of whether they should do it, at this point, but how—the logistics going forward. And there's plenty of time for all that. No need to figure it out right this second, when they have eight more courses to enjoy. So she says the one thing she knows will work: "That's probably a hundred dollars' worth of shellfish on your plate." Dan stares at her for a beat, then, resigned, lifts his fork and knife from the table and compliantly digs into his own barnacles. After chewing once, then twice, his eyebrows rise in surprise.

"Wow," he breathes.

"Right?" Jane smiles, taking that weird misplaced pride in convincing someone to try something and then being right about how delicious it is, as though you have cooked it yourself.

Dan swallows and, a little more eagerly this time, goes in for his second bite.

"I think I may have left the curling iron plugged in," Jane confesses.

Dan chews, swallows again, and looks at his wife. "You didn't," he says.

"Yeah, but—"

"I went back in the bathroom to check before we left. It was unplugged."

She stares at her husband, feeling both wistful and sad, as though she has already moved on, lives in the future as a divorcée, and is reflecting on how Dan once upon a time always double-checked these things that she worried over, not because he worried about them, too, but because he knew she did. She adds this to the list of things she will now have to do without Dan: *Take out the trash. Iron. Manage my own anxieties.*

"We're not getting divorced," Dan says, as if he's reading Jane's mind, which she supposes is a natural consequence of living with someone for nineteen years.

"Dan—"

"No," Dan says calmly. "This isn't about me. It never is. This is about—"

"Don't," Jane says, her muscles tensing. "Don't say it."

Dan ignores her. Plows forward. "Did you get another rejection today?"

Jane is simultaneously impressed once again that Dan knows her so well, embarrassed that she's so transparent, and livid that Dan is diminishing their wealth of relationship problems—including his own *affair*—and chalking them up to her personal career failures.

Sudden movement at the entrance of the restaurant draws

Jane's attention from her thoughts, from Dan, and she looks in time to see a number of people barreling into the dining room wearing an impressive array of earth tones, matching black gaiters shielding their noses and mouths.

"What in the hell," she hears Dan say, but she doesn't know the answer to this question, because everything is happening in slow motion and too quickly all at once, as if her brain can't catch up. At first she thinks it's some kind of avant-garde acting troupe, an art performance that she will pretend to understand but will have to look up on the Internet later to figure out what it means—like the movie *Inception*. Then she wonders if it's a flash mob. She's seen those on TikTok; maybe someone's going to propose, although this is a strange choice of attire for such a happy occasion, and wouldn't that be ironic? One marriage starting while another's ending. But wait . . . are those . . . *assault rifles*? Jane is no gun expert, but she did research various military-grade weapons when she was writing her novel *Tea Is for Terror*, about an evil gang taking over a high-end teahouse in London and holding everyone hostage and *oh dear God*.

She looks at Dan, her eyes wild, as one of the men stands directly at their table pointing his *assault rifle* inches from Dan's face, and Jane thinks perhaps those Insta influencers were right when they said, *Never underestimate the power of your intuition.*

A fever pitch of frightened screams fills Jane's ears, and that's when she knows: her sense of doom had nothing to do with the divorce or leaving her curling iron plugged in or her house catching on fire after all.

THREE HOURS AND
NINETEEN MINUTES
UNTIL THE END

CHAPTER

4

"WHAT IN THE HELL," DAN REPEATS UNDER HIS breath, even though it's clear what's happening when the barrel end of a gun is thrust toward his face. Not why or how, but what. He's seen enough *Die Hard* (that is to say, all of them) and James Bond and *Homeland* episodes to know—the restaurant is being taken over by terrorists.

Lucky for Dan, he has a plan for this precise scenario. He's never fancied himself the hero—he wouldn't go running toward the gunman or sacrifice his life to potentially save everyone else. He's not a risk-taker by nature. Or prone to violence in any way. He's not overly tall or strong or powerful (he has recently taken up jogging, but he's still a bit more doughy around the middle than he'd like). In short, he knows his limits. But when imagining this situation or one like it, he always planned to run. Or duck. Or, if he was with someone he loved (his wife, children, etc.), he envisioned throwing his body over theirs, and then ducking.

As it turns out, he wouldn't even do that. Instead of throwing himself over Jane or running for an exit or ducking beneath the table, he freezes, still as a statue chiseled from stone. Stares, with his mouth slightly open in confusion, his heart beating as loud as a thousand horses' hooves galloping in his ears.

It shouldn't really surprise him. At forty-three, he's old enough to know most things in life don't pan out quite the way you imagine they will, and you often end up with a feeling of vague disappointment: like the first time you have sex, or every New Year's Eve, or when you try to change the oil in the car yourself rather than taking it to a mechanic, because how hard can it be?

Or marriage.

And yet, here he is. Shocked at his inaction. Disappointed, too. But also, it cannot be overstated how utterly terrified he is.

"Nobody move," a large, chiseled man says—the last person to enter the restaurant. His voice is a deep baritone. Accented. Dan nearly laughs, as he's established he couldn't move if he wanted to. The man strolls confidently to the back of the room, in front of the expansive picture window, where the sun can be seen making its final descent—two more minutes, give or take, and it will slip below the waterline of the horizon. The sprawling beauty is nothing short of breathtaking, and incongruous with what is happening inside the restaurant. He's wearing an army camo vest and khaki cargo pants, the arm holding his rifle bent at the elbow, his naked brown bicep bulging, the muzzle of the gun pointing at an angle toward the floor. He looks like a life-size G.I. Joe figurine, a proper military leader (or a Hollywood approximation of a proper military leader, anyway). Even more alarming? His face is bare, uncovered. He does not wear the matching black gaiter donned by his co-horts, and Dan thinks it's either very cavalier, at best—or he plans to kill every single last one of them when he's done with whatever it is he's doing.

Regardless, Dan knows he will do whatever this man (these men!) holding the gun asks of him.

"Pardon the interruption to your meal," the apparent leader of the group continues, and with his accent—German, maybe? Dan's never had an ear for anything, music, accents—it almost sounds genial, gentlemanly. "My name is Brick and I'm going to lay down some ground rules. If everyone can kindly abide by them, we will be out of your hair and on our way and you can get back to eating your extraordinarily overpriced meal."

Dan hears a "Ha!" from behind him and turns in time to see Jane quickly cover her mouth at the inappropriateness of her response. Dan understands. It feels as though they're watching a performance and, as the audience, they should be fulfilling the duty of their role as polite spectators. Dan's both comforted by the fact that no one else moved either—that they've all been shocked into submission as easily as he has been—and also equally discomfited by this fact. *Who is going to save them?*

The man in charge—*Brick*—uses the barrel of his gun to point it directly at Monica, as though he's a CEO giving a speech at the company's year-end meeting and pointing out the top salesmen—people, Dan chides himself. Sales*people*— of the group.

"You," Brick says, and Monica flinches but doesn't other-wise move. "Take that ice bucket and dump the contents."

Again, the man gestures with the gun barrel toward a silver urn holding a champagne bottle on the table to his right. The two older women at the table flinch, too. Monica pulls the half-empty champagne bottle out of the bucket and then picks it up gingerly, as though it's a live hand grenade. She looks at Brick, unsure what to do next. "Dump it out," he confirms. She turns it over and dumps its ice water contents onto the floor, where they splash up on one of the female diners' stockinged legs. The woman lets out a small yelp.

Brick nods. "This waitress will be coming around with this bucket to collect your cell phones. As I'm sure you're all aware, there is no cell service, so any attempts to make emergency calls or texts are futile, but you can understand—we need to cover all our bases. You will get your phones back when we are done here."

As Monica begins to slowly move between the tables, performing her task as instructed under Brick's watchful gaze, Dan takes the opportunity to glance around the room at the rest of the people holding guns and finds himself surprised at the . . . diversity. A white guy, the Black man in charge, an indiscriminate tanned man who could be Latino or Indian or Hawaiian (or just a really tan white guy, for all Dan knows), and a . . . woman (A *woman*! White. Blond. How did he not notice her before?). Essentially, these *terrorists* are as diverse as the casting of an Old Navy commercial, and dressed similarly, too—all in browns and khakis and denim and greens, matching large hiking bags strapped to their backs—like as a group they were about to announce a sale on *jeans for the whole family!*

What could they possibly want? Dan wonders. If they've come to rob them, they'll be sorely disappointed with the paltry thirty-five dollars in his wallet.

"Once you've handed over your phone, Lyle and Caden"—he nods in the direction of the two guys—"will escort you, one table at a time, to line up against the window here."

As if to demonstrate, Lyle and Caden walk to the table with the two older women, who both stand up and walk toward the window where the female gunman (gunwoman?) stands guard, training a rifle on them. Once the women are seated with their backs to the floor-to-ceiling glass window, Lyle (or Caden? How is Dan to know?) kneels in front of the first woman and, with a practiced hand, zip-ties her wrists together and then her ankles. He repeats the process with her companion. One of the women is clearly terrified, her eyes round and wet, her face ashen, while the other looks simply irritated, wearing a scowl as though someone's abruptly changed the channel on her favorite television show without permission. Once the zip ties are firmly in place, Lyle (or Caden) stands up, and with that, it's as if a choreographed dance resumes. In an orderly fashion, Monica—who is visibly shaking so hard, the phones in the wine bucket are clattering—takes the phones from each table; Lyle and Caden (*Are those their real names? Dan wonders, and if so, isn't that a bad sign? Like seeing a robber's—or Brick's—full face*) swoop in behind and escort those cell phone–free diners to the wall, zip-tying each patron's wrists and ankles.

By the third table, it's all going so smoothly that Dan's heartbeat has slowed considerably and he's waiting for his turn to drop his phone and get in line, until a sudden commotion grabs his attention from two tables over. He turns in time to see the man from the couple he met at the outset of the evening (Rahul, Dan thinks, recalling his name from the recesses of his brain as if they met years ago and not twenty minutes earlier) get knocked in the head with the wrong end of a rifle by the female member of the group, who is half his size. The man's date screams, as his body flops like a rag doll back into his seat, then forward, the side of the table—and his bread plate— catching his head.

Dan winces.

Every person in the room—all ten other diners, two waiters, and three other gun-wielding men—freezes. Waiting. The silence that fills the air after the date's scream is somehow louder than the scream.

"GOD DAMMIT," the woman with the rifle yells through clenched teeth. "He stuck me with a fork."

That's when Dan sees the metal end of the silverware protruding from the woman's thigh. She plucks it out of her flesh and throws it to the floor, where it clatters and skids across the hardwood.

"Is he alive?" Brick asks.

Favoring her leg and holding her rifle in one hand, the woman bends over and uses her free hand to place two fingers against the neck of the man she incapacitated. She nods once.

Brick nods back and then tuts loudly, taking one step forward. "That leads me to the third rule: Do not try to be a hero. There's nothing to be heroic about. Appearances aside, we are not here to hurt anyone—though that gentleman will unfortunately have quite a headache when he wakes up."

"Then why are you here?" one of the older women against the window pipes up—the irritated one—giving voice to not only Dan's thoughts, but likely those of every person in the room.

Brick turns his head to look at her and then lets his gaze slowly span the room. If he's trying to build suspense, it's working. But it's the woman with the buzz haircut who speaks: "We're here to *save* everyone."

Dan stiffens. *Save us?* Oh God. Are they Christian extremists? After a particularly traumatic summer camp experience as a kid wherein Dan's mom signed him up for what she thought was a regular sleeping-in-a-cabin-and-building-campfires-and-swimming-in-a-pond experience turned out to be that shoved in between a very evangelical church service thrice daily—and terrifying to an eight-year-old Dan, who was told more than once quite forcefully by the preacher *and* other children that he was going to spend eternity in a fiery pit of hell for not being saved—Dan's since had a rather dim view of Christianity.

A small murmur passes through the group as people digest this news.

Monica approaches their table with the bucket, flanked by both Lyle and Caden. Dan's heartbeat pounds in his chest like a bass drum. Jane takes her phone off the table and drops it in the bucket, but Dan hesitates for a second—what if he kept his phone? What if he could slip outside somehow? He wonders how far he'd have to run down the road until he was in cell service range. He curses himself for not noticing on the long drive up when exactly they lost the signal. Then he spies his fork and knife crossed over his plate. Could he palm the knife some-how? He certainly wouldn't make the same mistake as the man now lying unconscious on the floor, but at least that guy did *something* instead of moseying along like a cow to slaughter. Maybe he could slip it up his sleeve to use later, catch one of their captors off guard, get ahold of the rifle—

"Dan!" He startles at Jane's voice and sees she's looking at him with part-exasperated, part-pleading eyes. "Give him your phone."

Dan reaches into the front pocket of his coat.

"Hey! Slowly." Lyle (or Caden) says, holding the gun muzzle inches from Dan's face.

Dan obeys, lifting his left arm up in an *I'm innocent* motion. Feeling the sweat trickle from his armpit, adding to what is likely a generous pit stain on his shirt, he grasps his cell phone with his right hand, pulls it out, and drops it in the bucket Monica is holding.

"Stand up."

Again, Dan does as he's told, following Jane to the wall, a deep disappointment and shame nearly rivaling his fear. He glances at the man on the floor and swallows down a flare of jealousy.

Once they're all seated, including Monica and Javier, backs against the glass window, ankles and wrists bound in front of them with white plastic zip ties, Brick walks methodically down the row, clutching his gun. He stops in front of the woman Jane pointed out what seems like hours ago, but some-how was only fifteen or so minutes. Time is funny like that.

"Mrs. St. Clair," Brick says in his deep baritone. *St. Clair!*

Jesus Christ. It's a last name as recognizable to every American—heck, probably anyone in the world—as Bezos or Buffett or Musk.

Jane leans over and whispers in his ear: "I *told* you she was somebody."

"Yes, because what's important now is that you were right," Dan hisses back. He doesn't mean to be harsh with Jane, but he's scared. He's also concerned that Jane doesn't appear to be. Maybe she's had some break with reality, Dan thinks, what with the aloof divorce talk, as though she were talking about someone else—one of their couple acquaintances that always seemed doomed to failure, and the mention of that failure didn't really have any impact on their own life. *Oh, did you hear Larry and Denise are splitting? Pass the chimichurri, please.*

But their own divorce? It would absolutely impact their lives, their *children's* lives, and Jane is behaving as though it's something as common and expected as brushing one's teeth. (Although, to be fair, while it seemed monumental at the time, a divorce *does* seem inconsequential compared to being taken hostage while dining out.)

Then again, Dan always forgets how good Jane is at dealing with emergency situations. It takes him by surprise every time. Like when Sissy was a toddler and split her head wide open on a boulder at a state park and—blood gushing everywhere the way head wounds gush—Jane just scooped her up and carried her to the car. No gasping. No panicking. She just did what needed to be done. He's never given her enough credit for it. She's probably as terrified as he is right now, but relying on her preternatural ability to remain calm in the face of danger. He moves both hands—since they're bound together at the wrists—and reaches for her pinky with his. He attempts to wrap it up, entwine it in his own like an octopus tentacle ensnaring a clam, to comfort her in some way, but she jerks her finger, shrugging him off.

CHAPTER

5

JANE DOESN'T NEED COMFORTING—NOT FROM DAN and his pinky finger or anyone else. What she needs is someone to explain to her why the entire opening act of her novel is playing out in front of her eyes, like some fever dream come to life. Or nightmare, more aptly.

Of course, it's not her book *exactly*, but still, what are the chances? She wrote a book about a hostage situation at a restaurant (well, technically a teahouse)—and is now in a hostage situation at a restaurant. If it weren't so absolutely terrifying to be held at gunpoint, it might even be funny. As it stands, it feels surreal—and not just a little regrettable: if Jane knew life would imitate her art, she would have written about something more fun, like winning the lottery or being marooned on a desert island with a shirtless Hemsworth brother. (Or all three of them.) And perhaps it's the shock that's keeping her from being as frightened as she knows she should be. After all, this isn't fiction. It's not something she wrote. It's real life! Those guns they are holding are real guns! With presumably real bullets! But the panic she knows she should be experiencing feels just out of reach. It's a bit like the time she took Xanax before a root canal—as though everything happening around her doesn't really have anything to do with her.

To be honest, what's most amazing to her is how many things she got right. The way they burst into the restaurant with face coverings, collecting the cell phones, the zip ties. Even the words they used. The first thing the guy said when he came into the restaurant was nearly verbatim from her book: *My name is Brick and I'm going to lay down some ground rules.* (Of course, her antagonist's name was Alek, not Brick, but on the whole she thinks Brick is probably a better name for a villain and she wishes she had thought of it.) She couldn't help it; she laughed. Mostly because she immediately thought of that awful Goodreads reviewer Stephen (which is such a pretentious way to spell Steven) who gave her book one star (*one star!*) and said—among other criticisms—that her dialogue was "ludicrous and inauthentic."

Though Jane probably gets more pleasure than the typical human from being proven correct (Dan always accuses her of that, anyway), she wishes she had her phone, if only so she could record the entire encounter and send it directly to that pompous asshat. *This is apparently* exactly *how terrorists talk*, Stephen.

Now she turns her attention back to Brick, who's calmly questioning Mrs. St. Clair on the whereabouts of her husband. "Is he in the toilet?" he asks, but pronounces it in that European way: *twal-lette.*

Brick glances to his right at one of his cohorts standing in the doorway between the dining room and hallway, and the man gives his head one sharp shake. "Empty."

Brick narrows his eyes. "Where is he? He was supposed to be dining with you tonight."

"How do you know that?" Vaughn St. Clair shot back, with the kind of righteous animosity of a person who is not used to being spoken to with anything but deference. Which is to say, a person who has billions of dollars at their disposal, like Vaughn St. Clair.

Had Otto been with them, Jane obviously would have recognized *him* right away, and therefore Vaughn and her daughter—Paisley, was it? Jane wasn't sure, but she had a mild recollection of it being a fabric pattern. As one of the wealthiest men in the world, and the founder of SierraX, one of the Big Five Silicon Valley tech firms, alongside Amazon, Apple, Microsoft, and Google, Otto St. Clair's name constantly dominated headlines, and he was well known for his eccentricities—like buying a chain of exclusive uninhabited islands off the coast of Belize just so he could create his own country, Ottolaw. His latest venture, self-flying electric helicopters, had been in the news for the last month since one of his prototypes had crashed on a test run in the San Fernando Valley, taking out three houses in a suburban neighborhood. Fortunately, no one had been home at the time, but a fierce debate sprang up in the aftermath regarding the safety of this enterprise.

"Stand her up."

Lyle grabs Mrs. St. Clair by her left upper arm and pulls her to her feet.

"Get your hands off me," Vaughn practically spits once upright, shrugging her elbow out of his grasp.

"Brick?" the woman who was stabbed with a fork says. She's older, tan, with sun lines on her face, her bleach blond hair cropped into a short pixie. "He's not here. Should we just go?"

Surprised, Jane swivels her head back to Brick. Could it be that easy? Maybe they'll leave as quickly as they came and she can throw back another gin, give her account to the police, and be in her bed watching an episode of *Queer Eye* by ten p.m.

Brick either doesn't hear the woman's suggestion or chooses not to. "Hey," he says to Vaughn's daughter. "It's OK. I'm not going to hurt you."

In that moment, Brick doesn't seem evil or even scary, though he's still clutching an AR-15 in his left hand. He almost seems . . . *gentle*? He doesn't *want* to hurt them; he's said it over and over. Perhaps that's a tactic: disarm your hostages with your accent and genteel, comforting demeanor. If so, Jane has to admit it's working. Objectively speaking, he's very appealing—more so than one would expect for a scary villain type, anyway.

But honestly, she's always had a thing for bad boys, Dan notwithstanding. Perhaps that's why she married him: not because he was nice, but because he was so different from what she was used to. It wasn't just polite that he called when he said he was going to. It was *novel*.

After nineteen years with nice, the novelty now is the passion behind Brick's calm demeanor. He means business. And Jane barely had the will to make it here for dinner. To be served. She can't imagine the self-motivation it takes to plan a coup—or is that just a governmental overthrow? Jane supposes you can't technically coup a restaurant. Although that Chef did seem to have some dictator-like tendencies, what with his no-cell-phones rule and all.

"Is a coup only when it's overthrowing a government?" she whispers to Dan.

"What?" he says, and whether he can't hear her or doesn't understand the question, Jane is annoyed and doesn't repeat it.

"Are you . . . OK?" Dan whispers.

Jane tears her eyes from Brick and looks at Dan. In a hushed voice that matches Dan's, she holds up her bound wrists and says: "Just ducky."

He frowns and she immediately regrets her sarcasm. It's become her default for talking to him ever since she found the text messages, and even though she keeps telling herself it doesn't bother her—that his cheating was a good thing, a relief—deep down, she knows she's hurt. How could she not be? Nineteen years of marriage. And this is what it's come to? A sleazy affair with a woman named "Becca"? He didn't even have the decency to change her name in his phone. So when he was in the shower one evening and it pinged on the counter, her first thought was *Who's Becca?* Out of curiosity, she picked it up, and the message—Will I see you tonight?—made her think Becca was a new colleague and she must be referring to an event, some podiatrist conference or dinner Dan had forgotten to mention. But as she scrolled up, it quickly became apparent with the You were on fire last night and the kicker even farther up: When are you going to tell your wife? To make matters worse, that evening, Dan put on his T-shirt and shorts, grabbed his keys, and said he was going for a run in the park. Who showers *before* a run? Jane couldn't decide if she was more upset by the affair or by how dumb Dan apparently thought she was.

"I mean . . . you don't seem frightened," he says now, his voice still low.

Jane considers this. She is scared—or at least knows she should be. But he's right. Fear is not her foremost emotion, and she tries to analyze why.

"I don't think they want to hurt us," she whispers slowly.

Dan raises his eyebrows. "I think the multitude of weaponry they're holding suggests otherwise."

"Yeah, but they didn't shoot him."

"What?"

"That guy with the fork. She hit him in the face with the butt of her gun instead of shooting him."

"And?"

"Ergo," she whispers, "they don't intend to hurt us."

"*Ergo?*"

Jane's skin pricks with irritation. She hates when Dan picks apart her words. She tries to ignore it. "Anyway, don't you think it's strange?"

"That we've been taken hostage? Yes. It's not how I anticipated our night going."

"No, I mean, how it's so much like my book."

"Your book?"

"Yes, Dan. The one I wrote and published six years ago?" Her aggravation grows.

"I know your book," he whispers.

"Don't you see the similarities? The face coverings, the guns, the zip ties . . ."

"Yes, I see the similarities," he says. "To your book and *Die Hard* and *Mission: Impossible* and *Inside Man* and every other movie where a group of people takes another group of people hostage."

Jane stiffens. "Yeah, but what about what he said when they first came in—about laying down some ground rules? It's what the leader in my book said, too!"

Dan raises his eyebrows, but it's a look more of pity than understanding. "Jane, I get that it's ironic, but—"

"Coincidental," Jane interrupts.

"What?"

"It's not ironic. It's coincidental."

"Really, Jane," Dan says, annoyance lacing his words. "Now's the time to be pedantic?"

Heat fills Jane's entire body, radiating from her belly outward, and it quickly dawns on her why she's not frightened—she's too angry. She thinks of the text messages. Of Dan lying to her. Of stupid one-star Stephen. Of her meal being so rudely interrupted by these gun-wielding maniacs, just when she was starting to enjoy the buzz from her gin and the surprisingly delectable goose barnacles. And suddenly the anger is all-compassing. It's all she can feel, all she can see.

"Pedantic! Oh, I'm *pedantic* now. Fantastic. Is *that* why you cheated on me?" She's not sure when her voice turned from a whisper to a full-on yell, but she can very clearly hear the overwhelming silence after her outburst and knows before she turns her head that every single pair of eyes in the restaurant is going to be squarely directed at her.

She slowly turns.

Yep. Every. Single. Pair.

Including Brick's.

"Are we interrupting something?" he growls.

"Um . . . no," she says, and then adds: "Sorry."

"Wonderful." He turns his attention back to the St. Clairs. "Now, when *exactly* will he be here?"

"I don't know," the girl says calmly, the tears on her face already dried and gone. "He just said after his meeting."

Brick nods. "Then we will wait for him." He claps his hands together, causing his biceps to twitch.

God, Jane thinks. The man really is unnaturally attractive. Maybe that's why she's not frightened. And then she remembers Patty Hearst. Isn't this exactly what happened to her? Jane's pretty sure Patty had *sex* with the man who took her hostage, and if he looked anything like Brick, Jane can see why! But maybe she's misremembering the whole Hearst situation. She would ask Dan, but she's still too angry to speak with him.

Even more irritating, she knows he's right, even if he used the wrong word. Face coverings and zip ties aren't unique to *Tea Is for Terror*—they're universal hostage-taking basics. Besides, in her book, the terrorists burst into the teahouse and shoot a patron right off the bat, to prove they mean business and subdue the other hostages. These captors haven't even used their guns for a warning shot, underlining her belief that there really is nothing to be frightened of. Maybe there aren't even real bullets in the guns!

Jane feels Dan shift beside her, and she turns as he dips his head closer to her ear and whispers: "For the millionth time, Jane, I am *not* ch—"

POP-POP.

The deafening crack of gunshots explodes in the kitchen, stealing the rest of Dan's sentence and startling Jane so much she nearly jumps out of her own skin. A loud bellow immediately follows. A woman screams, and Jane has no idea where it came from. It could have been her, for all she knows. Her heart suddenly feels like it's relocated to her throat, and her brain scrambles as though she can't quite piece together what's happening—but one thought is as clear as the glass window she's leaning against: Jane is scared now.

THREE HOURS
AND TWO MINUTES
UNTIL THE END

6

"WE NEED A DOCTOR!" A YOUNG MAN IN CARGO PANTS and a black T-shirt, with the same matching black gaiter over his nose and mouth, bursts through the swinging kitchen door.

Brick appraises him for a beat and then, instead of asking the questions Dan was curious about—*Who's hurt? What happened?*—Brick simply nods and turns to the hostages. "Is anyone here a doctor?"

There was a time, early on in his premed program, that Dan often fantasized about this moment. He would be on a plane or in a store or at a *restaurant* and someone would go into cardiac arrest or labor or have a stroke and someone else would shout (just like they do in the movies): *Is there a doctor here?* And Dan would stand up, hands on hips, chest thrust out in a stereotypical superhero pose (he could even see the breeze rustling his hair), and say, with full-throated confidence, *I'm a doctor*, before valiantly saving the person's life. And now, the moment has arrived and Dan remains mute.

"Dan!" Jane rams her shoulder into his, as if waking him up.

"What?"

"He's a doctor," she says. Her voice is screechy, and Dan would recognize it as panic if he wasn't so consumed with his own. Brick turns to them, eyes large and calm like an owl scanning for prey, and Dan is doubly unnerved.

"No! No, I'm not," he stammers. "I'm a *podiatrist*."

"What's that?" Brick asks.

"I specialize in foot and ankle injuries."

"So"—Brick crinkles his brow—"you *are* a doctor." It's a statement, not a question, but Dan feels the need to explain. Or defend himself further.

"Technically, but surely there's a . . . neurosurgeon in here? Orthopedist?" He names the top two highest-earning medical specialties. Doctors who could actually afford to eat in a restaurant like this. Doctors who would be infinitely more helpful in a trauma/gunshot/emergency situation. He knows the top two highest-earning medical professions because when he decided to go into podiatry, at every holiday for the next four years, his father slapped him on the back and said, *Sure you don't want to be an orthopedic surgeon? It's basically the same thing as podiatry but they make a lot more money. Second-highest income, in fact, right after neurosurgeon.* They get paid so much not solely because of the intricacy of the surgeries and the knowledge required, but because of the inherent risk— when you're tooling around in someone's *brain*, any number of things could go wrong. Dan has never liked risk. He doesn't drive above the speed limit or water-ski or skydive. (He's only ever even gambled once—on a trip with Jane to Vegas. He made one single bet at Jane's urging, and lost.) He doesn't like having the balance of someone's life hanging in his hands. So he became a podiatrist.

"He's a neurosurgeon," a woman's voice pipes up.

Oh, thank God. Dan's shoulders drop in relief. Until he sees that the woman who spoke is the food instigator (or whatever she called herself; Dan had never heard of that career before) and is gesturing to her husband, Rahul—the guy who was recently hit in the face with the butt of a gun. The man came to shortly thereafter, but is currently still supine; both of them are pressed against the glass wall of windows, his head in her lap, him groaning every few minutes as if to let everyone know he's still alive—and in a lot of pain. He's in no shape to help anyone else.

Dan's eyes next meet those of Brick, who is staring at him. Waiting.

"Was the gunshot in the foot?" Dan tries again.

Brick glances at the guy standing by the kitchen door, who gives his head one sharp shake. "We're wasting time."

"Cut his ties," Brick says to Caden (or Lyle). And the next thing Dan knows, he's being pulled to his feet and escorted to the kitchen.

"No! Wait." He stops moving and glances back at Jane, whose eyes meet his. Hers are filled with terror, and he mistakes it for fear for *his* life, which is to say—*love. See?* he thinks. *There's no way she really wants a divorce.* "I'm not leaving my wife."

Brick brings his gun up an inch in a way that seems to

71

communicate: *Remember who's in charge here?* "Yes," he says. "You are."

TWENTY MINUTES AGO, Dan would have sworn there was nothing more terrifying than someone pointing a gun in your face in the middle of dinner, but turns out it's much scarier when the person holding the gun is also terrified.

Lyle handed Dan off to the man who'd burst into the dining room shouting about needing a doctor. *Kid* was a more apt description, Dan thought, once he was able to drag his gaze from the barrel of the gun pointed at him and to the face of the person holding it. He's young, scrawny, maybe Sissy's age, eighteen, nineteen, his eyes wild, some kind of tribal tattoo crawling up the side of his neck, which does nothing to disabuse Dan of the notion that he *is* wild, unhinged. The kid's hand is shaking, and all it would take is his finger to slip on that trigger and Dan would be obliterated. He's contemplated his death before, of course, but there's a difference between knowing it's inevitable *one day* and staring it down.

There are two other people with guns in the kitchen, matching backpacks strapped to their shoulders, black gaiters covering their faces as well. If they're being worn as an attempt to appear menacing, it's working, Dan thinks. He registers each of them briefly, categorizing them in his mind by one standout feature—one is a woman in a baseball cap, one has wire-rimmed glasses, and one is tribal tattoo kid. Had Dan been thinking clearly, he may have recognized the woman—if not by her face, which is concealed by the hat and mask, then by

JANE AND DAN AT THE END OF THE WORLD

how completely still she went upon seeing him, which is to say he may have recognized her by virtue of her recognizing him. But his gaze has quickly and already moved on, directly to the man on the ground. A chef, it appears, based on the comically tall hat still perched on his scalp—one who was likely responsible for those delectable alien claws Dan has just been consuming—but Dan's brain doesn't make that connection either. His mind is on medicine—physiology, really—as he approaches the injured man.

Dan, his wrists still bound and helpless, drops to a knee, and a dreadlocked man—who appears to be a sous chef since he has the same white coat but does not have a ridiculously tall hat—who is administering aid shifts to make room for him, pulling the blood-soaked towel away. "No, keep it there. Press hard," Dan says, the rusty tang of fresh blood filling his nostrils. He tries to recall the names of the arteries in the shoulder—names he hasn't thought of since studying anatomy his first year of podiatry school. The *subclavian artery* feeds the *brachial artery* as well as the *brachial plexus,* the large nerve bundle that controls arm function. Dan makes eye contact with his patient. He takes in the man's pale face—made paler either by his shock at getting shot or by the loss of blood or both— the brown mole on the man's right cheek, and the tall, conic chef hat still somehow stuck to his head. Dan sees all these details at once without recording any of them, aside from one—the man's eyes are shiny. Alive. Scared, but alive. And that gives Dan hope. He gently removes the man's hat.

"We need to get this jacket off," he says, as if he and the other chef are a team, and then he remembers his own hands are conjoined, rendering him helpless. He lifts his arms, presenting them like an offering to his captor. "My wrist ties?"

The kid (tribal tattoo), still training his gun on Dan, just stares at him.

Nobody moves.

"Cut his ties," Wire-Rimmed Glasses says from behind, with bass in his voice. Dan presumes him to be Brick's counterpoint—the leader in the kitchen, not just by his commanding nature, but by his older presence—not older than Dan, but older than Neck Tat.

"I put all the kitchen knives in the van!" Neck Tat says.

"For the love of . . ." Glasses sighs. "Go get one of them!"

While Neck Tat takes off through the back door, Glasses swings his gun toward Dan, then apparently waffles between whether he should keep it on Dan or the hostages lined up against the wall. To Dan's great relief, he chooses the hostages. Dan turns his attention back to his patient, applying two of his fingers to the right wrist of the head chef until he feels the steady thump-thump of his pulse. *Good.*

"What's your name?" he asks.

"Lars."

Dan nods, pinching a fingernail on Lars's nail bed until it goes white, and then lets it go, watching it quickly turn back to red. *Good.*

"Lars, can you squeeze my hand?"

Lars grimaces as he gently squeezes Dan's fingers. *Good.*

"It hurts."

Neck Tat comes charging back through the door, clutching

a long serrated blade, a knife that—in other circumstances—would be used to slice a baguette. Dan holds up his wrists and the kid saws through the white plastic, freeing him. (Dan isn't sure when men in their twenties began looking like children to him.)

"His, too." Dan nods toward the sous chef, who is now his sous paramedic.

Neck Tat looks elsewhere for confirmation and, when he gets it, slices through the sous chef's wrist ties as well.

"My feet, too?" the man asks hopefully.

But Neck Tat jerks his head *no*.

"C'mon, man."

"Shut it," Neck Tat says, standing up and putting a hand to the gun in his waistband.

Dan glances at the sous chef and sees fire in his eyes. "What's your name?" he asks.

"Zay," the man says, rubbing his wrists.

"OK, Zay," Dan says as he unbuttons Lars's chef coat and tugs it off his unwounded arm. "On the count of three, we're gonna roll him gently on his side. You keep pressing the towel to his shoulder until the last possible second, when I need you to move it so we can get his jacket off." He looks at his patient. "Ready, Lars?"

The man nods, the muscles in his jaw clenching, and Dan and Zay roll him onto his good arm while tugging the jacket off his right side, revealing a white T-shirt underneath. There's no blood on the back of it, no exit wound, so Dan knows the bullet is still lodged in the chef's shoulder.

"OK, let's roll him gently back." When they do so, Lars grunts with pain and blood gushes up out of the small, quarter-inch wound, soaking the T-shirt even further.

"Pressure," Dan says, but Zay's head is turned and he's vomiting, the acrid scent immediately filling Dan's nostrils. He ignores it and takes the towel from Zay's hands, hastily pressing it back over the wound.

He glances up over his shoulder at Glasses.

"Have you called 9-1-1? This man needs an ambulance. A doctor."

"*You're* a doctor."

"I'm a pod—" He stops; it's unimportant. "He needs a doctor in a hospital. He's losing blood."

"No. That's out of the question."

"Do you want him to *die*?"

"Am I going to die?" Panic fills Lars's voice.

Dammit. "Not if we get you to a hospital," Dan says.

The bullet is deep in Lars's shoulder—an impossible place to create a tourniquet—which means there's no way to stop the bleeding, just stem it with pressure. But Dan knows eventually—in as little as one or two hours—the loss of blood will force Lars's pulse to get weaker while his heart will beat faster—a consequence of it working overtime to circulate the smaller volume of blood throughout his body. The color in his nail bed won't bounce back to red as quickly when he presses it. His breathing will become shallow, a panting, as his body tries to conserve the oxygen his brain and other vital organs so desperately need.

Dan wipes his brow, now damp with sweat. "Go get Rock."

"Who?" Glasses says.

"Your leader!"

"You mean Brick? He's not our leader. We're leaderless."

Dan, losing patience, scoffs. "Because that worked out so well for Occupy Wall Street?"

"What's that?" Neck Tat asks.

Dan shakes his head. These Generation Zers. Or are they Ys? They look so young, maybe they've started the alphabet all over again and they're As. Honestly, Dan can't keep up.

"Well, get the guy who's not the leader, then."

"Can't you just clean it with vodka or something?" Glasses says. "Dig the bullet out? That's what they do in the movies."

"This isn't the movies. The bullet is deep in his shoulder. If I try to dig it out I could do more damage. Not to mention, he'd bleed out even faster." Dan holds out his hand to Neck Tat. "Give me the knife."

"You're going to *cut* it out?" Neck Tat asks. His eyes grow wider, filling with an excitement that makes Dan uncomfortable.

"No. I need to cut this shirt off of him and it's too saturated with blood to rip it."

Neck Tat shoves his gun in the back of his pants again, grabs the bread knife from the table behind him, and kneels down with it. Dan lifts the towel to let Neck Tat have access.

"Hurry," Dan says.

Neck Tat works quickly, pulling the wet material away from Lars's skin and ripping it in two with the serrated edge of the knife. Dan presses the towel back to the wound, but it's already soaked with blood and isn't doing much to absorb more.

"I need a fresh towel," Dan says. "And gauze. Is there a first aid kit?"

Zay, now leaning against the fridge, the back of his wrist over his mouth, gestures to the stainless steel rack across the room and says: "On the bottom shelf."

Neck Tat retrieves the small blue plastic box with the red cross on the front and hands it to Dan, who opens it only to find three little squares of gauze that would hardly pack a paper cut, much less a bullet wound. His mind flashes to the home remedy his mom used on his nosebleeds as a kid.

"I need a tampon!"

In the silence, Dan feels most of the heads turn toward the one gun-wielding female he spotted when he walked into the kitchen.

"You think I brought period supplies?" she says.

The familiar voice grabs Dan's attention this time. Holding the kitchen towel firmly to the man's shoulder with his knee, he looks up, peering at the girl. He blinks once, then twice, as though his eyes can't thoroughly be trusted. And then his blood runs cold and hot from the shock of recognition.

"Sissy?"

CHAPTER

7

PULL YOURSELF TOGETHER, JANE.

The second Dan left, the fear that gripped Jane when she heard the gunshots grew exponentially, like a pot of water swelling from a simmer to a rapid boil. They actually shot someone! Which means they'd do it again. And any one of them could be next. If Jane wasn't so terrified, she might question the parallel to her book once more, but for now there are more pressing matters. Dan went toward the gunshots! She's scared for him, of course, but she's also scared for herself without him. It's the same as how she can never sleep by herself anymore—when Dan's gone on a work trip or she's in a hotel room alone. Every little creak of the house settling wakes her and she's sure a robber is seconds away from bursting into her room. When did she become this woman? She used to be independent. Confident. She used to relish sleeping alone.

Codependency, that was what all her self-help books called it, which made Jane laugh. How is it possible to be married to someone for half your life and *not* be codependent? The same way Dan is her arm but not her lungs, he's also a comfort, like a weighted blanket. The weighted blanket can't actually *do* anything—like protect her from a bullet, for instance—but it still feels better to have it on.

And isn't that partly why she needs to leave him? She doesn't remember who she is without Dan. It doesn't help that all those Christian mommy bloggers turned self-help gurus only found themselves *after* getting divorced. Jane's listened to their podcasts. They sound . . . happy. As if divorce was the best thing to ever happen to them.

Or maybe it's realizing you're a lesbian. That one sounds the happiest, to be honest.

Jane's often thought how much easier life would be if she were married to a woman. Especially in the middle of the night when she sits on top of the cold, hard toilet seat that Dan has left down. Or—God help her—every time Dan answers a question with the punch line to his very favorite dad joke for the seven thousandth time: "Very carefully." (As in when Jane seriously inquires something like: *How are you going to grill the steaks for dinner if we're out of charcoal?* and he grins and says: *Very carefully.*)

Anyway, she isn't naive enough to think it's all so easy. Take this pill! Get divorced! Find yourself! But she'd be lying if she said a little part of her didn't hope that it was. (Just like a little part of her hopes that she is secretly a lesbian, even though the only woman she's ever been seriously attracted to is Abby Wambach, and honestly, who *isn't* attracted to her?)

Now blanketless—or Dan-less, to be more accurate—Jane starts to a tremble a bit.

Get it together, she chastises herself once again. She straightens her spine and gives her head a shake, taking stock of her situation. She looks down the line at her fellow diners, who all seem as shell-shocked as she is. But they can't just sit there like lambs for the slaughter. They need to do something! They're being held hostage! They need to . . . call the police! Jane's gaze lands helplessly on the stainless steel bucket of cell phones, not that having hers would help her, since there's no service. She glances wildly around the room, and that's when she spies the camera in the far-right corner of the ceiling. Her breath catches.

She looks left and right to see if any of her fellow diners have noticed, and when it's clear they have not, she dips her head to the person closest to her—Ayanna, the food influencer who's holding her husband's head gently in her lap—and whispers, "There's a security camera up there."

Ayanna blinks slowly, as if in a daze, and Jane uses her eyes to direct Ayanna's gaze to the camera.

Ayanna glances at it and then back at Jane. "And?"

"Maybe someone's monitoring it? We could . . . I don't know, write a note that says *help* or something."

Ayanna raises one brow in the universal way that indicates she thinks Jane's an idiot. It's a look Jane is familiar with because she sees it so often from Sissy. "If someone *is* monitoring it, don't you think it's pretty clear at this point that we could use some help?"

"Oh," Jane says. "Right."

"It's likely closed circuit—surveillance for after-hours security to help prevent break-ins."

"Well, what should we do?" Jane asks. "We can't just sit here."

"What can we do?" Ayanna whispers, holding up her wrists. "You saw what they did to Rahul—" She glances down at her husband, gently putting a hand to his face. He winces. "And now they're shooting people? I vote for sitting here."

"Oy!" Brick shouts, and Jane jumps, jerking her head toward him and bracing for his ire. But he's not looking at her. He's looking at the opening from the dining room to the hallway.

"Where have you been?"

One of the captors, who Jane thinks is named Lyle, pauses under the doorjamb. Jane hadn't even noticed he was gone. "Bathroom," he says. "I had to go."

And like Pavlov's dog, by just hearing the word, Jane realizes she needs to pee. Dan always says she has to go at the most inopportune times, which really means at the times that are most inconvenient for him. She used to apologize for it. Every time they drove somewhere on vacation and she needed to pull over less than an hour into the road trip, or at a concert or show when they were inevitably seated in the middle of a row and she had to ask the surrounding strangers to stand in the middle of the performance so she could shuffle past them, Dan would sigh. *Can you just hold it? No, I can't, Dan*, she'd reply, irritation matching her embarrassment at her body's weakness. But honestly, it's just part of the series of mortifications mothers endure. She's birthed two children, and despite the pelvic-floor therapy and the Kegels, she still pees a little when she sneezes or laughs or coughs.

All of that to say, she thinks Dan may be right this time. Her bladder is fit to burst and it is wildly inconvenient.

"Psst."

Jane looks to her right, directly into the eyes of Javier, her waiter, who, less than thirty minutes ago, was telling Jane to *Let us know if there is anything we can do to make your experience more enjoyable.* Now *that* is ironic. She wishes Dan was here so she could tell him.

"You want to do something?" he whispers.

Jane nods.

"There's a silent alarm in the chef's office right under his desk, down the hallway. It alerts the police. We need to get to it."

Jane feels her heartbeat pick up speed. "Yes, OK! Good, good. How?"

Javier looks helplessly at his bound wrists and feet and then at Jane's and shrugs.

Monica pokes her head over Javier's shoulder and whispers: "What if one of us says we need to use the bathroom—they'll have to let us, right? And maybe we can manage to slip into the office?"

As far as plans go, it's not great. But Jane *does* need to use the bathroom, and she doesn't have a better idea. She looks at Ayanna.

"Don't look at me! I told you, I'm not messing with them."

She looks back at Javier. "I'll do it," she says. She takes a deep breath and opens her mouth. "Excuse me," she squeaks, looking at Brick, who doesn't appear to hear her, as his head remains bent in conversation with Lyle.

"Hey!" Jane shouts.

This time, nearly every head swivels in her direction, including Brick's.

"Yes?" he says in his deep voice.

"I need to . . . use the restroom."

He looks at her, half-curious, half-irritated, as if he hadn't planned for this interruption either. Slowly he nods.

"Anyone else?"

"I do, too," Paisley says, her voice barely audible, and Vaughn immediately raises her cuffed hands as one. "Me, too," she says, even though it's clear to Jane she simply wants to be wherever her daughter is. Who can blame her? It reminds Jane of that children's book she used to read to Sissy and Josh when they were little: *If you run away, I will run after you, for you are my little bunny.* Her heart squeezes.

Brick nods once, as if he's made a decision. "Stand up," he says to Jane, and he watches as she struggles to her feet, her balance off-kilter due to her wrists and ankles being zip-tied together, coupled with her ingrained desire to remain modest and not flash anyone. Finally, she is upright, on two feet. Brick nods to Lyle, who comes over, drops to a knee at her feet, and slices her ankle ties in two.

"Couldn't have done that before I stood up?" Jane mutters.

"Let's go," Brick says, gesturing for her to join Vaughn and Paisley and then walk ahead.

"Brick!" the same pixie-blond woman who mentioned leaving earlier shouts, and Jane stops and turns along with Vaughn, Paisley, and their captor. "What is the *plan* here?"

"I am escorting them to the toilet."

"And after that?"

"We will wait for our guest of honor."

"How long are we going to wait? We've been here nineteen minutes already," she says. "We need to go."

Brick pauses, and the silence is so pure and tension-filled, Jane's reminded of that one time in Vegas, pre-kids, when Dan had too many mai tais and put two hundred dollars they couldn't afford on black at the roulette table and she nearly passed out waiting for the ball to drop. "As long as it takes," he says. "We've come this far."

Shit, Jane thinks. *Red*. Just like in Vegas.

Then he looks dead at Jane and says "Walk," his intonation so deep, she cannot distinguish if it's a flutter of fear she feels in her chest or the vibrato of his voice. Vaughn and Paisley lead, and Jane follows with Brick close behind, through the doorway opposite the kitchen.

The hallway they enter is narrow, dark compared to the light airiness of the dining room, thanks to the black paisley print covering the walls, peppered with an eclectic mix of framed paintings and drawings. At the end of the hallway sits a red landline telephone with a spiral cord and push-button numbers on a narrow, waist-high table. It looks like an art installation. A relic, Jane thinks, even though she had a pink one just like it in her bedroom growing up, and she stares at it desperately. She regrets not using the phone earlier to call Sissy. What if that was her last chance to hear her daughter's voice? Morbidly, she tries to remember the last thing she said to her, to Josh, and thinks it was probably something rote and banal as they both headed out the door into the night, like *Make good choices!*

Doors on either side of the phone stand guard like sentries, each with small matching gold placards declaring: GENDER NEUTRAL. But Jane's gaze falls to the only two other doors in the hallway, to the right of her. They both bear signs that say: EMPLOYEES ONLY.

Which one is the chef's office? Jane panics as they pass the first one, missing her opportunity to open it, even as she's terrified to try. This is her only chance! If she can just get in and remain a step ahead of Brick, she can press the button. She hears Ayanna's voice in her head—*And now they're* shooting *people?*—and tries to tamp it down. As she passes the second door, she takes a deep breath and—her heart beating so hard in her throat it feels like she swallowed a baby bird trying desperately to fly—grasps the knob with her bound hands and tries to turn it, throwing her body into the door at the same time. Neither the knob nor the door budges.

"Oy," Brick shouts. "What are you doing?"

"Sorry," Jane says, straightening her body. "I tripped."

Brick raises his brow at her once again. "Move," he says.

When they reach the phone table and bathroom doors, Jane and Vaughn and Paisley stop and look at one another, not sure what to do next.

"Well, go on," Brick says.

Vaughn holds up her cuffed wrists again to Brick. "A little help?"

Brick looks from Vaughn's bound hands to Jane's as if it's just occurred to him that they are restrained, and then says: "You can help each other."

Jane momentarily forgets her need to pee as it dawns on her that he means for all three of them to pee together.

To her credit, this doesn't seem to faze Vaughn. "Fine," she says, pushing the bathroom door to the right of the phone open with her shoulder, holding it open for Paisley. Jane follows her in and is surprised at how simple the room is: white walls, marble floor, charcoal-slate farmer's sink next to the toilet.

Jane nearly wets herself in relief.

"Go on," Vaughn says to Paisley, and Jane clenches her thigh muscles and her mouth. Of course they need to let the child go first. Though with her pouty lips and abundant cleavage, there isn't much that's childlike left about her.

When Jane hears the familiar sound of urine streaming into the bowl, she clenches her own pelvic floor even tighter. To take her mind off it, she whispers: "That didn't go well."

"What were you doing?"

"Trying to get into the chef's office. There's a silent alarm under the desk."

Vaughn eyes her. "And you thought you could reach it without him noticing?"

At least I was doing something, Jane thinks, but bites back her retort.

When she's finished, Paisley shimmies her pants back up and then steps toward the sink to wash her hands, and Jane wastes no time moving into her place. She knows she should offer that Vaughn go next, but her bladder won't allow her to waste time on pretending to be polite.

She's already anticipating the relief before quickly realizing she can't both hold her dress up and pull down her underwear with hands tied together. She abhors asking for help but sees no other choice.

"Um, can you hold up my dress?"

"Sure, let me just . . ." Vaughn closes the gap between the two women and grasps the back of Jane's dress, looking at the wall to give her privacy.

When Jane is finally seated and her most pressing problem is being solved, she turns her attention to the next. "Should we try something else?" she whispers.

Vaughn jerks her head back toward Jane's, locking eyes with her, and Jane has a flash that this is it—some female synergistic moment like a movie scene—and the two of them are going to come up with a plan to save not only their lives, but the entire restaurant.

"Like what?"

Jane considers this, hoping something—*anything*—will come to her. She imagines barging out of the bathroom, the two of them attempting to overpower Brick, whose name is an apt descriptor for his body—sturdy, strong, impenetrable. It's an absurd image—like two flies trying to pass through a pane of glass. Futile.

"I don't know," Jane admits. She glances around the small bathroom and her eyes light on the long rectangular window above the toilet. It's frosted glass and doesn't appear to have a latch or any way to open it, but Jane thinks if they could break it, perhaps they could squeeze Paisley through it. Vaughn also glances at the window, then pops an eyebrow in skepticism, and without any words, Jane knows they agree it's a fool's errand, and the sliver of hope that they might be able to escape is gone.

"What do you think they want?" Jane whispers.

Vaughn shrugs and sighs. "Otto has nutters threatening him all the time." And then she mutters, more to herself than to Jane: "He's going to kill me for giving security the night off."

"You have a security team?"

Vaughn nods.

"Like the Secret Service?"

"I think that's just for presidents, but yes. Otto doesn't like us to go anywhere without them. But, I mean, I thought this of all places . . ."

"Mom." Paisley's voice cracks behind Vaughn. She's barely talking above a whisper, but it startles them both. They turn to look at her, and Jane sees her face crumple like an accordion. "I'm so sorry."

"Paisley-girl," Vaughn croons. "What for? It's not your fault."

"It is. It is my fault." Tears are streaming down her face and she's working to get the words out.

"What? No. Why do you think that?"

"We're only here for my birthday."

That's what they're doing here? They came to the most expensive restaurant possibly on the whole of the earth, and most definitely the most expensive one Jane has been to in her forty-six years of life, for a *child's* birthday? Jane tries to remember what restaurant they went to for Sissy's last birthday. Maybe P.F. Chang's? It's quite possible they simply ordered pizza.

"You didn't *make* us. We wanted to come here. And your dad wants to be here, too."

At that, Paisley's crying turns into downright sobbing. She's snotting everywhere, unable to get it together. Jane might think it dramatic if she did not also have a teenage daughter who wore her emotions so close to the surface. And, Jane reasons, they are being held hostage by gun-wielding bad guys, so maybe it's the exact right emotional reaction to have. Maybe Jane is the one who's behaving peculiarly.

Vaughn, as though reading Jane's mind, says: "It's been a week. She just broke up with her boyfriend."

"We didn't break up," Paisley says. "He *ghosted* me."

Vaughn looks at Jane and shrugs. Jane tries to approximate a look of empathy in return.

As Jane is finishing up, Vaughn—still holding the hem of Jane's dress up so it doesn't slip into the bowl—accidentally brushes Jane's arm with her own, and the cool, sleek feel of Vaughn's blouse on her skin reminds Jane of the question she had earlier. "What's mulberry silk?" she asks as she stands upright.

If she's surprised by this turn in questioning, Vaughn doesn't show it. Without missing a beat, she says: "It's silk made from the larvae cocoons of the *Bombyx mori* moth, which are grown in captivity in China and fed a diet exclusively of *Morus alba* leaves—Latin for 'white mulberry.'"

Jane lets out a sharp "Ha!" She didn't expect Vaughn to be funny. It reminds her of those memes spoofing Ina Garten: *If you can't get butter infused with the tears of Dutch milkmaids, any good quality sweet cream butter will do.*

She looks at Vaughn's face and realizes she isn't laughing with her. "Oh my God," she puffs. "You're serious."

"Yes. It's the highest-quality silk in the world."

This only sets Jane off harder. In high-stress situations, Jane often has trouble regulating her emotions—or expressing the appropriate one. Or, to be more accurate, her entire body is racked with fear disguised as laughter. Vaughn stares at her with a stern curiosity.

The door rattles from a fist banging on it, and Paisley lets out a small scream. "Hey," Brick intones through the door. "Time's up."

Still trying to control her waves of giggles, Jane hurriedly scrubs her hands at the sink. She dries them on a fresh hand towel, and then Vaughn opens the door and they reenter the hallway single file and stand in front of Brick, Vaughn standing protectively close to her still-shaken daughter, waiting to be told they can return to the dining room.

But Brick doesn't move. "Call him," he says, nodding to the phone.

"Otto?" Vaughn asks, as if there could be another *him* Brick would want her to call.

"Yes."

"What do you want me to say?"

"We're going to make sure he's coming."

"But he *is* coming. He said he was, so he will."

Brick pauses, studying her. And then: "Find out when."

"OK." Vaughn lifts the receiver on the phone with both hands, cradling it between her ear and shoulder, and hesitates a moment before deliberately pressing a succession of numbers with her right pointer finger, her left hand just along for the ride. Though Brick is staring at the keypad, Jane hopes Vaughn is secretly calling the cops, or her security team. Jane can hear the faint ringing, and they all wait for Otto to pick up.

"He doesn't know this number, he's not going to—"

A voice comes through the line and Jane leans forward without knowing it. Brick does the same.

"It's his voicemail."

"Leave a message," Brick growls. "Tell him it's an emergency." He says this as if that would be a lie and Jane nearly laughs again. Since when is being held at gunpoint *not* an emergency?

"Hey, it's me," Vaughn says, light at first, but Jane can detect the tremble in her voice. "Please call me back at this number. At the restaurant." She pauses, glancing at Brick, and then adds: "It's an *emergency*."

CHAPTER

8

DAN'S HEAD GOES LIGHT, AND IN HIS CROUCHED position, he rocks back on his heels, sitting down hard on his bottom.

"You OK, man?" Zay asks.

Dan is absolutely not OK, but he can't find the words or the breath with which to respond. His thoughts are a tangled jumble and he can't take his eyes off his daughter. His daughter, Sissy. Who is supposed to be at a friend's house watching some show—isn't that what Jane said?—and making up dances on TikTok or whatever it is they do, yet is somehow standing across the room from him, wearing a black gaiter across her nose and mouth and a baseball cap on her head and holding a *gun*, which, if he had to rate the level of astonishment for each revelation, might be the most shocking piece of information of all. The image is so absurd, in fact—like a chicken wearing pants or those AI-generated pictures that give humans four hands instead of two—he thinks he must be hallucinating.

"Wait, who's Sissy?" Glasses says. "Goldie, you know this dude?"

Her eyes, locked with Dan's, go wide, and she gives her head a small, nearly imperceptible shake.

Why are you calling her Goldie? Dan wants to shout. Sissy's real name is Sarah, but when Josh was born, Jane jokingly started calling her Sissy, making fun of how obnoxious it was when other families did that—and it stuck, and they became the obnoxious family. Sissy's friends have given her their own various nicknames over the years—Brooksy (for her last name), S.B., and Rah-rah, for starters—but Dan is certain that *Goldie* is not one of them. She doesn't even have blond hair!

"Of course not," Sissy says, breaking her gaze with Dan and looking at Glasses pointedly, but Dan can hear the tremble in her voice. "I must look like someone he knows."

Dan wants to object: *Sissy, it's* me! *Your* dad!

He wants to shout:

What is happening?

Are you OK?

WHY DO YOU HAVE A GUN?

But the way she's staring at him now, it reminds him of when she was three or four and had those night terrors. Dan and Jane would go running into her room, and her eyes would be wide open, her body stiff as a board, the most awful screams emanating from her mouth. Dan would turn on the light, stand her straight up, holding her tight. "You're not supposed to startle her!" Jane shouted the first time, no doubt having read about night terrors in one of her many parenting books. But Dan didn't know what was happening; he knew only that he

94

needed it to stop immediately, and it worked. She always woke up, confused as to why her parents were there, why the light was on, why she was standing up and not sleeping in her bed.

He feels the same way now. Confused. Maybe he's the one having a night terror.

But Sissy's the one who looks scared, and it occurs to him that she must not be here of her own free will. Obviously. He nearly laughs with relief. She would never choose to do this. She makes straight As. She's in the National Honor Society. She got accepted to Stanford, for Chrissake. She didn't even cut school on Senior Skip Day. They—whoever *they* are—are *making* her do this. She hates guns. She abhors violence of all kinds! She once cried at a National Geographic special when a cheetah caught a rabbit for dinner. He remembers her tear-stained baby-fat cheeks, her hair in two braids. Her sticky fingers squeezing Dan's. Dan knows it was years ago, but it feels like only months. How do they grow so quickly? One day they have trouble pronouncing spaghetti (*pasketti!*) and they grasp one of your fingers with their entire chubby hand as they cross the street, the next they're holding you hostage—at *gunpoint*—in a restaurant.

Dan looks at his daughter again, wanting to let her know he understands she is being made to do this against her will, that he will help her out of this, but she's purposefully not meeting his gaze.

The kitchen door swings open and the woman with the blond crew cut walks in. She scans the room, her eyes landing on Dan and the supine head chef.

"Isaac, what the fuck?" she says, addressing Neck Tat.

"I didn't mean to!" Neck Tat, whose name is apparently Isaac, says.

The crew-cut woman just glares at him.

"Did Brick do it?" Glasses asks Crewcut as she walks toward Dan, favoring her left leg. "Are we done?"

Crewcut gives her head a firm shake. "Otto's not here."

"What do you mean he's not here?"

"He's not here. Wife and daughter are alone."

"But the girl said he'd be here."

"Brick's taking care of it."

"Taking care of it how?" Sissy pipes up. "If he's not here, what are we still doing here?" Eyes wide, Dan swivels his head to his daughter and the way she said *we*, like she is a *part* of this group. Voluntarily. And not being held against her will. *Is she on* drugs? he wonders now. He's never felt so bewildered staring at his daughter—counting the time he took her to see Taylor Swift at SoFi and she screamed so hard and for so long, he thought she was having some kind of manic episode and worried for her health.

"He's taking care of it," Crewcut says, louder.

Glasses nods, as if this is enough for him, and then he notices Crewcut's slight limp. "Are you *bleeding*?"

"Oh. Yeah. Some Bruce Willis wannabe stuck me with a fork."

"Ouch."

The woman nods. "Glad he didn't have a steak knife."

Dan, tuning back in to this exchange, has a thousand questions on the tip of his tongue, but the woman comes to a stop in front of him and asks her question first.

"How's he holding up?"

In a fog, Dan takes a beat to realize she's speaking to him. He blinks and then turns to the patient in question, looking to where Zay has dutifully been holding a fresh towel to the chef's—*Lars's*—shoulder. Dan gently takes over and pulls the towel back from the wound, expecting another small gush of blood, but nothing comes out.

"Huh. Well, that's weird." He checks Lars's nail bed again. The color is still good and Lars is surprisingly alert.

"What?" the woman asks.

"What?" the chef repeats, except the word is decidedly louder and more panicked coming from him.

"The bleeding has slowed significantly," Dan says.

"That's a good thing, right?" the woman says.

"Yeah, I mean . . . the bullet obviously missed the subclavian artery," Dan muses, mostly to himself. "Or he'd be dead by now. Those things bleed out in a matter of minutes."

"*Minutes?*" Lars says.

"I wonder if the bullet is somehow stemming the blood flow," Dan continues. Granted, he doesn't have a lot of experience with gunshot wounds. In podiatry school, he did one rotation in the ER, and the first night, after he nearly passed out tending a man who lost half his face to the gravel in a motorcycle accident, and an angelic child of a patient projectile-vomited the pot roast she'd eaten for dinner on him, he knew trauma (or pot roast) was not for him. He also had been around enough ER doctors to know that inexplicable medical miracles happened all the time—a bullet that stops mere millimeters from the heart, a man with a traumatic brain injury waking from a coma and walking out of the hospital mere days after doctors assured the family they'd likely be planning his funeral. Maybe Dan is witnessing his own medical miracle.

"So he's going to be OK."

"Well, the bleeding seems to be under control, which is good, but he still needs medical attention. If you wait too long, infection can take hold. And it's hard to say what's happening internally without an X-ray." He waves in the vicinity of Lars's shoulder. "If the bullet's lodged in the brachial plexus—"

"English, please."

"He could lose the use of his arm and/or hand."

"My hand!" Lars shrieks. "I can't lose my hand. How am I supposed to cook?"

"That's worst-case scenario," Dan says, hoping to reassure him, and then realizes his error. "Well, *dying* is worst-case scenario, I suppose."

"God dammit, man!" the chef shouts, looking at Isaac. "My shoulder? *Really?*"

Dan looks from the chef to Isaac. He thinks it's bold of the chef to yell at the man (well, kid) who shot him. The same kid who still has a gun trained on both of them. But then again, Dan has never been shot, and from the looks of it, it's quite painful. Lars probably isn't completely in his right mind.

"It was an accident." Isaac repeats his earlier denial, but Dan doesn't see an ounce of regret in his face. In fact, from the way he's glaring at Lars, if Isaac could do it all over again, it looks as though he would.

"OK, I'll let Brick know."

I thought you were leaderless, Dan wants to say, but he manages to hold in his snide comment.

"You. Stay with him," Crewcut says to Dan. "Let me know immediately if there are any changes."

"I will," Dan says, and is comforted by the concern in her voice. She clearly doesn't want the chef to die. Dan's reminded of what Jane said: *I don't think they want to hurt us.* And— aside from Isaac, whose wild eyes make him look like he not only wants to hurt somebody but would *enjoy* it—Dan thinks she might be right. Much to Dan's consternation, Jane often is—with the exception of when her anxiety gets the best of her.

Like the time she was worried about Sissy going to public high school because she might join a gang.

"A gang?" he said to Jane back then, laughing. "Like the Bloods and the Crips?"

"It's not funny, Dan! Being a teen is completely different now than when we were kids."

"OK. But seriously, this is Sissy we're taking about. And secondly, we live in the suburbs."

"Dan, do you even read the news? They arrested six teens at the mall last week for stealing sneakers at knifepoint."

"Really? Well, those Converse she wears couldn't have cost more than forty-five dollars, so I don't think she's going to be in any danger there."

"Dan."

"Look, there are plenty of things to worry about in high school," he conceded. "But Sissy being in a gang is not one of them."

Dan's eyes go wide as he takes in his daughter once more. In a *gang*. He swallows. He really does hate it that Jane is always right.

9

BRRRR-IIIIIING!

The piercing trill of the telephone nearly makes Jane come out of her skin. Even though they'd all been standing there with the sole expectation of it ringing, it's been at least ten minutes, which was just long enough to be lulled into the sense that perhaps Otto wasn't going to call back at all. Vaughn certainly was convinced he wouldn't. "He's in a meeting near San Francisco," she had said to Brick as they waited, her voice shaking. "He's not going to check his messages."

Does anyone? Jane thought. She couldn't remember the last time she'd actually checked her voicemail.

"He will call," Brick said, confident, as though he knew Vaughn's husband better than she did.

For the next few minutes, Jane had waffled. She had so many questions, and though she typically had no problem speaking up, she had never found herself in quite so intimidating a situation. And while Brick's demeanor seemed genial in the dining room, his mood had definitely shifted to a more serious tone.

More intense. Who knew what would set him off? She dug deep for courage and finally uttered her one pertinent question out loud—albeit in a very tiny, timid voice: "Why Otto?" She cleared her throat in an attempt to free the shake from it.

Brick leaned against the wall, his gun resting on his chest, the barrel pointed up toward the ceiling, and she fully expected him to ignore her. She wasn't even quite sure she'd said her question out loud until he cut his eyes to her and said: "He's a billionaire."

Something clicked in her brain: the most recent thing Otto had been in the news for, aside from the electric auto-piloted helicopter fiasco and the Ottobyte cryptocurrency—something about pledging to make his company carbon-neutral by a certain date. "Yeah, but . . . isn't he one of the good ones?"

Brick barked one loud "Ha!" His lips curled into a genuine smile. "That's the problem, isn't it?"

"What is?"

"That you think any of them are good."

"Oh," Jane breathed. She offered an apologetic glance to Vaughn and Paisley, as if *she* had insulted their husband and father. She half expected them to jump to his defense, but Vaughn just scowled and Paisley continued looking—understandably—fearful.

Jane wasn't sure what to say next, but she wanted to keep him talking. Isn't that what people who are kidnapped or held hostage are supposed to do? Attempt to befriend their captor? Make them see you as a fellow human, so they are less likely to hurt you.

"I have children," she blurted out.

"I'm so happy for you," he said. If she didn't know any better, she'd think he was teasing her.

"I'm just saying—can't you let the rest of us go? We're innocent." It wasn't until the words left her mouth that she realized she was parroting her own hostages in her book.

"I could," he said. "But then only one of us would get what we wanted."

Jane cocked her head as the words struck her. Narrowed her eyes. It made sense for *her* to echo her book. She'd written it. It did not make sense that Brick's response was the exact same line the captor in her book gave. This time word for word. She remembered writing that line specifically, because she thought it was so clever.

She could tell Brick thought it was clever, too, the way he was grinning.

There were only two possibilities she could think of: 1) Her line wasn't really as unique and clever as she thought, if Brick had thought of it, too. 2) Brick was somehow one of the three hundred people in the world who had actually read her book, and the lines had wormed their way into his subconscious memory (which is honestly the basis of her greatest fear when writing—that a line she has read has stuck in her brain and she will plagiarize it without even knowing she's plagiarized).

She opened her mouth to speak. Closed it. Opened it again. "Do you read often?"

It was his turn to tilt his head at her, and she could tell the question genuinely caught him off guard. He frowned and then straightened his back. "Enough talking," he said gruffly.

Now Brick stares at the ringing phone, a college boy playing a mind game with a girl he likes. Or maybe he just wants the time to bask in the fact that he was right when he said with such confidence that Otto would return the call. On the fourth ring, Brick lifts the receiver.

"Hello," he says. And then his face changes, confused at first before slowly morphing into anger. He slams the receiver onto its base, triggering a faint ringing sound to echo in Jane's ears.

"What happened? What did he say?" Vaughn asks.

"Nothing," Brick says. "Wrong number. Let's go." He takes off down the hall. Jane and Vaughn look at each other and then take off after him, Paisley trailing. When he enters the dining room, he starts barking orders.

"Bring me the cell phones!" he says. "Tink, the booster."

As Lyle rushes over with the silver ice bucket, Jane scans the wall of hostages for Dan. He must still be in the kitchen. She locks eyes with Javier and his brows raise in question. Jane gives her head a quick shake.

Brick takes the bucket and shoves it toward Vaughn. "Find yours," he instructs. Jane's eyes widen—she can see her cell phone! It's at the top of the bucket and is now just a foot or two from her hands.

The woman with the blond G.I. Jane haircut, whose name is apparently Tink, walks over to the table Brick is standing near and rapid-fires questions at Brick.

—"What do you need the booster for?"

—"Is Otto coming?"

He turns to look at her, and Jane seizes the moment, inching closer to Vaughn. Her cell phone is right *there*. At the top.

"Brick, what's the plan here? I don't think it's safe to stay for too much longer," Tink says, and though Brick ignored the first two questions, at this third one, he replies: "Then leave."

Tink stares back at him defiantly for a beat and then takes her book bag off and slings it onto the table. As she unzips it, she continues talking, low. Her voice is even more muffled by her gaiter. Jane leans in to hear. "We've got a problem. The chef? He needs a doctor. A real doctor. In a hospital."

Without thinking of the consequences, Jane shoves her hand in the bucket and grabs her phone. Vaughn eyes her but doesn't say anything.

The relief Jane feels when she palms her cell phone is brief—overtaken by sheer panic when she realizes she has nowhere to put it. God, why doesn't every dress come with pockets? She stares at the back of Brick's head and considers dropping her phone back in the bucket before she gets caught, but at the last second slips it down the neck of her dress and into her bra, where she hopes the hard angles don't protrude in too suspect a manner. Her heart is thudding against her rib cage so hard, she's worried it's more noticeable than the outline of the phone.

Jane takes a deep breath to steady herself. She has her cell phone. Now to figure out how to use it without getting caught.

"Where is the bullet wound?"

"Shoulder. The bleeding has slowed, but the doctor guy said he could lose the use of his arm."

Jane realizes the *doctor guy* is Dan.

"Dammit," Brick says, and while the concern seems genuine, Jane wonders if he's concerned about the chef or if he's just annoyed about another unexpected kink in his plans.

104

Vaughn, holding a phone up in her hand, says: "This one's mine."

Brick cuts his eyes to her as if he almost forgot she was there. Then he grabs the booster Tink produced from the innards of her book bag. He plugs it into the nearest wall outlet.

After about thirty seconds, the ice bucket full of cell phones starts dinging and buzzing, coming alive with text messages and notifications that have been missed since the customers set foot on the property.

Jane feels hers buzz against her breast and tenses, her face turning red, sure Brick is going to notice any second that her chest is vibrating, but he doesn't even look at her. Relieved, she longs to fish her phone out and see whom her messages are from. What if Sissy tried to call? Or Josh. She misses her kids with the intensity of a parent who thinks they might never see them again. Why did she have to fight with Sissy this evening? Why does every conversation of theirs turn into a fight? Jane swears to herself if she gets out of this, she'll be more patient with Sissy. With both of her children. More present.

"Now," Brick says, nodding to the phone in Vaughn's hand. "Call him."

"What do you want me to say?"

"Find out when he plans to arrive," he says. "And make sure he's flying his helicopter."

"Of course he is. Driving would take too long."

"Make sure," Brick growls, and then adds: "And act normal— no funny business, understood?"

Vaughn's face goes steely. "Or what?" she says. Jane's eyebrows pop in surprise, and she notices Vaughn's do a little, too, as if she is also surprised by her words. Jane glances at Brick, who closes his eyes and sighs loudly. When he opens his eyes, Jane can see the actual shift in his countenance. With one hand, he takes Paisley's arm and pulls her off her mother. "No!" Vaughn shouts, trying to keep hold of her daughter's arm, but Brick's strength wins out.

He holds the girl tight to his chest in the crook of his right arm and moves the barrel of his gun toward her face until it's scraping her cheek.

Jane yelps, but the sound is overtaken by Vaughn's own.

Jane doesn't blame her. One slip of Brick's finger and Vaughn's child will die right before her eyes. Jane wishes she could do something. Intervene. She feels helpless. And nearly as terrified at the prospect of seeing Paisley's brain matter spray out of her head as she's sure Vaughn is.

Paisley whimpers.

"Or you will regret it," Brick says. "Understood?"

Vaughn nods weakly. She holds up her phone and, fingers shaking, scrolls through the screen until she gets to "OTTO CELL." With her thumb, she presses his name and then puts the phone up to her ear. The room is so quiet, Jane can hear the ringing emanating from the earpiece of Vaughn's phone and then the tinny voice of a man answering.

"Otto!" Vaughn says, her voice cheerily fake. "Is your meeting through?"

She listens, her eyes growing wide. "Oh! Right, yes, the emergency." She chuckles, staring at Brick. "Hold on one second, darling."

She covers the receiver with her hand and hisses. "He listened to his messages. He wants to know what the emergency is."

Brick stares at her. "I thought you said he never listened to his voicemail."

"He doesn't! What do I say?"

Brick blinks, seeming unsure of himself for the first time in the evening.

"Tell him there was an accident," Jane says. They both swivel their heads and look at her. Her mind races as she does the one thing she's always been good at: making up a story. "A car accident on the road that leads up here. Oh! And that's why he has to fly his helicopter. The road's blocked with emergency vehicles."

If Brick is surprised at Jane's outburst, he doesn't show it. He stares at her for a beat and then nods deeply. He shifts his gaze to Vaughn. "Tell him that."

Vaughn puts the phone back to her ear. "Sorry, the waiter was . . . asking me a question. Yes, everything's fine, but there was apparently a fender bender—" Jane shakes her head and mouths *Worse*. "A terrible car accident," Vaughn amends, raising her eyebrows at Jane, and Jane nods encouragingly. "On the road leading up here, and I just wanted to make sure you were coming in your helicopter and not driving."

She pauses as Otto speaks. "Yes, so sorry to alarm you. We're fine. How long until you think you'll be here?" *Pause.* "Ninety minutes?" She raises her brow at Brick this time, and he presses his lips into a firm line. "OK, well, do hurry up if you can; we'll hold dessert for you."

She hangs up and immediately says: "I did it. Let her go."

"Phone back in the bucket," Brick says. Vaughn tosses her cell on top of the others, and Brick releases Paisley, who collapses into her mother's arms.

Jane lets out a breath as if it was her own daughter being held at gunpoint. She lets up a silent prayer of gratitude that at least her kids are safe.

"Unplug the booster," Brick says to Tink. "And tie them back up."

Dammit, Jane thinks, eyeing the device. She needs it to stay plugged in if she has any hope of using her phone, but Tink yanks the plug with force and then hisses through her teeth. "Brick, what are you doing? This isn't what we agreed on. We don't have time for him to *fly* here. We're all going to get caught."

"Then we get caught."

"*What?*"

Division in the ranks, Jane thinks as Lyle comes over to lead the three of them back to the wall. This should excite Jane. If this were a novel, it would represent her opportunity, an opening, to somehow get free. But this is real life, and it only scares her further. Things are not going according to plan, which means people are getting desperate. Or, more specifically, Brick seems desperate. And she's no expert, but she thinks it best when people who are holding guns do *not* feel desperate.

"We came here for a purpose," he says. "You are either in this or you are not in this. What good is it to be halfway committed? Who wants to leave?" Brick bellows to the room as loud as a lion's roar. "You want to go?"

Ever the good girl, Jane urgently wants to raise her hand, as if it could be that easy. *I would like to leave, please, sir! I would no longer like to be a hostage, thank you.*

But, of course, Brick is talking to his fellow gun-wielding gang members.

"Otto is on his way here. I am waiting for him. You do not have to stay. You can go back to your meaningless lives, waiting until it is the right time to do something, waiting until everything goes perfectly according to plan, or you can do what we came here to do. So tell me now: Do you want to leave?"

Jane has to admit: it's a rousing speech. Not the words, necessarily, but the conviction with which he says them. Brick waits, boring his gaze into one captor and then the next, daring them to speak up, to move, to leave. No one does.

"Bring the others in here! I want everyone in one room where we can see them."

"Even the chef? I don't know if we should move—"

"ALL OF THEM," Brick thunders.

Lyle leads Jane and Vaughn and Paisley back to the wall to sit down, this time together, which Jane is somehow comforted by, and she supposes it's only natural that she should feel a bond with the women, even if the bond is through experiencing the same paralyzing fear together.

As Lyle re-zip-ties Jane's ankles, Jane notices her own body is trembling and wonders how long it's been doing so. Her teeth start chattering, the molars clacking together like one of those dental windup toys, and she knows it's her body's reaction to not only the fear of seeing Brick put a gun to a child's temple, but the exhaustion of the countless conflicting emotions she's experienced in such a short amount of time.

Lyle looks at her. "I'll see if I can find some blankets," he says—not kindly, but not unkindly either. Jane's impressed that someone so young—he can't be more than nineteen—would be so caring. She starts to tell him she's not cold, but then she thinks a blanket would be nice, and why would the underlying reason matter at all?

"I have to go to the bathroom," Javier says from his place, now many people down from Jane. They catch eyes, and Jane wants to tell him the door is locked, but maybe she just tried the wrong one. Maybe Javier will have better luck.

Lyle looks around and his gaze falls on Caden. "Caden—take him to the bathroom." Caden nods and hops down from his perch.

"Could we get some ice?" a voice emerges from down the line. It's Ayanna, her voice as soft as the carefully pressed shiny black waves in her hair. "In a plastic bag? He has a real knot on his head."

Lyle nods and stands, then he looks at Jane once more, his eyes dropping to her breast—where her cell phone is. Everything stops—her heartbeat, her breath; her mind goes blank, and then Lyle's eyes meet hers again. His left eye winks and he turns toward the kitchen. Jane stares after him. Wait, did he really just *wink* at her? Or no, he must have had something in his eye. Or it was a trick of the light. Jane leans her head back on the glass.

Maybe she really is cracking up.

It wouldn't be the first time.

CHAPTER

10

THE FIRST TIME INVOLVED A CHRISTMAS TREE farm.

"A Christmas tree farm," Dan repeated when Jane presented him with the idea. She had seen it on Instagram that morning in the three minutes she had to herself on the toilet. A picture-perfect farm in Vermont that looked like it was the movie set for every Hallmark holiday film ever created, and the couple who owned it wanted to retire and sell the entire operation, including their gorgeous six-bedroom Georgian farmhouse built in the 1800s, for the bargain price of $1.2 million.

"Yes! We can sell our house and—well, we'll have to take out a business loan, but can't you just envision it? The kids can have a hot chocolate stand—"

"Josh isn't even walking yet."

"In the future! And we'll give horse-drawn sleigh rides and have bonfires with s'mores and—"

"Jane, be serious," Dan said. "We don't know anything about farming. Or . . . horses."

"We can learn!"

"OK," Dan said, but it was placating, not an invitation for further consideration of the idea. "Should we get pizza for dinner, or Thai?"

So Jane didn't mention it to Dan again—but she didn't put it out of her mind. She couldn't. When Sissy was at preschool and Josh was napping, she was glued to the Internet for hours, staring at the listing for the farm, visualizing herself kneading dough on the butcher block island (never mind that she had never baked bread before and had no idea how). And then the fantasies started to bleed over into when she was *with* the kids—changing diapers and making bottles and filling sippy cups and having arguments with a three-year-old over the wrong-color spoon that often ended in tantrums that Jane felt ill-equipped to handle, she would find herself drifting off, her mind on the Christmas tree farm. She wasn't so naive to think that all those parenting trials wouldn't also exist at the farmhouse, but they seemed more manageable for some reason in an ideal setting, instead of her and Dan's cramped two-bedroom starter home, the only place they could afford on Dan's salary, every closet and cabinet overflowing with little-kid detritus.

She knew it was unhinged, obsessing over a farmhouse she couldn't afford in a state she had never been to, but sometimes she also felt like it was the only thing keeping her afloat. She didn't know how to explain it, but she couldn't remember who she was before she was a mother. She'd had a job once—one at a marketing firm that she was competent at but didn't love—and she and Dan decided she should quit after Josh was born, when they realized her entire paycheck would simply be turned over for day care. She didn't miss working, necessarily, as much as she missed having an identity outside of being a caretaker for two very demanding children. And maybe the Christmas tree farm was a new identity she was trying on for size.

One afternoon when Josh was sleeping and Sissy was enthralled in an episode of *Little Einsteins*, Jane called the number on the listing and spoke to the real estate agent in quiet tones, asking serious and important-sounding questions: *How old is the roof? How much do the monthly utilities cost? What are the schools like in the area? How much income do the Christmas trees bring in?* She dutifully recorded the answers in a notebook that she'd later slip in her bedside drawer like a keepsake or a middle school diary. *Would you like to make an appointment to come look at it?* the real estate agent asked. *I would*, Jane said, which wasn't a lie. *I'll look at my schedule and call you back*, she said, which was.

And though she knew logically they would never buy the farm, that it didn't make sense financially or otherwise, and therefore never once brought it up again with Dan, irrationally, she started to resent him. When she lay in bed at night, staring at the ceiling and four walls of their cramped bedroom that seemed to be pressing in on her, going over the mental checklist of the day ahead—was the green T-shirt for Sissy clean for Earth Day?; they were out of cheese sticks and running low on Goldfish; she'd forgotten to call the insurance company for the fourth time; the Subaru needed an oil change;

was the mole on her left breast getting bigger or was it her imagination?—she would stare at Dan snoring beside her and feel like she was in somebody else's bed, living someone else's life. Her life—her *real* life—was out there, waiting for her. Maybe on a Christmas tree farm, maybe somewhere else altogether, and she was desperate to go find it.

THE KITCHEN DOOR swings open, jolting Jane out of her thoughts, and a young man in glasses, army green pants, and a black tank top, clutching a gun, walks through first. He holds the door open and a man in a chef's coat comes through next, shuffling backward as he carries the end of a white tablecloth that's been turned into a sling or a hammock for a supine body. Jane's eyes widen, wondering if it's a *dead* body, until she sees its face—very much alive and grimacing. Dan is holding the other end of the tablecloth at the man's head and shouting commands: *Careful. Watch the door. Don't jostle him.* He looks tired, and his hands and his white shirt are covered in dried blood.

Paisley gasps beside her, and Jane says "It's not his blood" before she realizes it's likely not Dan the girl is concerned about. Regardless, it comforts Jane to have said it out loud.

She doesn't remember Dan taking off his jacket, but makes a note to herself to find it and retrieve it before they leave, as if they are merely at a work holiday party and don't want to leave anything behind. His captor leads Dan and the chef to the far wall, away from Jane, and she finds that she's disappointed. Not only because she was worried about him and wants him by her side (She needs her arm back! Her weighted blanket!), but because she also wants to tell him what's happened, fill him in on what he's missed, like they used to do routinely in the evenings after a day apart—back in the beginning, when things were good.

She would tell him about peeing with Vaughn and Paisley. About the mulberry silk and how she laughed so hard she thought perhaps she was having a nervous breakdown. She would tell him about Brick holding the gun to Paisley's head and how terrifying it was. The girl could have *died*! Right in front of Jane's eyes.

Though she's staring at Dan as she thinks about all these things she would tell him, it takes her a minute to realize he's trying to tell her something. He's sitting beside where the chef lies against the wall, and he's staring at her intently; his mouth is moving up and down, repeating the same unintelligible phrase over and over, while he keeps nodding his head to where the men with guns who had been in the kitchen are now conferring with Tink and Brick.

Jane can't make out what he's saying, but he looks absolutely unhinged and she wonders if it's something to do with the chef. She frowns. The chef's skin is quite pale.

What? she mouths back. And that's when she notices the proximity of the cell booster to Dan. It's on the table closest to him, not more than five feet away. And though it would be risky for him to move, to close the gap, grab the cord, and plug it in at the wall, it wouldn't be impossible. And then Jane remembers the noise of all the phones coming to life, which would certainly alert their captors. Still, maybe she'd have time

115

to dial 9-1-1 before they unplugged it again. But who knows what the consequence to Dan would be?

As her mind buzzes with the risks versus benefits, the pointy end of an elbow connects with Jane's stomach, and she thinks it's an accident until she looks to the left at her fellow diner and finds Vaughn staring directly back at her. "Do you still have the phone?" she whispers.

"Yes," Jane says, ever aware of the weight of it against her breast.

"I need to text Otto."

"OK," Jane whispers back, though if she got the phone to work, the first thing she'd do would be call the police. "I need to figure out how to get the booster turned back on."

"What about the Wi-Fi?"

"What Wi-Fi?" Jane's eyes dart around the room again as they speak, ever vigilant of their captors. It reminds her of elementary school—the heightened anxiety of passing notes to her friends without getting caught by the teacher, but with obviously more catastrophic consequences.

"This place must have Wi-Fi, so they can run credit card charges and the employees can use their cell phones."

"Oh," Jane says. She hadn't thought of that, mostly because she doesn't really understand technology at all. She relies on Sissy and Josh to help her with even basic tasks, like setting up her iPhone when she finally bought one six years ago. "How do I get on it?"

Vaughn stares at her a beat, and Jane braces for the judgment at her technological ineptitude, but Vaughn simply whispers: "Go to settings? Wi-Fi? And click on the one for the restaurant."

"OK," Jane says. She tries to swallow, but finds her mouth is too dry. "Keep a lookout." She glances up first, making sure no one is looking at her—and they're not. Brick is at a table, deep in conversation with Tink. They've all shed their backpacks, which now sit in a heap in the middle of the floor.

The few guys who had just been in conversation with Brick are—to Jane's surprise—nowhere to be found, and she wonders if they went into the kitchen to get food. Her stomach growls, and she presses her hand to it, slightly embarrassed, as though she shouldn't be thinking of eating at a time like this. But they hardly got to eat anything before their meal was so rudely interrupted.

Even though no one is paying any attention to her, her underarms dampen and her heartbeat revs as she awkwardly reaches into the top of her dress with her bound hands and grasps her phone, quickly pulling it out and holding it down at her side between her and Vaughn. She enters her passcode and maneuvers her way through the steps with her thumb. Aha! She sees the network pop up: LaFinduMondeNet. She clicks it, and Vaughn says "You might need the password," at the same time Jane's screen says "Enter Password."

"Shit," Jane says. "How do I get that?"

"The people on staff should have it," Vaughn whispers. She nods at Monica, tied up at the far end of the row. Javier hasn't returned from the bathroom, and Jane hopes he's somehow been able to trip the alarm and trying to get cell service to her phone will be moot. Before Jane can ask her to do it, Vaughn turns and whispers to the woman to her left, and Jane watches as each hostage sends the message down the row, like a game of telephone. She's hopeful this yields better results.

While she waits, she pulls her knees up to her chest and nestles the phone between her thighs to block the view of it from others—even though it means her underwear is likely on display. She quickly maneuvers with her thumb to the text screen and decides to punch out a text to 9-1-1 so it's ready when she gets the password.

> Help! In La Fin du Monde. Man has been shot. We are being held hostage by men with guns. Send help!

She stops. Reads it over. Considers. Technically it's not just men. Should she change it to *people*, maybe? Also, she said *help* twice, which is redundant.

She shakes her head. Occupational hazard. Now's not the time for edits. It's succinct and gets the point across. But . . . do they need to know who she is?

She types: This is Jane Brooks.

Deletes it.

Types it again.

She presses send, even though there's no service, and waits, glancing nervously around the room again, making sure no one is looking at her, but this time, someone is. Brick's gaze locks on hers and he tilts his head curiously.

Shit. Shit, shit, shit. She blinks and casually continues her gaze around the room, hoping that it wasn't plainly obvious what she was doing, and knowing she looks guilty as sin. Her stomach in her throat, she waits for him to approach her, to find the phone, and then . . . what? She can only imagine how angry he'll be, what he'll do. She closes her eyes and swallows, tries to slow her breathing. When she opens them, she expects Brick to be hovering over her, but his gaze has moved down the row of hostages.

"Oy," he shouts. "No talking." He glares until he's sure the hostages have complied and then turns back to his conversation with Tink. Jane exhales a long, shaky breath and glances down the row, where it appears no one is continuing to pass her message along. And who can blame them?

Her stomach growls again, and Jane's not sure if it's acid eating away at her innards from nerves, or hunger, but she realizes she's no longer under the impression that this whole matter will be wrapped up quickly and she'll get back to her table for the remaining eight courses. This is not a blip, a small interruption to dinner. This is the trajectory of the evening now. A train she has gotten on and is unable to get off—even though she's unsure of where it's taking her.

She feels the hard edge of her cell phone with her hip and wishes for the hundredth time she could call her kids.

"They don't know it," Vaughn whispers, her lips barely moving.

Jane tenses. "What?"

"The password. Says the chef changes it every day and doesn't give it to them so they don't get distracted by their phones."

"Seriously?" Jane mutters. God, the man really is a dictator. And then she remembers that dictator who knows the password is sitting—well, *lying*—across the room from her . . . and right next to Dan.

She looks at her husband and finds he's staring at her, like he's been waiting for her to look to him again—and she feels that buzz of connection. Of course! They've been married for nineteen years; *of course* he would know she needed him.

But instead of waiting for her to say what she needs, he mouths the unintelligible phrase he was trying to tell her earlier—this time a vein is throbbing in his neck; his eyes are wild. She knows it's a stressful situation and he's worried about the chef, but she shakes her head, trying to convey that her need in this moment is more pressing.

He stops and looks at her, waiting.

She darts her eyes around the room again, and, satisfied no one—namely Brick—is paying attention, she mouths *I have my phone*, exaggerating each word.

His eyes go wide.

Emboldened, she continues: *I need the Wi-Fi password.*

He narrows his eyes and nods.

From the chef. She points at the chef.

He points at the chef, as if to underline what she's saying.

Yes! She nods, waiting for him to ask, but Dan stares back at her blankly.

Ask him, she mouths.

He scrunches his nose. And then mouths the same phrase he's been mouthing since he first sat down. Jane closes her eyes and clenches her fists and tries not to scream. *Of course* Dan can't understand her. He can't even read her facial expressions at his god-awful work parties, once leaving her for more than

an hour trapped in a conversation with Bob, an older podiatrist in his practice who was telling her all the particulars of his
latest trip to some New Jersey toy train museum. Bob was a
miniature-train enthusiast—also known as a "railfan," Jane
learned against her will that evening—and his entire basement
was home to his overwhelming collection. Jane understood at
this point why Bob had never remarried—and why his wife,
Camilla, had divorced him. Jane had been making eyes at Dan
for the entire conversation to come save her, but when he finally approached and she began to feel a sense of relief and
gratitude, he merely dropped off a fresh glass of champagne
and said, *Didn't mean to interrupt! Carry on,* and promptly
left Jane alone for another thirty minutes of statistics about
the museum that Bob had apparently memorized when he was
there (8 miles of track! 403 tunnels! 260,000 figurines!) that
Jane had to pretend to be enthralled by. When really, the only
thing that impressed her was the seemingly masculine ability
to hold such mounds of trivial data in their brains but have no
idea where they left their wallet.

All that to say, Jane doesn't have hope that Dan will suddenly be able to read her lips, and she's no closer to getting the
password for the Wi-Fi.

Javier appears at the doorway, jerking Jane's attention from
Dan. Caden leads him back to the wall next to Monica, and
Jane wills him to look at her. Was he successful? Did he trip
the alarm?

"Mom," Paisley whispers.

"Yeah?" Vaughn says.

"I have to tell you something."

"OK," Vaughn says. "What is it, baby?"

Paisley swallows and then: "That's Isaac."

"Who?"

"Isaac!" she says, pointing at one of the younger guys who was in the kitchen and now sits alone at a table, one hand on his gun and the other up to his mouth, where his teeth are nibbling a hangnail. "*That's* the guy who ghosted me."

"What?" Vaughn says, straightening her spine.

"He's the one who suggested I come here for my birthday!" she whispers. Jane watches as Paisley's shock morphs into anger and then embarrassment and self-flagellation. "This really is all my fault." And though Vaughn of course contests it, assuring her it's not true, Jane has to agree with Paisley's assessment. Had Paisley not fallen for Isaac's deviousness, Jane would be on her second gin and halfway through the nine courses by now.

"Hey!" Brick shouts in their direction. "I said no talking."

Paisley buries her head in her mother's shoulder, and Vaughn locks eyes with Jane, who tries to keep her schadenfreude-esque grin at bay and force a sympathetic frown in its place, the universal one that conveys from one parent to another: *Kids, huh?*

It's not that she takes pleasure in Paisley's mistake—she's a kid, after all, and Jane did all kinds of dumb things as a teenager. It's that motherhood is hard, and sometimes the only bright spot is when you see someone having a harder time at it than you are, and you can momentarily dwell in the comforting reminder that comparatively, you're doing just fine. While Jane may not have the money to take her children to ridiculously expensive restaurants to celebrate birthdays, and Josh plays too many video games, and she can't seem to have a simple conversation with Sissy lately without it blowing up into an outright war—at least Jane can say with 100 percent certainty that none of her children are consorting with criminals.

TWO HOURS AND THIRTY-SEVEN MINUTES UNTIL THE END

CHAPTER

11

WHEN THE CALL COMES OVER THE RADIO, DEPUTY
Kip Grayson is staring at the glowing white backside of a naked young man and trying to ignore the sharp scent of oregano
and red wine vinegar tickling his nostrils. It's his turn to patrol
Baker's Cove Beach, where teens notoriously sneak off to make
out, drink cheap beer, and skinny-dip. He parked his car so
that it's hidden behind a dune but still affords him a partial
view of the shoreline, and is trying to decide if he has it in him
to ruin the night of these kids, who, while breaking the laws of
public decency, really aren't hurting anybody. His partner,
Sandy, is biting into an Italian hoagie, the mix of mayo and oil
dripping down her hand and onto her blue pants. "Dammit,"
she says. "I just had these dry-cleaned."

When dispatch announces a 10-71 at La Fin du Monde, Kip
stifles a yawn and sits straight up at the mention of the famous
restaurant. He does a double take at the radio as it hits him. A
10-71! It took a second for his brain to make the connection,
because he has never had a gunshot-wound call before.

The "World's Safest Beach"—the stretch of California coast ninety minutes north of L.A. that Kip and the eight other officers in his division cover—had seen its share of emergencies. A baby seal stuck on the rocks. Public urination. A missing person, once! Though the husband was found in mere hours at his boyfriend's home. But never a gunshot wound. And never an incident at La Fin du Monde, a haven for celebrities and the wealthy. In fact, the closest Kip had come to celebrity was the time he pulled Emilio Estevez over for speeding—and he didn't even realize it was him until he looked at his driver's license. Starstruck, he rambled on about *The Mighty Ducks* being his favorite movie as a kid (truthfully, it was his favorite as an adult, too), then told him to slow down, as these curvy roads could be quite dangerous. It wasn't until Emilio pulled off— squealing tires and speeding away—that Kip realized he'd forgotten to ask for an autograph.

Suffice to say, though he'd sat through hours of mind-numbing video training for active shooters and hostage situations and protest-crowd control and violent encounters with various weaponry, this was his first call for a real-life, bona fide emergency. Someone had been shot. With a gun! And Kip feels like the benched quarterback pulled into the game when the starter tears his ACL. This is what he trained for! This is why he became a cop! Not to arrest harmless skinny-dipping kids but to *save lives*. To be a hero.

He puts the CB to his mouth and holds down the button to speak.

"This is 92 Grayson. I'm at Baker's Cove, three miles from the road to La Fin du Monde. Over."

"We've got a male victim gunshot wound. Two ambulances en route. Officer Groebner is en route as well. As the senior-most officer, can you take command? Over."

Kip swells with excitement. With Sheriff Cesar Guillermo out of town in South Carolina visiting his newborn (and first) grandbaby, Kip knew he was currently the senior-most officer in the precinct, but he'd not heard anyone say it out loud until now.

"Ten-four," he says. "Moving out now. Over."

He flips on the lights and siren (his inner child still getting a thrill, even after all these years) and throws the car into reverse, peeling out of the parking lot. The kids on the beach scatter, hearts pounding, a flash of their future selves explaining to their parents on their one phone call why they're in jail lighting in their brains. But fortunately for them, tonight, that vision won't materialize.

"Lucky kids," Sandy says, but Kip doesn't look back.

He's got a job to do.

EXASPERATED, DAN PRESSES HIS HEAD BACK INTO the wall behind him.

To be fair, he couldn't understand what Jane was trying to tell him either. Reading lips has never been a strength of his, nor reading Jane's expressions. He can't count the number of dinners and work parties they've been to where Jane's given him a look or mouthed something and he's misinterpreted it. Often their conversations on the way home consist of some version of: *How was I to know that look meant you didn't want to talk to Bob about his model train collection anymore? I thought you wanted another glass of champagne!* He suddenly understands Jane's frustration at being misinterpreted— or not understood at all.

Now Jane's attention is on Vaughn and Paisley, and he's no closer to letting her know that Sissy is right in front of her. Holding a gun! He glances over at where Sissy is sitting at a table with her other . . . *friends*? Is that what they are? And though she's pulled the ball cap lower over her eyes and the mask is covering the rest of her face, it's so clearly Sissy, he can't believe Jane can't see it. It's like one of those magic eye three-dimensional pictures—it took Dan a minute to recognize Sissy in the kitchen, but once he finally did, now he can't unsee her.

He sighs. He doesn't know what good it will do, once Jane does realize it's her. He just knows it's information he doesn't want to be privy to alone, like when he had the weird mole on his back and felt compelled to show her. Jane's not a dermatologist—it's not like she could analyze it or remove it—but it felt better for her to know about it, too, so Dan didn't worry about it alone. And though he often complained and made fun of her for her myriad anxieties, the truth was—if Dan ever thought deeply enough about it—that Jane worrying about so many things took the burden off Dan. He didn't *have* to worry, because he knew she would worry enough for the both of them.

Dan glances back at Jane, who's still enthralled with a con-versation between Vaughn and Paisley, so he turns his atten-tion to the chef, diligently checking the wound, pressing Lars's fingernail and counting the pulse at his wrist.

"How am I doing, Doc?"

"Good," Dan says. "How are you feeling?"

"Like I've been shot in the shoulder."

Dan offers a sympathetic grin.

"I can't die, though."

"You won't," Dan says, an automatic kindness—he has no idea if *anyone* is going to make it out alive, and it stands to reason that the person who has a bullet wound certainly has the least chance, statistically speaking.

"Good, because I yelled at my wife this morning and that can't be the last thing I say to her."

"What'd you yell at her for?" he asks, less because he's curious and more because the answers to the questions he really wants to ask—*What do these people want? What is my daughter doing with them? When is Jane going to recognize Sissy? How am I going to get us all out of this?*—are not forthcoming, and certainly not held by the chef.

"It was dumb. Two days ago she parked too close to my Bentley Bentayga in the garage, and when she opened her car door, she dinged my passenger door. I just got it wrapped and I found out this morning it's going to cost twelve hundred dollars to fix."

Dan isn't sure he knows what a Bentley Bentayga is, except for a car he won't ever be able to afford, and he thought wrapping a car was something only professional athletes and rappers did. Still, he murmurs nonsense words to let Lars know he's listening.

"God, I never used to be this way. Who cares? It's just a car. But it's from working here. Serving these . . . *people*. I'm becoming one of them. Insufferable."

Dan raises his brow. In his experience, men who spend a lot of time and money on expensive sports cars (mostly plastic surgeons in Dan's orbit) are often not aware of how insufferable they are.

Lars clocks his reaction and mistakes the reason for it. "Oh, I don't mean you. You're obviously not . . . one of them."

This only causes Dan to be more surprised. "How could you tell?" He's not sure whether to be offended.

"The way you carry yourself. It's not pretentious."

Dan opens his mouth to say thank you, but Lars isn't done.

"And your suit. Looks like something you'd get at Men's Wearhouse."

Dan closes his mouth. He looks down at his white shirt (now covered in dried blood) and gray pants. He probably did get them at Men's Wearhouse. He realizes he left his suit coat in the kitchen and wonders if he'll get it back.

He glances at Jane again, then over to his daughter. Someone has brought dishes out from the kitchen and a few of the hostage takers are sitting around digging in, careful to slip forkfuls beneath their gaiters lest anyone see their full faces. Instead of eating, Sissy simply looks on, keeping her head tilted down, and Dan feels sure she's doing what she can to make sure Jane doesn't notice her. He wonders, not for the first time, what she's thinking. What could she *possibly* be thinking?

Dan also wonders what they're eating, and his stomach rumbles. Is it the barnacles? Or another delicious course they had yet to get to? If he was a different kind of person, he might stand up and ask for a plate. Demand that everyone else in the restaurant be fed as well.

But Dan is not that kind of person. He will not stand, mostly because his wrists and ankles are re-bound. He will not make any demands. He has already run through the risk-benefit analysis of tackling a terrorist or trying to steal a gun or thwart what's happening in any way. And he's determined that one man has already been shot and he wouldn't be able to live with himself if his actions caused anyone else the same fate. Especially his own daughter. Or his wife.

133

He sighs again.

"What's your wife's name?" he asks Lars. And this is the instigating question that prompts a waterfall of information wherein Dan learns more about Lars, the head chef of La Fin du Monde, than he imagined he would ever know. Lars is a new father to a three-month-old boy. Finn. His wife, Amhara, is Ethiopian. They had two weddings, a small ceremony on the cliff outside this very restaurant and a large three-day affair in Addis Ababa. A talented prima ballerina, she was a principal in the L.A. Ballet for three years before a severe tibial stress fracture ended her career. Amhara now teaches dance for a local nonprofit dedicated to bringing the arts to underprivileged youth. She is a terrible chef but an excellent gardener, and when she was pregnant, her ankles and toes swelled so much they lovingly called them her Flintstone feet. He wishes he hadn't overreacted about the Bentley Bentayga. He has a problem with overreacting. Finn smiled at Lars within hours after he was born—a big toothless grin that the nurse said was gas, but Lars knew it was because he recognized his papa. Lars thinks vanilla is the best flavor of ice cream (pure, simple). Lavender does not belong in dessert. Cream cheese absolutely does not belong in sushi, and the fear of cultural appropriation is killing culinary inventiveness.

It's a mishmash of information, due to both the random nature of Dan's questions to keep Lars talking and the rambling and sometimes incoherent thoughts of a man who both is in shock from unfolded events and also very much likes to hear himself talk.

Dan looks past Jane and Vaughn and Paisley at the ten

other diners turned hostages. The neurosurgeon is now sitting up next to his wife, holding an ice pack to his head. The two elderly women are leaning on each other, but they're both stiff and appear as uncomfortable as Jane. The one four-top group—a graying older couple, their adult son, and his blond wife or girlfriend—is whispering among themselves, not urgently, just a few words here and there. And while Dan knows they're likely benign phrases—*I'm hungry. Is the zip tie digging into your ankle? Here, have my water*—he secretly hopes they're coming up with a plan to help them all escape, since he can't seem to come up with anything himself. Javier and Monica sit next to each other in silence, both staring off into space.

Enough time has elapsed that people are settling in for the long haul, like when a flight is canceled and would-be passengers start making themselves comfortable at the gate—stretching out on dingy carpet or propping feet up on suitcase ends. Like Jane, most of the women have removed their shoes; men—even with bound hands—have managed to loosen their ties or ditch them altogether. Everyone seems to be making themselves at home, as it were. The hostages, while not completely relaxed, are no longer on a knife's edge, likely because the captors themselves have become lackadaisical in their . . . captor-ing.

Lyle and Caden, finished with their meal, are playing some kind of game involving forks and a glass. Dan can't tell what the end goal is or what the rules are, but there are a lot of forks falling, clattering onto the table, causing the boys to guffaw, gently shove each other with taunts, and it's incongruous, the scene. Boys with guns slung across their chests or stuffed into the backs of their army cargo pants, behaving like children at a party.

"Are they eating the ravioli al uovo?" Lars asks at one point, his gaze looking past Dan at the few terrorists still sitting at the table, Sissy included.

"The what?"

"It's ravioli with an egg yolk center. I top it with Grana Padano and shaved Alba truffles."

Dan turns and cranes his neck, wishing, too, that he knew what they were eating. "Looks like . . . rolls?"

"Good. Those fuckers don't deserve my truffles."

Dan feels someone standing over him and looks up to find Caden looming. "Brick sent me over to check on . . . him," he says, gesturing to the chef.

"His name's Lars," Dan says.

Caden nods. "Does he need anything?"

"A hospital," Dan says.

"Oh, I mean, anything I can get him right now?"

"Do you need anything?" Dan says to Lars.

"I need to not be shot in the shoulder," he says dryly.

Dan turns back to Caden. "Nope." As Caden steps to leave, Dan says: "Hey, wait a minute." There are so many questions he wants to ask, namely: *What is my* daughter *doing here?*, but instead he says: "What were you doing over there? With the forks."

"Oh, that?" Caden says, glancing at the area where he was standing with Lyle. "Some magic trick Brick tried to teach us once. We still can't do it."

"Brick's a . . . magician?"

"I mean, I think it's just a hobby. Card tricks, the whole bit." Caden pauses. "He may have used to do kids' birthday parties, now that I think about it."

Dan gapes at the kid, at the incongruency of the Brick he knows—a menacing man with an AK-47—and one that knows fun card tricks and entertained children with them. He furrows his brow, confused at the entire exchange. "Are you supposed to be telling me this?"

Caden's eyes widen, like he forgot for a minute he took people hostage until Dan reminded him, and then, without another word, he trots off, heading back to the table with Sissy, leaving Dan to shake his head in disbelief over the events of the evening.

"Hey, keep talking to me," Lars says. "It's keeping my mind off the pain."

Dan doesn't point out that of the two of them, it's Lars who's done the majority of the talking. Instead, he thinks for a beat and then asks the next question that pops into his mind. "What's with the cell phone thing?"

"You mean why I ban them?"

Dan nods.

Lars sighs, as if it were perfectly obvious. "You don't take pictures of the Sistine Chapel, do you? The *David*?"

Dan inwardly rolls his eyes at the frankly egomaniacal suggestion that the chef's food is on par with the greatest works of art in the world, but is simultaneously impressed with the endless bounds of the man's arrogance. Dan can't remember a time he ever felt so sure of himself. Maybe in the beginning with Jane. The way she looked at him. "Everyone takes pictures of the *David*, actually. I know I did," Dan says, thinking back to when he studied abroad in Florence in college and he and his friends took turns taking photos at such an angle that it looked like *David*'s twig and berries sat directly in the palm of their hands.

"OK, but you didn't capture the magnificence of it."

That much, at least, is true. Dan remembers looking through his photos, after getting his rolls of film developed once he got home, and thinking that they didn't do any of what he saw in person justice—including Lina, the Italian girl who was the best and most unexpected surprise of his trip. His gut twists with guilt, thinking of this girl from twenty-plus years ago. He and Jane had just started dating before he left for study abroad, and while they weren't exclusive, he'd still felt like he had cheated, and he never told Jane the truth, even when they were going through his pictures when he got home, for fear she would leave him. "Who's this?" Jane asked, stopping at a smiling Lina posing at the Basilica of San Miniato in front of a panoramic view of Florence. "I don't know," Dan said lamely. "Just some girl." He could tell Jane knew, but to her credit, she let it go.

He swallows past the lump in his throat, reminding him he's been lying to Jane once again and she doesn't deserve it. He glances at her only to see she's staring at him, as if impatiently waiting for him to look her way, when she was the one who tuned out in the first place. She's mouthing words to him again, and he squints, determined to understand this time.

She repeats her phrase two more times and Dan focuses, really trying to concentrate on what she's saying, as she gestures to the chef. It looks like: *Get the fast food.* Which obviously can't be right, but maybe it's close.

Are you hungry? he mouths back, and Jane's face turns into yet another silent scream and he knows that's not it. He shakes his head and opens his mouth to once again try and tell her that Sissy is there—certainly more important than whatever Jane is trying to tell him—but she shakes her head, and her lips move again in slow, exaggerated words: *Hit the bathroom.*

He squints. That can't be right.

"The truth is, people are so distracted all the time," Lars says, and Dan is only half listening. "They're spending hundreds of dollars to come eat my food—" Lars pauses, trying to get a breath. His words are growing wispy, like those thin clouds that eventually float apart. "Shouldn't they surrender fully to the experience?"

"Shit." Dan snaps to attention, sitting up and pinching Lars's nail bed again. The nail turns white, but when he lets go, the red doesn't come back nearly as quickly.

"*Dammit.* Lars, how you feeling, man? You doing OK?" he says as he removes the towel from Lars's shoulder to check the wound again. His shoulder is swollen, round and purple, which means even if the blood isn't coming out, it's going somewhere.

"I'm a . . . little . . . tired, actually," Lars says.

This is what finally springs Dan into action. "Help!" he yells, but it comes out quieter than he intended, so he shouts "HELP!" once more, louder. The restaurant falls silent and multiple guns are swung in his direction, but in his heightened state of panic, he can't be bothered to care. His gaze locks on his daughter, who's staring at him with wide eyes, and he has the sudden urge to rush to her, grab her and then Jane, and run clean out of the restaurant with them both. He jumps to his feet with no plan; he knows only that he needs to do something— except he's forgotten about his bound ankles, and standing throws him completely off-kilter. The next thing he knows, he's falling and has time to think *Oh shit*, but cannot catch himself (his wrists are bound!) before his head slams into a table.

And then everything goes black.

CHAPTER

13

"DAN!" JANE SCREAMS AS HER HUSBAND'S BODY flops to the floor. She's not even sure what just happened, except that one minute she was trying to tell Dan for the eight hundredth time to get the password from the chef, and the next her husband yelled "Help!" and tried to stand, then instantly dropped to the ground like a tree felled by Paul Bunyan, slamming his head into the two-top dining table in front of him with a *THWACK*.

At first, no one moves—including Dan.

"Help him!" Jane screeches, and starts crawling toward her husband, though her bound wrists and ankles make this challenging. Tink rushes over to Dan as he starts to come to, which would be a relief, if not for the line of red blood gushing down the side of his face.

"Oy!" Brick yells, and Jane stops her weird army/worm crawl and looks up at him. "Back to the wall." He indicates where he wants her to return with the barrel of his gun.

"No!" Jane says. "That's my husband."

"The one who's cheating on you?" Brick smirks.

Someone in the room gasps, but Jane can't turn to look. She exhales an irritated breath but refuses to move.

Brick rolls his eyes, then walks toward Jane, his army boots thumping on the wood floor. When he reaches her, he holds out one of his meaty paws and she flinches, which sends Brick's eyes heavenward once more. "I'm not going to hurt you. I'm helping you up. Unless you want to crawl the rest of the way there."

"Oh," Jane says.

She lifts her bound wrists to him like a damsel in distress (she is in distress!) and he slips his thick, warm hand between hers. She tries not to look directly in his eyes, but fails, and the intensity of his gaze sends a jolt down her spine as he easily lifts her to her feet as though she weighs no more than a child. She grasps his arm for balance as she shuffle-steps with her bound feet over to her husband.

"Dan?" She peers down at him. "Are you OK?"

He blinks at her. "I'm fine," he says. "Help him."

"Who, honey?"

"Lars." He winces. "He needs help." Jane and Brick both turn to look at the chef, who is pale and very apparently struggling to breathe. Dan tries to sit up. "I think he's got fluid in his lungs."

"Shit," Brick mutters under his breath. "Go get him ice," he says to Tink, and then releases Jane and steps closer to the chef, hands on his hips. "Lars, you OK? Stay with us, man." To Dan: "What does he need?"

"He's having trouble breathing. Maybe a fragment of the bullet lodged in his lung?"

"OK—so what does he *need*?" Brick repeats.

"A doctor."

"I thought you were a doctor!"

Dan sighs heavily. "I'm a podia—"

"I can help," a deep baritone croaks out from the wall of hostages, cutting Dan off. Jane and Brick turn to see the man who stabbed Tink in the leg with a fork and subsequently got knocked out. He's still holding a half-melted ice pack to his head.

Brick gestures to Lyle. "Bring him over." He cuts his eyes back to the man. "But keep him tied up."

Jane drops to the floor beside Dan and reaches for the cut bleeding profusely at his hairline.

Tink arrives with another bag of ice and a kitchen towel in her hand. "Here," she says, handing both to Jane. "Can you move?" she asks Dan. When he nods, she says: "Let's give them some space."

Dan slowly scoots on his bottom to a spot on the wall Tink has indicated about fifteen feet from Lars. Jane follows, resuming her challenging army crawl. Breathing heavily, she finally reaches Dan and pushes herself up to sitting beside him. Tink has moved on to where Brick and the neurosurgeon are attending Lars. Jane watches as the neurosurgeon assesses the chef and then starts shouting orders.

"I need a knife and a tube—something long and flexible. Both sterilized. And a needle and thread."

"Oh God, he's going do a thoracostomy," Dan says to Jane.

"Is that bad?"

"It'll either save his life," Dan says, "or kill him."

Jane feels her entire body tense—not only because she has never seen anyone die before, but because if the chef dies, she'll definitely never get the password. And then she remembers the booster. She passed the table it was on when they moved down the wall, and now she's about ten feet from it. A farther distance than she would like, but the chef is certainly providing a distraction that might enable her to move unnoticed.

"Go," Brick says to Tink.

"Where am I supposed to get a needle and thread?" Tink asks.

"See what you can find," says Brick, waving his hand to dismiss her.

"I've got a sewing kit in my purse," one of the older women sitting against the glass window says.

"Which purse is yours?" Brick asks.

"The green one at that table." She gestures with her bound hands to where she was sitting.

"Caden," Brick says. "Get the sewing kit. Tink, the knife and tube."

"Where am I supposed to get a tube?" Tink says.

"There's one in the kitchen," a sous chef chimes in. "We use it to infuse food with smoke flavor."

"Take him with you," Brick says.

As Tink rushes past them with the sous chef, heading back into the kitchen, Jane gently presses the towel to Dan's cut. It's bleeding profusely, as head wounds tend to do, but the cut itself looks small. "Are you really OK?" Jane asks, glancing back at the booster.

He winces again. "A little embarrassed."

Jane replays in her mind's eye the ridiculous image of Dan standing and falling, and she exhales a laugh. "What the hell were you doing?"

"I don't know. I was . . . I was trying to save you. I was trying to save Sissy!"

"Sissy!" Jane nearly laughs again, but then furrows her brow in concern. Dan clearly hit his head harder than she thought.

"Yes," Dan sighs. "Sissy."

Jane stares at her husband. "Do you know where we are? What year it is? Honey, Sissy's at Jazz's house watching *Yellowjackets*."

"No." Dan looks Jane directly in the eyes and then says gently: "She's here. Well, over there"—he points with his bound hands—"at that table."

"What?" Jane says, still not quite believing what Dan is telling her, but enough to glance wildly around the room until her gaze lands squarely on a girl Dan's pointing toward, and Jane finds that she can't stop looking at her. Her black ball cap is pulled over her eyes and the gaiter covers the rest of her face, but her hair—Jane knows that hair, the curly ponytail, sticking out of the back of the cap, that Jane has combed and tamed and conditioned and smoothed for the better part of ten years, before Sissy could care for it herself.

"That's what I was trying to tell you."

"What?" Jane croaks, repeating herself, unable to take her

eyes off the girl. She doesn't even know what she's asking, but her brain is scrambling and her mouth is on autopilot, a broken record, speaking of its own accord. "No," Jane says, slowly shaking her head. "No! Sissy's at Jazz's house watching *Yellowjackets*." Not because she believes it anymore, but because she thinks if she says it enough times, she can force it to be true. Though the girl is too far away to hear them, it's as if she senses she's being talked about, because at that second, she glances up, locking eyes with Jane, the jolt of recognition sending ice through Jane's veins. She gapes at her daughter as though she is looking at a complete stranger, and she might as well be, as this person—dressed, like the other terrorists, in a black tank top and camouflage army pants, and clutching a gun in her hands, a *gun*—is a stranger, completely unknown to Jane.

"What," she says for the third time, but it's lost in her exhale of breath. All air has left her lungs. She feels weightless, unmoored. "Sissy?" she whispers. And then, as the pressure from the shock builds and the questions mount on top of each other like blocks in a Jenga game, she hisses it. "Sissy!"

Her daughter shoots her a stern look—as though Jane is the one who has done something wrong!—before dropping her eyes.

Dan squeezes Jane's arm with his hands. "Jane, no," he whispers. "Don't make a scene."

"Don't make a— What is she doing here? Have you talked to her?"

"No, but I think she's with . . . them."

"What do you mean *with* them?" Though Jane knows exactly what he means, considering Sissy is dressed like *them*

146

and very clearly did not come here as a patron to eat dinner—it's just that it can't be true.

"Sissy!" she hisses again, and the two sous chefs tied up nearest them and a few of the other terrorists at the dining table turn their heads from the excitement with the chef toward Jane quizzically, but Sissy doesn't look up.

"Jane," Dan says urgently in her ear. "Listen to me. I don't know what she's doing, but we can't draw attention to it. To *her*."

"Why *not*?"

"Think about it," Dan whispers, with the annoying patience of someone who's had time to digest the shocking information that you have just learned. "All of the people in this room are *witnesses*. When this is over, do you want them to be able to identify her? To the *police*? She'll go to jail, Jane."

"Oh, jail is the *least* of her concerns right now," Jane says. She stares daggers at her daughter, but when she notices Isaac in particular staring at her with intense curiosity, she glances away.

"Ohmygodohmygodohmygodohmygod." She's panicking now, spiraling a little bit, and longing for the regular anxiety she felt just an hour earlier when she thought she had left her curling iron plugged in and her house was going to burn to the ground with Sissy in it. "She can't go to jail, Dan, she's going to *Stanford*!"

Tink returns holding a steak knife in one hand and plastic tubing in the other. "I boiled them in hot water," she says.

As she hands them over to the neurosurgeon, Brick levels the barrel of his gun at the man's head. "Don't try anything funny," he says.

Dan and the rest of the room collectively hold their breath as the surgeon, with shaky hands, begins to press on Lars's rib cage with his fingers, presumably looking for the right spot to make the incision.

Jane watches, too, but her mind isn't on the procedure. "What are we going to *do*, Dan?"

"I don't know," he says. "But we have to try to remain calm."

Calm, she thinks, and then she says it out loud: "Calm?!"

"Yes," he says. "Panicking isn't going to get us anywhere." He gestures to his head. "We will figure this out."

While Jane typically enjoys—and even relies on—Dan's pragmatism, in this moment she finds it wildly exasperating. "Our daughter is holding a gun, Dan—*a gun!*—and you think we should remain calm?" Her heartbeat revs again, her fingers tingle.

"Yes," Dan says.

A loud, mangled scream that's so animalistic it sends chills down Jane's spine emanates from the chef, and then silence.

"Is he OK?" Brick asks.

"Passed out from the pain," Rahul says.

The stillness is somehow even worse than the screaming. Not knowing what else to do with the anxious energy running rampant through her body, Jane growls and then twists her wrists, trying to loosen the zip ties that are chafing her skin and that she can't stand to be bound by for a second longer. She knows there's an easy way to pop them off, she just doesn't know what it is. She scrolled by it on TikTok once—or was it Facebook?—a video teaching people how to break free of them. She regrets not clicking on it now, but it didn't feel pressing. It was enough to know the information was out there should she need it; something she could and probably would learn eventually, like how to fold a fitted sheet, or create the perfect cat-eye with liner, or season a cast-iron pan.

Giving up, she stills her hands in her lap, leans her head back on the wall behind her, then rolls her head to the left until she can see Vaughn, who has Paisley's head in her lap and is gently smoothing her daughter's hair with her bound hands, murmuring soothing nothings every so often. Jane finds herself simultaneously embarrassed at her earlier musings of parental superiority and overcome with rage and jealousy. All Paisley did was date a guy in a terrorist group—she didn't up and *join* one! Who's the bad mother now?

Jane slides her gaze back to Sissy once more. Where did she go wrong? She thinks of the untold number of conversations she has had with her children over the years about not touching firearms—*whether they are loaded or not*—and wonders if she should have added a don't-hold-people-hostage lecture into the mix. Parenting is full of your children doing things you never imagine you need to warn them off of—like putting raisins up their noses or trying to open a car door while you're driving seventy-five miles per hour down a highway—but this, Jane thinks, truly could not have been anticipated—could it? Were there clues she missed? Perhaps she inadvertently scrolled by a BuzzFeed article titled "Ten Signs Your Child Has Joined a Terrorist Group."

A loud noise—a mix between a yelp and a wheeze—snaps Jane's head in the direction of the chef. "There he is," Brick says. "You OK, mate?"

The chef looks at him, bewildered. "Fucking . . . hurt!" he manages.

Brick offers what could be considered a small sympathetic nod, and then looks at Rahul. "Is he gonna be OK?"

"I'll stitch the tube in place—"

"Oh God," Lars breathes, staring at the needle.

"—and he'll be stable for now. But he really needs a hospital."

"That's what I've been saying," Dan mutters.

"Great," Brick says. "Caden, get the knife. The rest of you—let's get set up," he says to no one in particular. "He'll be here soon."

A few of the hostage takers stand up at once. Tink grabs her bag from where it was abandoned in a heap and slings it over her shoulder. "Where are you thinking?"

Brick gestures toward the wall next to the kitchen door where a four-top table sits. "Here's good."

A couple of the boys push the table out of the way and Brick positions one chair in the center of the wall.

Meanwhile, Tink sets up a laptop and a large ring light on the table across from the chair and then goes back into her book bag. Jane realizes that, between the cell booster, laptop, and ring light, Tink is not only the mother hen but the tech guru of the group. Or at least the tech Sherpa.

"We have to talk to her," Jane whispers to Dan.

"Jane, I really don't think—"

"Get her attention."

Dan sighs. "How? How do we do that without getting everyone's attention?"

Jane's not sure, but she feels an urgency to do something, anything, if it could possibly help reach her end goal of talking to Sissy. "God, I always thought it would be Josh, you know? I mean, not that he'd be a terrorist, but . . . *Sissy?*"

"I know," Dan says. "She's our *good* one. I don't understand."

"Well," Jane mumbles. "Maybe if you weren't the fun dad all the time." She immediately regrets it, pressing her lips together as if it would create a vacuum to suck the words back in. Why must she say everything she's thinking out loud?

"What?" Dan asks, but Jane knows he heard because he follows it with: "Are you saying this is my fault?"

Don't say it, Jane thinks. Nothing good will come of it, and it doesn't even matter! What's done is done. "You're so permissive with her all the time!" she whisper-shouts, years of resentment at being cast in the role of the enforcer, the mean parent, the stick-in-the-mud, bubbling over. "Always trying to be her best friend, never giving her consequences for anything. Of course she thinks she can do whatever she wants."

"Are you serious right now? If anything, this is *your* fault. You're so controlling all the time, always micromanaging her every move—no wonder she rebelled."

"*Micromanaging?*" Jane hisses.

"Yes! Take Stanford. Does she even want to go? It's hard to tell with the way you shoehorned her into applying."

"Of course she wants to go! What kind of a question is that? Everyone wants to go to Stanford. And *someone* had to be in charge of college applications. Lord knows it wasn't going to be you."

"What's *that* supposed to mean?"

"ARE YOU TWO QUITE FINISHED?" Brick thunders, startling Jane. She slowly rotates her head, taking in first Brick's murderous glare and then the numerous pairs of eyes trained on her and Dan yet again.

"Um, yes," she says, wondering exactly how much Brick and everyone else heard. She doesn't dare look at Sissy, and she notices Brick hasn't either, which makes her hopeful no one has connected the dots.

"I knew I shouldn't have let you go over there," Brick says, mostly to himself. "Alright—you," he says, pointing to Jane. "Back to the other wall."

Jane gapes at him, thinking of an excuse to stay right where she is. As infuriating as Dan is, she'd rather be by his side in this whole mess than across the room trying to mouth to him phrases he can't possibly comprehend, but before she can conjure any words, she notices Brick's countenance change. He tilts his head, really studying her. Then he takes three long strides, closing the gap between them, and points directly at her breast. Jane freezes; her stomach hollows; all saliva leaves her mouth in an instant as though she were chewing cotton.

"What is that?"

"What?" she squeaks, panic rising like bile in her throat. Or maybe it actually is bile. She tries to swallow it back down, but her mouth is too dry.

"That." He points directly at her breast. "The square thing that looks like a phone."

"Oh! This?" Jane says, widening her eyes to feign innocence. "Oh, I forgot that was in there."

"What. Is. It?" he asks, enunciating each word.

"It's a . . ." Jane racks her brain trying to think of what it could be, but the stress is too much and she falters, exhaling the truth in one breath. "It's my phone, yes."

Brick holds his hand out. "Give it."

Jane raises her bound wrists and digs the cell out of her bra, under the entire restaurant's gaze, and places it in Brick's up-turned palm.

"Did you call anyone?"

"No!" Jane says. "I couldn't! No service."

Brick studies her face, as if he has a lie detector processor in his brain and is waiting for the verdict. He grunts, shoves Jane's phone in the side pocket of his cargo pants.

"Now, back to the—" he says, when a thunderous *BOOM* of an explosion fills the air, fracturing his sentence, shaking Jane's vision, and vibrating the dining room so hard, the silver-ware and the glass beads of the chandeliers rattle, turning Jane's entire world into a confusion of sound.

CHAPTER

14

AT FIRST, JANE THINKS IT'S AN EARTHQUAKE.

She's been through enough of them to know she should not be sitting out in the open. Instinct guides her to scramble toward the dining room table closest to her—awkwardly, with her bound ankles and hands—but she makes it only a few inches before the deafening noise and shaking stop as quickly as they started.

And then: silence.

Jane glances at Sissy first—mother's instinct—to make sure she's OK, then at Dan, and then Brick, who has left his position in front of her and is now at the glass front door, peering out into the dark night. Then she glances around the room at the rest of the bewildered faces mirroring her own. She knows they're all thinking the exact same question: *What the hell was that?*

But, as the shock wears off and Jane realizes everything and everyone in the restaurant is unharmed, she notices Brick's calm demeanor—as if he's not only unsurprised by the explosion, but *expected* it—and it dawns on Jane that she knows exactly what it was.

A bomb. A bomb in a van, to be precise, triggered by opening the van door.

She knows because it's exactly what the terrorists in her book did—create a booby trap, in a van half a mile down the entrance road to the teahouse, to stall any police that might try to come to the rescue. And she knows without a shadow of a doubt, the same way she knows her own name or knows the exact way Dan sticks his tongue in his cheek when he's concentrating, that these terrorists have done the same.

What she doesn't know is *why*. She remembers reading somewhere a few years ago that humans think coincidences are really rare events, when actually they happen all the time. You meet someone and realize you share the same birthdate or that your parents were born in the same small town, or you always happen to glance at the clock at the exact same time every day, and you think: *What are the odds?*

What are the odds her daughter is at the same restaurant—taking it hostage, no less—the exact same night that she and Dan happen to be dining there? And what are the odds that the events throughout the night have been eerily similar to a book she wrote? And that it all feels a little more calculated than two people realizing they have the same birthday? She doesn't think it's a stretch to say, objectively, that added together it feels like much more than a coincidence. It all must be related somehow, but how?

And more important, if someone—if *Brick*—is following

the plot of her book, then . . . this is bad. Oh, this is really, really bad.

She doesn't know she's said it out loud until she hears Dan saying, "It's OK. We're all OK." And Jane doesn't know if Dan's trying to convince her or himself.

"No," Jane whispers, crawling the few inches back to Dan. "No! It's not OK. We're not OK. We have to get out of here. We have to get *her* out of here."

"I know. I know!" he says. "But look, we're all OK."

Before responding, Jane surreptitiously glances around so as not to attract Brick's attention again, but in the aftermath, he seems to have forgotten about Jane and Dan altogether, confidently pacing like a military commander and shouting orders.

"Lyle—the roof. See what you can make out," he says, and Lyle nods and heads out the front door.

"Tink, are you set up?"

"Almost."

"How much time until Otto's arrival?"

"Forty minutes, give or take."

Brick nods, and Jane keeps her head straight forward, whispering out of the side of her mouth, "We're not OK, Dan. Don't you understand? I think that was a . . . a bomb."

"A bomb?"

"Yes. An IED made from two propane tanks rigged to a Taser in the front seat of a van."

"That's . . . oddly specific."

"I know. Because it's *exactly* what happened in my book."

Dan carefully keeps his face trained forward as well, but

she can feel the concern waft off him and then senses it turning into full-blown irritation. "This again?"

"Yes, Dan! I think they're . . . following it or something."

"Really, Jane?" Dan hisses. "Were there two people in your book out for tea on their anniversary and then their *daughter* showed up with a gang of hoodlums, taking everyone hostage?"

"No, of course not, but—"

"And did a chef get shot and nearly *die*?"

"Well, no," Jane admits. Her brain is working overtime. "But that had to be a bomb, right? A booby trap to keep people away, just like in my book. And maybe . . . I don't know, maybe Sissy gave them the book?" She's mostly thinking out loud at this point, but even as she says it, she knows how unlikely that is. Sissy was twelve when Jane's book was published, and she was utterly disinterested in reading (a heartbreak on its own to Jane, an avid reader)—and it's even more unlikely Sissy's picked it up since.

"For the love of God, Sissy's never read your book," Dan hisses, confirming Jane's own thoughts. "*No one's* read your book, Jane! This can't be like your book because no one has read it."

Jane stares blankly at her husband. Dan isn't an unkind man. He rarely even raises his voice. Like any married couple, they've had their arguments over the years, of course, and Dan has said some terribly mean things in the heat of the moment, but Jane thinks this might be the cruelest thing Dan's ever said to her, even if it is true.

"What is going on with you?" he continues. "I know you're in a . . . weird place, but is this some ego thing? It's like you

want this to be about your book because you need the validation or something."

Welp, Jane stands corrected. *This* is the meanest thing
Dan's ever said to her.

"An *ego* thing?" she breathes, all at once furious with Dan
while simultaneously wondering if he's right. Is she seeing similarities because she wants to? And worse—is this what he
thinks of her? That she's fragile and selfish and egotistical? It's
an unflattering portrayal, to say the least. And it's what she
fears, deep down, is true. That she yearns for success with her
novels because she needs the external validation. There's nothing worse than the person you've been married to for half your
life holding up a mirror to your worst characteristics and hat-
ing what you see.

And if that's what Dan really thinks of her, no wonder he's
cheating.

Dan exhales a deep breath. "I'm sorry," he says, his voice
once again calm, soothing. "I'm worked up. It's this whole . . .
situation."

Jane says nothing, because what is there to say?

Suddenly, Sissy stands up, grabbing both Jane and Dan's
attention, and takes a few steps to the center of the room. Her
fists are clenched, her eyes are closed, her feet are rooted to the
ground, and her body is vibrating, quivering. It's a familiar
stance to Jane, one she's seen hundreds of times since Sissy was
a toddler. Dan had even named it: the Teapot, as it's similar to
the bubbling and rattling and steaming of a kettle, right before
it announces its boiling with its high-pitched scream.

"Oh no," Dan says.

"Uh-oh," Jane says.

"Brick!" the girl shrieks. The same shriek Jane heard just recently—hours before, actually, in relation to Sissy's losing her phone charger—and she gets a small jolt of delight that she is not, in fact, the only person in the world to be on the receiving end of Sissy's anger. "What the hell *was* that? You said the bomb was fake. Just in case the police were called, so they'd have to call the bomb squad. You said no one was going to get hurt!"

"See?" Jane hisses. She feels a jolt of righteous energy at being proven correct. Again. "It was a bomb."

Brick remains calm in the face of Sissy's vitriol and puts a hand up. "Listen. I had to put it there as a precaution. And it's a good thing I did, otherwise whoever detonated it would be up here by now."

"And what if whoever detonated it is hurt? What if they *died*?"

Jane has been watching their exchange like a spectator at a Ping-Pong match, as though waiting to hear something that is going to suddenly explain what her daughter is doing with these . . . these . . . gun-wielding maniacs.

Brick waves her off. "It's mostly a flash-bang—more bark than bite. I'm sure whoever it is is fine." Sissy glowers at him, but Brick just flashes her his overly straight-toothed and glowing smile. Then he winks. "Trust me," he says in his muddled but charming brogue. And suddenly Jane understands. Oh, does she understand. Sissy's in love with him. In *lust*, technically, but to an eighteen-year-old girl, the words are often one and the same. Jane knows because she used to be one.

"Well, shit," she mutters. She can't exactly blame Sissy. She wouldn't be the first young woman in the history of the world to make terrible decisions based on brooding good looks and an accent.

"What?" Dan whispers.

Jane gives her head a small shake as she continues studying her daughter. Sissy doesn't look mollified, exactly, with her hands still on her hips, her brow still low and furrowed over her fiery eyes, but she sets her mouth in a straight line, apparently done pressing him for now.

Lyle comes bursting back into the room, clearly winded, like he ran all the way down from the roof. He stands with his hands on his knees, trying to catch his breath.

"Well?" Brick says.

"There's a fire. From the explosion," Lyle says. "And flashing lights. Police lights."

The police! Relief floods through Jane—someone managed to call the police! She blinks. Wait—was it her? Did her text message somehow go through? She sits straight up as it hits her that the police coming would be the worst possible outcome for Sissy. And it could be all her fault.

No, wait! It had to be Javier, right? She glances in his direction, but he stares straight forward, not looking at anyone.

"The police," Brick repeats, frowning. "The van *just* detonated. How did they get here so fast? Unless—"

"The police!" Sissy shrieks, cutting Brick off. "We were supposed to be in and out in fifteen minutes and now the police are here?"

"They're not *here*," Brick says. "They're halfway down the

160

hill. And they won't be coming up anytime soon, as protocol will dictate they bring in the bomb squad to sweep for more IEDs before proceeding. And the nearest bomb squad is at least ninety minutes away in Santa Barbara." His brow furrows, and Jane can see the wheels in his head turning. "But it is very interesting they've turned up so soon. It means someone has called them." He jerks his head toward Jane.

"Me?" Jane says, startling at the sudden attention. Though she has to admit, any other person would likely come to the same conclusion. She had a phone. The police were called.

Brick levels the barrel of his gun even with her face, and Jane wilts. "The truth!" he demands.

Her vision narrows to only the black hole from which a bullet could exit at any second, and she suddenly understands the difference between general fear and acute. She swallows. "I didn't have service." Then she adds: "I would have! I wanted to." She stops short of admitting to the text message, but she hopes the half-truth is enough to make Brick believe her. Anything to remove the gun from her direction. The barrel's gaze bores into her.

"Do you think it could have been Otto?" Tink says.

Brick shakes his head, still eyeing Jane. "No. I doubt he suspects anything. Besides, if he did, he would have called his private security, not the police."

"You can check my recent calls!" Jane says, taking care not to say *texts* and hoping he doesn't call her bluff and check it all. "It wasn't me."

"You could have deleted them."

"I don't know how to do that!" Jane retorts. This, at least, is 100 percent true.

Brick stares at her a beat more, then—finally—lowers the gun. "Search them all again," he barks. No one moves.

"Who?" Caden asks in a small voice.

"I don't care! One of you."

Caden jumps to action, approaching Vaughn and Paisley first.

"Do *not* touch my daughter," Vaughn says. And though she isn't the one with the guns and the power, Caden freezes. Vaughn looks across the room at Tink. "*You* may search her."

Brick rolls his eyes in an exaggerated display of irritation. "Goldie, you search the women; Caden, the men."

To Jane's surprise, it's Sissy who nods.

"*Goldie?*" she whispers to Dan as Sissy walks over to Paisley.

"Apparently that's her nickname," he replies.

"She doesn't even have blond hair!"

"My thoughts exactly!"

Jane watches her daughter stand the women up against the window one at a time and pat them down—and her heart flutters as she realizes Sissy will likely come to search her as well. She mentally prepares for what she'll say when Sissy is in front of her. Time will be limited, and she'll need to focus on the most pressing questions—but which are those? There's so much she wants to know: Why? When? How? But those aren't nearly as important as getting her daughter out of this situation she's in altogether. Out of harm's way.

Finally, Caden comes over and helps Dan to his feet. And Sissy is ten steps behind him.

Given the circumstances, Jane can't help the morbid thought

that creeps in—what if this is the last time Jane gets to speak to her daughter? There are so many things she wants to say:

You are my literal heart walking around outside my body. Please be careful.

I love you. I love you. I love you.

What she actually says—or hisses, more accurately—when Sissy crouches down in front of her: "A *gun*, Sissy? Seriously?"

Sissy's eyes flash with defiance—which Jane recognizes as the default reaction to any words that come out of her mouth lately—but behind it she sees something else: Fear? Regret? Or maybe Jane just hopes that's what she sees.

Truth be told, Jane's had trouble deciphering Sissy's expressions for months now. It's something Jane has worried about relentlessly, or maybe *grieved* is the more accurate term—the happy-go-lucky child Sissy once was, who wore all her emotions so plainly on her face. Fell and bumped her knee? Pure agony and tears. A spontaneous stop at a drive-thru for a milkshake? Oh, the joy! But lately Sissy's face has been a crossword puzzle for Jane to solve, a hard one like the Sunday *New York Times*, with no answer key to flip to. And while Jane knew it was the natural order of things—teenagers needed to have their own private thoughts in order to cleave themselves from their parents, create their own separate identities and lives—now it's clear she didn't worry about it enough.

Instead of responding, Sissy stands and takes a step backward.

"Wait," Jane says, trying and failing to keep the desperation out of her voice. "You didn't search me. She didn't search me!" she says, realizing at once the absurdity of telling on her own daughter to the apparent head of the terrorist organization she's a part of.

Dry amusement crosses Brick's face as he flicks his eyes toward Jane. "Are you hiding *another* phone?" he asks.

"No," Jane says.

Sissy smirks and pops an eyebrow, and Jane is once again amazed at Sissy's innate skill for making her feel like *she* has done something wrong, when Sissy is holding a gun. And to make matters worse, Jane *has* done something wrong! She had one chance to talk to Sissy and she said the wrong thing. Jane can't remember the last time it felt like she'd said the right thing to her daughter. "Mine are all clear," Sissy says to Brick.

"Same," Caden says, after finishing with Dan and telling him to sit back down.

Brick stares at them both. "You sure?"

Caden nods. "No phones."

"Then who called the police?"

Caden shrugs, and Brick growls. "OK, well, we need to finish setting up. He'll be here soon. We have to get everyone back to their tables."

"What?" The skinny man with glasses who was in the kitchen with Dan steps forward. "Why? That's not part of the plan."

"Plans change," Brick says. "Otto's coming by helicopter. Presumably he'll be able to see directly into the restaurant through this giant picture window here—and if he sees a line of handcuffed people sitting against it, he *may* become suspicious."

"Oh, good point."

Brick gives a sharp nod, as if to say: *Thought you'd see it my way.*

"Isaac, Goldie, make sure all forks and knives are off the tables. Jeremy, Lyle, we're going to keep people's ankles tied, hands free. Anyone tries anything, they get dealt with. Let's move."

Jane stares at Sissy as she begins gathering all the forks and knives off the tables, and as the countless questions rattle through her mind again—Why? When? How?—a new one takes center stage: *Who?* And Jane thinks it's astonishing that though she's been with Sissy for every single day of her entire eighteen years on earth, it's quite possible Jane has absolutely no idea who her daughter is.

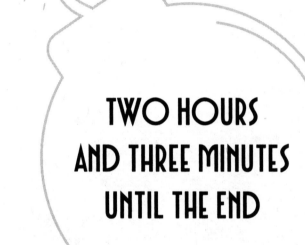

TWO HOURS
AND THREE MINUTES
UNTIL THE END

CHAPTER

15

"FUCKITY-FUCK-FUCK!"

Kip has made plenty of mistakes in his four-year career on the Coastal Bureau police force, but he's fairly certain that this is the biggest one yet. The only thing on his mind as he led the charge of two police vehicles and two ambulances, sirens blaring and lights flashing, up the long, winding hill to La Fin du Monde was reaching the victim. Saving his *life*. When he came to the obstacle of a white van parked sideways, effectively blocking the road, Kip knew—or should have known from the hours of endless video training—protocol said to wait. Do not approach the van. Assess the situation.

But it was an emergency! A man's life hung in the balance beyond the van, and Kip felt the urgency and made the call. Stationed behind his open police car door, gun drawn and pointed at the van, Kip sent Groebner, the newest man on the force, to clear the vehicle, first the back and then the front.

Kip literally—embarrassingly—didn't even think of the possibility of an explosive device, until his partner, Sandy, said to him over the hood of their car, right when Groebner's hand reached for the van's door handle—*Wait . . . what if there's a bo*—and the night around them shattered in a burst of sound and light and flame.

Now he sits in the back of an open ambulance, being treated for the ringing in his ears and the growing knot on the back of his head from where it slammed into the pavement when he was thrown from his feet, and he clutches a cell phone, trying to explain himself to Franklin Zimmerman, the LAPD chief of police, whom Sandy called—along with the local fire department—in the aftermath of the bomb. Thank God for Sandy.

"Fuckity-fuck-fuck!" he repeats.

"No need for all the language, Grayson," Zimmerman chides him like a patient grandfather. "Now, just slow down and tell me what happened."

How to explain? Kip looks at Sandy, his mind replaying the entire incident. "Is Groebner dead?" Oh God. Please don't let Groebner be dead. It's all his fault.

"They got him in the other ambulance. Luckily, the door blew off and shielded his body from most of the blast," Sandy says. But thanks to the ringing, all Kip hears is a low mumbling. He stares at his partner's lips, as if he's suddenly gained the power of reading them, but alas, he has not.

Kip lets out a half sob. "He's dead, isn't he? Oh God."

"No—can you not hear me? Grayson!" Sandy snaps her fingers to get Kip's attention, at the same time Zimmerman yells through the earpiece, "Grayson!"

"I'm tryyyyying." Kip stares at Sandy. He doesn't mean to

whine, but he's in shock. And the ringing. Well, it's getting slightly better now. She points at the phone Kip has to his ear and mouths, *Start talking.*

Right, Kip thinks, nodding. He's senior officer. He's got to take control of this situation. He gives his head a firm shake, trying to clear his mind.

"You need to run me through this," Zimmerman says. "Your partner says it was a 10-71. At the restaurant. And now you've got a van on fire? Possible IED? What in tarnation is going on there?"

"I don't know! I don't know."

"Walk me through the dispatch."

Kip takes a deep breath, closes his eyes, then speaks: "Nine-one-one got a call. Ten-seventy-one, like you said. Gunshot victim in the restaurant. Needed medical attention immediately. That's it. About halfway up the road to the restaurant, a white van was perpendicular, blocking the route. Upon approach"—Kip sees no need to rehash the fact that he instructed Groebner to open the door—"the van detonated."

Zimmerman pauses, as if he's analyzing the information, and then: "Something's not right."

Seeing as how Zimmerman is technically his superior, Kip has to swallow a sarcastic *What was your first clue—the bomb?* Plus, considering he set the bomb off with his clumsy police work, Kip doesn't exactly have a high horse to sit on. He merely mumbles "mmhmm" in agreement.

"I'm calling in SWAT and the bomb squad. ETA about two hours. Set up a perimeter. Don't go near the van or past it—we're gonna have to sweep for secondary devices. And call the restaurant. Find out what in the hell is going on up there. Ask if they need a medevac. Santa Barbara's got a chopper. Keep me posted."

"Yes, sir." Kip fills with relief, grateful to have a plan, to have someone telling him what to do. He hangs up and relays the information to Sandy and McLeod, the officer from the second police car, directing them to set up the perimeter. Then he types La Fin du Monde in the search bar of his cell. It takes a minute to load—service is shit out here in the woods—but the number finally appears. He clicks it and listens to the phone ring eight times before he hangs up and tries again. Then he lets it ring ten times. He waits a beat and tries again. Seeing as how this is his only duty, he has all the time in the world.

While Kip waits, phone to his ear, he watches Sandy and McLeod set up the crime tape, giving the van and the firemen putting out the blaze a wide berth while simultaneously sweeping for evidence, marking anything, without touching or moving it, that could possibly aid the bomb squad in their investigation. The bomb squad! Of course, Kip thinks, they wouldn't have to hold and wait for the bomb squad if Guillermo had only listened to him when he suggested adding a Range Rover Sentinel to the force's fleet of vehicles. A few years ago, Kip had been tasked with coming up for ideas on how to allot the extra half a million surplus dollars in the Coastal Bureau's government-allotted budget.

"An armored vehicle that can tolerate a thirty-three-pound bomb exploding less than seven feet away," Sheriff Guillermo read aloud when Kip presented him with the list.

"Yes."

"Grayson," Guillermo said, peering at him over his glasses. "In the four years you've been on the force, how many bomb threats have you been called to?"

"Well, just the one, sir, but—"

"And was it real?"

"No, sir." Turned out, an innovative eight-year-old at the local elementary school didn't want the cafeteria's beef nachos for lunch and thought pulling the fire alarm and yelling *Bomb!* throughout the halls would be the most expeditious solution to that problem. Kip remembered how the child kept giggling every time the handcuffs slipped off her tiny wrists, as if they were playing a game, and Kip was getting so increasingly frustrated, he fired off a self-righteous memo that evening asking how he was supposed to do his job properly if he didn't have the appropriate equipment, namely youth-size handcuffs.

"Exactly," Guillermo said. He scanned the list once more. "We'll go with the robot dog that can take folks' temperatures in the event of another pandemic."

"But, sir—" Kip had just included the robot dog as a filler option because Guillermo had asked for five ideas and he could come up with only four. And then he remembered his then-wife mentioning the dog offhandedly one evening, after reading an article about the controversy it stirred in Honolulu, when the police force there had bought one with their extraneous Covid funds. The robot dog *was* cool—don't get him wrong—but Kip could see how it also could be viewed as a waste of government funds. The Range Rover Sentinel, on the other hand—well, a serious bomb threat was more likely than another pandemic, wasn't it? Seeing as those only seemed to come around every hundred years or so. Regardless, Guillermo wouldn't hear another word of it.

Now Kip wishes Guillermo were here to see just how right he was. A real bomb! That almost took out Groebner!

Kip sighs and keeps redialing until, on his seventh try, someone—finally—picks up.

"Hello?"

CHAPTER

16

DAN STARES AT HIS WIFE, SEATED ACROSS FROM him once again at their table, squeezed between the hostess stand and the kitchen door. She's holding her watered-down gin up to her mouth with both hands and taking large gulps.

It reminds him of the very first time he laid eyes on her— standing at a bar in a poorly lit hotel conference room, down-ing a neon-green appletini. He was a senior in college, a guest at his boyhood friend's wedding, and he was stunned not so much by Jane's beauty as by her prepossession. The full-body confidence of her stance. It didn't surprise him later to learn she was three years older, a woman of the world already. It did surprise him to learn she had been invited not to this wedding, but a different wedding across the hall. "This one has an open bar." She shrugged and grinned, and Dan, ever the rule fol-lower, was immediately drawn to her bold insubordination.

Now when Jane sets the glass down next to her plate with a thud, it's empty and there's a kind of a crazed look in her eye. The high-pitched ringing of a telephone somewhere in the restaurant is muted by the busyness of everyone getting settled back at their tables under the watchful eyes of their captors (including his daughter!), and it feels surreal, as though they are on a movie set, pretending to be diners at a high-end restaurant, which Dan supposes in a way they are. It's just for show.

He wishes he could rewind time to ninety minutes ago, when he and Jane were enjoying a nice anniversary dinner, exchanging witty barbs about the exorbitant price of the meal and eating surprisingly delicious barnacles. OK, it wasn't all picture-perfect. She did ask him for a divorce as well, and Dan suddenly flashes on another moment from the night they met, when she rolled her eyes at the overly sentimental wedding toasts and informed Dan in a side whisper she never had any interest in getting married. At the time he thought it was just something girls said to appear breezy and casual to prospective partners, but now he wonders—perhaps twenty years too late—if she actually meant it. Regardless, Jane's desire for a divorce, while troubling, seems insignificant in the grand scheme of the evening, and besides, Dan has always been the type to focus on the good. The silver linings.

For instance, the sharp relief he feels in his lower back now that he's finally sitting in a chair instead of against a wall. His wrists are no longer tied together. He is starving—and still has one and a half barnacles on his plate! He pinches a piece of spongy meat with his fingers and pops it into his mouth, regretting it immediately. It's cold, rendering the texture and flavor not nearly as pleasant as when the dish was fresh. He pulls a face and looks back at Jane.

"We need to come up with a plan," she whispers, rubbing her wrists.

"Yeah, I know."

"Well?"

"Well what?"

"Do you have a plan?"

"In the two seconds since you told me we needed one?" Dan says.

"I would have hoped you'd been thinking about it for more than the past two seconds," Jane hisses, and even though her request is patently ridiculous (Of *course* Dan's been thinking about it! Does *Jane* have a plan?), irritation rips through him. Isn't this the crux of their difference? To any problem that crops up, Dan prefers a calm, logical, gather-the-facts-and-analyze-the-data approach in order to come up with a solution, while Jane's constantly ready to act, rationality and sensibility be damned! Still, Dan hates the idea that he's letting Jane down somehow, though it's a feeling he's far too familiar with.

"How are we going to get her out of here, Dan?"

And because Dan would give anything to make her smile, he grins and says: "Very carefully."

Instead of smiling, Jane pinches the bridge of her nose with her thumb and forefingers, closes her eyes, and mutters something that sounds a lot like: *Oh, forthelove.*

Dan frowns.

The sharp trilling sound emanates again from the hallway for the eighth or ninth time in the past five minutes. Dan starts to think he's the only one who can hear it—or that maybe he's

177

hallucinating it—when Brick finally barks: "Can someone answer the goddamned phone?" and Caden goes running out of the room.

"We have to get her over here somehow," Jane says, talking so quietly it's unclear to Dan if he's part of the conversation. "Though you should probably be the one to talk to her."

"Me?"

"Yes, you. She never listens to me."

Dan can't remember the last time Sissy listened to anyone.

"How can we get her over here?"

Dan blinks. While he wants answers as much as Jane does, he doesn't see how drawing attention to themselves and Sissy is going to do anything but cause trouble. "Jane, I really don't think—"

"Maybe if we need something?"

"For now, let's try to keep a low profile. Wait until an opportunity presents itself."

Jane squints, as if considering Dan's words, and then bobs her head slowly. Dan folds his hands together on the tabletop, pleased he's made his point so clearly and gotten Jane on the same page.

Then Jane abruptly breaks eye contact and says "Excuse me!" to the room at large.

Every muscle in Dan's body tenses. "Jane!" he whispers. "What are you—"

"Excuse me!" Jane repeats, waving her hand like a rude patron.

Heads turn this time, including Brick's, who, upon registering that it's Jane talking, gets such a look of exasperation, Dan feels almost a kinship with him. "What," Brick says flatly.

"Could we possibly get some food? None of us really got to eat before you . . . came in."

Brick's gaze is steely and intense—a look that would cause any normal human to wilt and shrink, but of course his wife keeps talking. "Plus, if we're eating when Otto arrives, it will look . . . more authentic."

Dan holds his breath as Brick's brow changes in a way that looks like he can't argue with that. Dan also knows that feeling.

"Fine," Brick says through a clenched jaw. "Goldie, why don't you see if you can scrounge up something in the kitchen for our guests to eat?"

"Do I look like a chef?" she fires back, and Dan flicks his eyes to the ceiling—why do his wife and daughter have to be among the most stubborn women in the world? Would it kill Sissy and Jane to just put their heads down when dealing with the unstable head of a *terrorist* group? It's like poking a grizzly bear—which, come to think of it, they both probably would actually do, if the bear said something that could even remotely be construed as sexist.

"No," Brick says, "but our head chef is currently . . . indisposed and the others are tied up. Maybe you could find something simple—"

"Roquefort almond sourdough rolls are in the warmer." The sous chef, Zay, speaks up from where he is still tied up against the wall, along with Javier, Monica, and the supine Lars—all just out of view of the picture window.

Brick acknowledges him with a brief nod. "Goldie? Could you procure the rolls?"

"I can help!" Jane screeches.

"No," Brick says, barely looking at her before his attention is drawn by Caden appearing, frantic, in the doorframe between the dining room and hall. "It's the police!"

While he's distracted, Dan nudges Jane's feet with his own under the table, trying to get her attention, to remind her that taking time to come up with a good plan is preferable to acting without thinking—and will likely yield better results.

"What?" Brick says.

"The police," Caden says. "On the phone?"

He nods, as if he assumed as much. "What'd they say?"

"They got a call . . . about a man being shot." Brick's gaze darts to Jane, and Dan's does, too. *Did* she call the police? Dan can't imagine when she would have had time, but Jane is nothing if not resourceful (not to mention tenacious and stubborn and foolhardy)—and while he's not great at reading her expressions, he's fairly certain the one currently written all over her face is guilt mixed with a touch of fear. "They want to know if we need an ambulance or medevac," Caden continues. "What do you want me to say?"

Yes! Dan thinks, trying to telepathically give Brick the correct answer, but it doesn't work.

"Nothing," Brick growls. "And rip that phone out of the wall."

No! Dan thinks, but it's Jane who screeches it: "NO!"

Caden freezes, and in the silence that follows her outburst, every head turns toward her, for maybe the seventy-fifth time that evening? Dan can't keep track. And he wonders—not for the first time—if the inability to keep one's mouth shut is actually a bona fide medical condition. If so, he's certain Jane suffers from it.

Brick raises his brow at her. "Is there a problem?"

"Yes."

"And what, pray tell, is it this time?"

"You have to talk to them."

"Who?"

"The police."

"Why is that," he says in a monotone Dan understands to mean Brick doesn't actually want the answer. Jane does not interpret his words the same way.

"Because it will keep them from bursting in the door at any second."

"They'll have to wait for the bomb squad to come up from L.A. or down from Santa Barbara," Brick says, repeating what he said to Sissy earlier. "Either way, it's bought us at least two hours. By the time they come and clear the hill, it will be too late."

Dan wonders if he's the only one for whom the words *too late* caused goose bumps to crawl over his skin.

"What if they don't follow protocol?" Jane says, her words tumbling out in a rush.

Brick cocks his head, as if this is something he hadn't considered. Then he narrows his eyes. "Is it my imagination or are you trying to *help*? I thought you wanted the police to come—and now you . . . don't?"

"I just . . ." Jane pauses and Dan closes his eyes, intensely hoping it will occur to her at some point to close her mouth. "I just don't want anyone to get hurt. And if the police come charging in here, I imagine it's not going to end well. For anyone."

Brick studies her, but Jane—of course—keeps talking. "You can negotiate with them."

"For what?"

"For whatever it is you want."

"I don't want anything from them."

"Well, you could ask for something."

"How about pizza?" Caden says, clearly warming to the idea.

Dan's stomach growls again.

Brick looks at Caden with disdain. "What is this—a child's birthday party?"

Caden shrugs. "That's what they always do in the movies."

"THIS ISN'T A MOVIE."

"If you ask for something, it will help stall them," Jane says, nearly pleading. "Of course, they'll want something in return. Probably a hostage."

"The chef!" Dan says. "Please give them the chef."

He didn't know he was going to do it, but now that everyone's attention is on him, he continues, determined. "Lars needs a hospital. Right?" He glances at Rahul, who is still sitting with Lars, monitoring the drainage of the tube. "Tell them."

The neurosurgeon nods heavily. "He does."

"Please," Dan says, and searches the room until his eyes land on his daughter. His daughter who couldn't stand to see a bunny rabbit suffer, much less a human. "He could die," he says, looking directly into her deep brown eyes, a mirror of Jane's.

Sissy blinks, slightly nods, and then stands. "Let's give them the chef," she says, and Dan's chest blooms with pride—only slightly dampened by the reminder that his daughter is holding a restaurant full of innocent people hostage. But at least she isn't completely hardened. "I don't want him to die."

"Yeah, same," Lyle agrees. "Please, Brick. That's not what we came here for."

"Why are you all begging him?" Isaac pipes up from where he's been sitting—observing everything and everyone—since he came in from the kitchen. He's young, not just in appearance but in attitude. His eyes and voice convey a sneer of disdain that Dan has now gotten used to seeing on Sarah's and Josh's faces—that universal teenage expression that they know everything and are merely tolerating your own ignorance. "Aren't we leaderless? You all kneel down to Brick like he's some god. The great wizard everyone lives in fear of. You want to give over the chef? Let's give over the chef. Brick doesn't own us. Let's take a vote. All who want to release the chef, raise your hands."

Dan shoots his right hand straight up like a dart. Brick sighs as though he's the impatient caregiver of a child. "You don't get a vote."

Sissy and Tink raise their hands. Then Caden, Lyle, and Jeremy, the wire-rimmed glasses guy from the kitchen.

"Isaac?" Brick turns to the insolent teenager, the only one who didn't raise his hand. "You don't want the man you shot to be saved?"

"I don't care one way or another. I'm just tired of the spineless sniveling," Isaac says.

183

Brick shoots the kid a look of annoyance, then pauses, hands on his hips. After a beat, he nods as though he's decided something. "You," he growls, pointing at Sissy. "Get the rolls. The rest of you—" He eyes Tink, Isaac, Jeremy, and Lyle. "Anyone moves, deal with them." Then he storms out of the room, following Caden down the hallway.

Once Brick is gone, it feels like the entire dining room exhales—like it's a living organism with a heartbeat and emotions, the foremost one being relief. Until Isaac jumps off his perch on the table and swings his gun around in the air, laughing whenever anyone flinches.

"Knock it off," Tink says.

Dan kicks Jane under the table again, this time harder. She looks at him, annoyed. "What was that?" he hisses.

"What?"

"I thought we agreed to keep a low profile."

"I couldn't just let him *not* talk to the police, Dan," she says evenly, as if any sane person would have done the same thing.

"Yes! That's exactly what you could have—*should* have done."

"They need to know it's a hostage situation, so they'll create a command center and keep their distance."

"A *command center*. How do you have any idea what the police are or are not going to do? What, do you moonlight as a cop in your spare time?"

"Well," she says, dropping her gaze.

"Well *what*?"

"I did interview that hostage negotiator for my book."

Now it's Dan's turn to pinch the bridge of his nose. "Well, I've watched a lot of terrorist movies, and I don't know about a command center, but the second Brick tells them he's keeping everyone hostage, that hill"—he points dramatically toward the door—"is going to be swarming with cops and the FBI—the FBI, Jane!—and that *definitely* never ends well for the terrorists. The terrorists, which include our daughter."

As if on cue, the door to the kitchen swings open and Sissy comes back in carrying a metal tray. She passes Jane and Dan without a glance and starts at the table farthest from them. He notices Jane following their daughter with her eyes. Then she turns to Dan, as if he hasn't even spoken, and whispers: "When she gets here, you do the talking."

He stares at her, waiting for her to at least acknowledge his point, and when it becomes apparent she's not going to, he nods curtly. "Fine."

"Ask her what on earth she's doing."

"Right," Dan says.

"And thinking," she says. "And why! Why is she doing this? And is she being held against her—"

"Jane," Dan whispers her name sharply. "I've got this."

They sit, staring at their plates, waiting. Jane straightens her water glass and napkin, lining them up with the plate, as though she'll be graded on it later by an etiquette judge. Finally, Sissy approaches their table. Balancing the metal tray on her left hand, she uses the tongs in her right to grab a roll and place it on Jane's bread plate. Dan clears his throat and Sissy glances at him. He opens his mouth.

"Sissy, are you on drugs?" Jane hisses.

"What the—" Sissy's face screws in disgust and she glances around. "Keep your voice down."

"Jane!" Dan whispers. "Let me handle this." He looks at Sissy. "Are you on drugs?"

She stares at her father, her face hardening even more. "No, Dad. I'm not on drugs."

"Then what are you doing here?" Jane says. "What *is* this?"

"What are *you* guys doing here? I thought you were going out for your anniversary."

Dan looks at Jane, waiting for her to respond, since she so clearly wants to handle it herself, but she's staring at him. "Oh—now you want? OK." He turns to Sissy. "We *are* out for our anniversary!"

"Here? You always go to the Macaroni Grill."

"We do not!" Dan says, and he feels Jane's severe gaze on him. "OK, maybe we do, but your mother loves the chicken scalo—"

"Dan!" Jane says.

He softly clears his throat and tries to get back on track. "Sissy, what are you doing with these . . . these . . . *terrorists*?"

"We're not terrorists!"

Dan opens his mouth, but Jane once again beats him to it. "The guns you're toting like it's the goddamn Wild West would suggest otherwise. Guns, Sissy! Who even are you?"

Tears spring to Sissy's eyes. "It wasn't supposed to be like this."

"Oh, Sissy," Dan breathes, his heart melting at once. He's never been able to stand seeing her cry.

"Oh, good Lord, Dan. She's faking it," Jane says, and then, to Sissy: "You came barging into a restaurant armed to the teeth and it wasn't supposed to be like this? What did you think was going to happen?"

Sissy wipes a tear but doesn't respond.

Dan glances around, nervous that someone is listening in on their conversation, but thankfully the hostages are busy eating their bread, and the other terrorists are in their own clumps of conversations and paying no attention to Dan and Jane's little corner of the restaurant.

"Honestly, Sissy. What have you gotten yourself mixed up in? Are they *making* you do this? Are you in trouble?" Jane whispers, and then, before giving her a chance to respond, says: "Is this because of him—because of Brick? Are you in . . . love with him?"

Dan blinks. Where did *that* come from? Sissy, in *love*? Dan feels his hackles rise, heat forming in his belly. He knows Sissy gets to make these choices for herself, that he has no say-so—nor does he *want* any say-so—in her love life. (He can't even think the word *sex* in the same context as his daughter.) But Brick is old enough to be her . . . well, not her dad, but her much older brother, at the very least. He's a grown man. And Sissy's a child!

Sissy's expression morphs from sadness to shock to anger. "Oh my God, Mom. Gross. He's like, *thirty*!"

Dan exhales.

"But he is *very* good-looking," Jane continues, and Dan's head snaps toward her. "I mean what with the accent and those eyes and the biceps—good Lord, you'd have to be blind not to . . . Anyway, it would be understandable—"

"Uh, hi," Dan says, offering a little wave. "Remember me? I can hear you."

Sissy's nostrils flare. "Yes, because as a woman I can't possibly have any opinions or motivations of my own, right? It all must be wrapped up in desire for a man's attention. Sexist much, Mom?"

"OK," Dan says, "I think we've gotten a little off—"

"Oy!" Brick shouts, and Dan, Jane, and Sissy freeze. He's standing in the doorframe of the hallway, glaring at them. "What's going on over there?"

For once, Jane keeps her mouth shut.

"Nothing," Sissy calls over her shoulder. "This lady is saying she, uh . . . needs to go to the bathroom."

"*Again?*"

"I have an overactive bladder," Jane says. Dan can't disagree with that.

The faint chop-chop-chop of a helicopter approaching from a distance fills the air and Brick grins. "Fine," he says, waving a hand. "Take her. Just make sure you're back for the main event. Tink," he says, turning his attention away from their table. "Plug in the booster. I gave the police your burner number if they need to get in touch with us again."

Tink leans over and inserts the plug into the outlet, causing the bucket of cell phones to come alive once again.

Then Brick points directly at Dan, and Dan's heart nearly stops. "You," he says. "And you." He points at Rahul, the neurosurgeon. "We're letting the chef go. How do we move him?"

Dan closes his eyes in relief and swallows. Then he opens them and takes a deep breath. "Very carefully."

CHAPTER

17

EIGHTEEN YEARS AGO, AFTER TWENTY-SEVEN AND a half hours of labor, Jane took a deep breath, clenched every shaking muscle in her legs and stomach with all her might, and finally—*finally*—expelled her infant daughter from her womb. When the nurse placed the striped-hospital-blanket bundle in the crook of Jane's elbow, Jane stared into those brand-new gray eyes, waiting to be overcome with all-consuming love and joy, with the life-changing magic of motherhood she'd read about in so many books. But inside she felt . . . nothing. Chalking it up to exhaustion and sure the correct feelings would strike her at any second, she affixed her face adoringly. She exclaimed: *Greige-blue, like yours, Dan!* She rubbed the pad of her thumb gently over the baby's impossibly soft and delicate cheek. But Jane remained as hollow as her belly now felt. Carved out. And all her latent fears were confirmed: Jane was a bad mother. Or worse, she wasn't a mother at all. She was an impostor. A fake.

Dan smiled over her shoulder, already the patient and loving father, buying Jane's act, but she thought this new baby, whom they had dubbed Sarah (Did she look like a Sarah? Who was she to give someone a name they would have for the rest of their life? Who was she to say who someone *was* when Jane suddenly didn't even know who she herself was?), and her all-knowing eyes could see right through it. Her eyes seemed to say: *You?* You're *who they stuck me with? Where's my real mother?* And then Jane did feel something—sympathy for this poor child who was unlucky enough to acquire Jane as her mother.

For days, and then weeks, Jane went through the motions of new motherhood: feeding, holding, rocking, singing off-key pop songs in a gentle voice because she couldn't remember more than the first verse of popular nursery rhymes (See? An impostor!). And the only emotion that grew greater than her sympathy for this helpless creature was resentment for how this tiny human, with all her needs and inability to communicate in anything but cries, had so thoroughly upended Jane's life.

Jane can't remember when it happened—six weeks? eight? Those first months all swim together in her mind—but one morning she was clipping Sissy's impossibly tiny fingernails and accidentally caught the skin on the pad of Sissy's finger in the sharp clipper, cutting it when she pressed down and causing Sissy to scrunch her face tight in pain. But it was the cry—animalistic, raw, a cry that was different from hunger or discomfort from a wet diaper or exhaustion—that struck a chord deep within Jane. She bundled her daughter to her chest, rocking her gently, whispering against her wisps of hair, *I'mso sorryMommy'ssosorryS'okS'okYou'reOK* over and over while tears rained down Jane's cheeks.

And that's when something exploded inside of her. Or maybe bloomed is more accurate. Love, yes. So much love. But also guilt for having injured her baby, and fear of all the other unknowable and unpreventable dangers in the world that could cause Sarah harm. Jane would soon come to understand these were the three pillars of motherhood: guilt, anxiety, and love. But in that moment she only knew, without a shadow of a doubt, she would do anything to protect her daughter.

Including, apparently, doing everything in her power to help her escape a hostage situation in which Sissy is on the wrong side of the hostages.

For the second time that evening, Jane finds herself in the hallway walking toward the red landline telephone on the pedestal. The phone! She would have given anything to have unfettered access to it in the first thirty minutes of the evening, but now what good will it do her?

"Did you just text me?" Sissy says. Jane looks up at her daughter, relief coursing through her body—relief she finally has her daughter to herself, away from the immediate danger. And though she has a thousand questions, she is solely focused on getting Sissy even farther away from the terrorists—completely out of the restaurant and somehow home safe in her own bed.

Then she notices the cell in Sissy's hand. "You have your *phone*?"

"Of course."

"Great," Jane mumbles, nodding. "Just great. One more piece of evidence putting you at the scene of the crime." Moments like these make Jane wonder how Sissy got a 1590 on her SAT.

Sissy frowns. "Did you leave your curling iron plugged in?"

Jane stops. "You got that text?" She thinks of her phone, ensconced firmly in Brick's pocket, and wonders if Tink plugging in the booster allowed her texts to be sent.

It feels like a lifetime ago, that concern—and now Jane has a thousand more pressing ones, namely getting Sissy out. That's when she remembers the window in the bathroom! Then she immediately frowns, as she realizes it's likely too small to get Sissy through.

Her eye lands on the two EMPLOYEES ONLY doors. Maybe there's a bigger window behind one of them. She reaches for the knob on the first door and it opens immediately. She pokes her head in and realizes it's the chef's office. No window, though. She grabs the handle of the second door—the one she tried to open earlier—and jiggles it, but it's still locked.

"So did you leave it on?" Sissy asks.

"What?" Jane says, distracted. "No. Your father says he unplugged it."

"What are you doing?" Sissy asks.

Jane ignores her. The door handle is standard: a cheap knob with a small hole in the center. The exact kind of door handle she's had years of experience unlocking in her own house when Sissy barricaded herself in her room, a handwritten KEEP OUT sign serving as an ominous warning to anyone (mainly Josh) who'd dare try to enter. She slides a bobby pin out of her hair and pushes it in the doorknob, jiggling it until the knob gives, turning easily in her hand.

"Mom!" Sissy says as Jane pushes the door open, blinking into the pitch-black room beyond. It takes her a second to realize it's not a room but a staircase, leading down.

"A basement?" she mutters to herself, surprised there would be anything underground on a cliff this high up.

"A wine cellar," Sissy says. When Jane looks at her questioningly, Sissy drops her gaze. "Brick had the blueprints."

Jane ignores for now the reminder that Sissy is, in fact, in league with Brick and was plotting this . . . debacle . . . *with* him, and focuses on the fact that most basements have a hatch that opens to the outside for easy loading and unloading—particularly in the case of a restaurant. She gropes on the wall for a light switch, and, finding it, illuminates the stairs, then charges ahead.

"Where are you going?" Sissy demands. Jane doesn't wait for her daughter or command her to follow, because she knows Sissy won't have much of a choice. Sure enough, when she reaches the bottom, she hears her daughter's footsteps pad behind her.

The ceiling is low, the stone-walled room smaller than she expected. It looks like a relic—a leftover remnant from a previous era, and Jane remembers reading somewhere that La Fin du Monde used to be the quarters of a lighthouse keeper in the 1800s. Though the lighthouse itself had long been demolished, this building was repurposed multiple times over the decades. Jane looks around the dim room, each wall covered with bottles and bottles of wine and champagne—some of them so old they're caked with dust. In front of her are more rows of wine shelving—so many she can't see to the other side. She takes off around them, her daughter calling after her.

Upon reaching the other side, Jane fills with relief when she finds what she's looking for—a rickety wooden ladder reaching up to a two-flap cellar door on the ceiling, held together with a thick padlock. Jane climbs the rungs, Sissy's voice drifting up to her.

Jane yanks on the padlock, but it doesn't budge. She tries her bobby pin—to no avail. She glances around below her for something—anything that she could use to hit the padlock and knock it loose. A rock, a crowbar. She considers a bottle of wine, but is fairly certain she'll just have shards of glass to show for her efforts.

"ARGH!" she shouts in frustration as Sissy continues her stream-of-consciousness, one-sided conversation. "And what was Brick talking about out there—is Dad *cheating* on you?"

This turns Jane's head. "What? No—" She stops herself. She doesn't want to lie to her daughter. "That's not important right now."

"So that means he is. He's *cheating*? Daddy?"

Jane pinches the bridge of her nose for a beat and then climbs down the ladder and stands eye to eye with her daughter (though Sissy reached Jane's height during a seventh-grade growth spurt, Jane still finds herself caught off guard at times at her daughter's stature). "Sissy," she says. She hears the plaintive pleading in her own voice and does nothing to suppress it. "What are you *doing*? What is this?"

Sissy looks away, refusing to meet her mother's gaze.

"Sissy!"

Her daughter takes a deep breath, as if she knew this was coming. "We're trying to save the world, OK?"

"Save the world," Jane repeats, letting out a puff of laughter. What a ridiculous, childish phrase. She studies her daughter and throws her hands up, deciding to bite. "From *what*?"

Sissy exhales, and then: "We're an underground environmental action organization called Force of Nature."

"What?" Jane stares at her daughter, as if waiting to see if she's joking. When it's apparent she's not, she says: "This is about . . . *climate change*? What, does the restaurant not recycle their cooking oil? Are those barnacle things endangered?" Then she remembers Otto. "What's that got to do with Otto St. Clair?"

"You're kidding. You do read the news, don't you?"

"Of course. He makes electric helicopters! He drives some ridiculously expensive *electric* sports car! And didn't he build the world's biggest solar farm or something?"

"Oh God, Mom, you would believe that."

"Why wouldn't I believe that?"

"That's all a publicity stunt. Optics. You know what he's really done?"

Jane racks her brain for other headlines and remembers the one Dan mentioned when she was getting ready in the bathroom. "He made his own crypto! Apparently, it's worth more than Bitcoin now."

Sissy rolls her eyes. "After publicly committing years ago to using one hundred percent renewable energy, like building wind and solar panel farms, to run SierraX's massive data centers, he hasn't. He still uses fossil fuel energy to run them! And then, as if that's not bad enough, he's been secretly working with oil and gas companies—getting paid *billions* to automate their operations and create tech that helps them extract even more oil out of more wells. His company is doing more to single-handedly destroy the earth than they are to help it. He doesn't actually care about the environment! All he cares about is lining his pockets."

"Hm," Jane grunts. None of it really surprises her. She's old enough to understand the way the world works and that the people in power often do whatever it takes to get more money and more power, no matter the collateral damage. "OK, so Otto's awful. I get it. But you thought you could just bust into a restaurant guns a-blazing and make him see the light of day? This isn't like you, Sissy!"

"Isn't it *you* who's always telling me if I don't like the way things are going I should do something about it?"

Jane's eyes go wide. She did say that the few times Sissy lamented the state of environmental affairs, crying when she found out that recycling trucks didn't actually recycle most of the plastic they collected and threw it away instead.

To be fair, Sissy's always been sensitive and was equally upset about homelessness and LGBTQ+ rights and the ubiquitous use of Roundup that was killing off honeybees in droves. She belonged to so many clubs at her school last year, Jane couldn't keep them all straight. Nevertheless, it was something she always admired in her daughter—the passion of her convictions. Mostly because Jane couldn't remember the last time she had been so passionate. She just knew she had been—at

one time—like the sun, burning with the ferocity of a thousand opinions, injustices, ready to scorch the earth in the name
of what was right. And then, at some point, apathy started to
take its place, along with fear and anxiety and the feeling that
she would rather shrink back down, not say anything, than
stand up for what she believed in. Part of it, Jane knew, was
the natural evolution of becoming an adult and realizing you
don't know as much as you think you do. But part of it, Jane
feared, was that she'd stopped believing in things. She'd stopped
believing in herself.

She stares into her daughter's eyes, the eyes that began
greige-blue at birth but darkened over time into an exact mirror of Jane's own deep brown. Her daughter, who is still the
sun. And Jane thinks of the many restless nights she suffered
over the years wondering how to hold Sissy's flame in her
hands just so—that impossible balancing act of reining in
her daughter's fire without extinguishing it.

Now she wonders if she erred too far in the wrong direction. Maybe she should have doused Sissy's fire completely
with a ten-gallon bucket.

"I meant start a composting co-op in the neighborhood!"
Jane says. "Or join a Save the Sea Turtles campaign!" And
then something else dawns on her. "OH MY GOD—is *this* the
climate-change anxiety support group you've been going to every
week?"

The chop-chop-chop of helicopter blades growing louder in
the distance fills the silence.

"It *was* a support group at first!" Sissy says, and then lowers
her eyes. "That's where I met Brick."

Jane's head goes light at the realization. "You've been planning to do this for *months*." She'd always been a little judgy of parents whose kids ended up in the hospital after drug overdoses or who ran off with some stranger they met on the Internet. How do you not know what your own children are doing? She suddenly has a flood of empathy for those parents, because apparently she *is* one.

"And guns, Sissy!" Jane can't help it; her brain keeps coming back to this salient point. "You hate violence."

"I know. I know! But mine's not even loaded!" she says. "None of them were supposed to be. Brick promised they would be blanks."

"Oh, Sissy." Jane's heart squeezes at her trusting, naive, completely idiotic daughter. "Just like he promised the bomb was fake."

She nods weakly. "I thought we'd be in and out. I didn't think anyone would get hurt."

Jane puts her hand on Sissy's shoulder lightly, but—as Jane anticipated—the girl shrugs her off. Jane sighs and turns to climb the ladder again. "Come on. Help me figure out how to open this. We have to get you out of here."

Sissy gives her mother a confused look. "What do you mean? I'm not going anywhere."

"You're joking."

"No! What do you think I'm going to do—run and hide in the woods?"

Jane didn't actually think it through past getting her out, but it was as good a plan as any. "Yes! You can hide in the woods.

Dad and I will come find you when all this"—she waves her hand—"is over."

"No, that's ridiculous. I *want* to be here. Otto's almost here. We're almost done."

"Done with *what*? What's the plan? Are you trying to convince Otto to stop consorting with fossil fuel companies? Because that's never going to work." Jane grabs the padlock again, yanking it one way and then another in the vain hope that it might budge. The helicopter blades are purring so loud now, it swallows the thuds of her ministrations. Jane groans.

"No, that's not—"

"Then what are you doing?"

Sissy averts her gaze once more, looking at her feet, the walls, anywhere but Jane's eyes. She mumbles something unintelligible.

"What?"

"I said: We're setting things right."

"How?" Jane asks, and then she goes completely still. Her vision blurs, and she thinks this time she really might pass out. "Oh my God. You guys are *stealing* from Otto St. Clair. That's what this is all about." She can't believe she didn't put it all together before now. And then she realizes what she's just said.

"YOU'RE STEALING FROM OTTO ST. CLAIR?!" she roars.

"We're going to anonymously donate the money to all the grassroots, on-the-ground organizations who really need it. Who can really make a difference in their communities and the environment. Groups that Otto would be giving to himself if he actually cared about making an impact. It's like . . . Robin Hood."

"Oh my God. Oh my God, Sissy." She steps down from the ladder, putting her feet on the cement ground once again because she really does think she's going to pass out. "Like Robin Hood," Jane breathes. "I don't think that defense actually holds up in court, Sissy." She sits on the cement floor of the cellar and pulls her knees up to her chest.

And though Jane knows it's unlikely, that Dan is probably right—she's the only one who sees it, and it's all in her head, or worse, some weird ego trip—she has to ask. "Have you read my book?"

Sissy looks at her blankly. "What book?"

"*Tea Is for Terror*! The only book I've ever written and had published?"

"Oh, right." She cocks her head. "Yeah, I did. Why?"

"Wait—you did?"

"Yeah, remember that time I lost my phone for like, three days? I was soooo bored, and so I picked it up." She grins, proud of herself.

"My book."

"I mean, part of it, anyway."

"How much did you read?"

"I don't know! Like the first . . . ten pages, or something?"

Jane sends her eyes heavenward and sighs heavily.

"Sorry, Mom. It was reaaaaally boring."

Jane bobs her head. She really should have expected nothing less. Her own husband didn't even read the book; why would her child? "You didn't—I don't know—give it to Brick or anything, did you?"

"No. Why would I do that?"

"I don't know. I don't know! Everything is just so similar. I'm worried they're following it or something. And if they are—if it's the same—then this is really bad, Sissy. It's *evil*. Since when are you OK with *hurting* people? Killing them?"

Sissy cocks her head. "Why do you keep saying that? Nobody has died and no one is going to. That's why we put blanks in the guns. Well, obviously Isaac didn't, but—wait. What happens in your book?"

"All the hostages *die*, Sissy!" Jane says. "The thieves set off a bomb to blow up the teahouse to cover their tracks!"

Sissy's jaw drops. "*What?!* That's the ending?"

"Yes!"

"Mom, that's awful! No wonder the reviews are so terrible. What kind of ending is that?"

Jane's eyes flash. "It's a metaphor!" she shouts. To be fair, it was what most of the negative reviews pointed out: What was the point of the book if the bad guys just got away with it? And Jane wanted to scream at them (especially that Stephen with a *ph*) that that was the point; it was a metaphor, a social commentary highlighting how the real bad guys—the politicians, the CEOs, the lobbyists—always get away with everything.

Jane can see the wheels of Sissy's brain turning as she says: "Wait, so you think Brick is going to *bomb* the restaurant? Kill everyone in it?"

Jane lets out a loud clap of a laugh. "You *don't*?"

"No! He's not like that, Mom, I swear. We've got a plan."

"A plan. Wasn't the plan to get in and out? And now you've been here for what—ninety minutes? And the police! The only way out of here is down that hill. How are you going to get past the police, Sissy?"

Sissy hesitates, and Jane can see the uncertainty in her eyes. "You think that man—who didn't even blink when the chef got shot; rigged a van with high-powered explosives, possibly *killing* whoever set it off down there; and is stealing money from one of the richest men in the world—cares whether those people in there live or die?"

Sissy blinks. "I really don't think—"

"There are witnesses, Sissy. *I'm* a witness. Your *father* is a witness. What choice does Brick have?"

Sissy frowns but doesn't respond. The whir of helicopter blades is suddenly so loud it sounds as if the machine is in the cellar with them. And then a man appears behind Sissy, and Jane screams. Isaac offers a devilish smile as he briefly takes note of Jane's fear—and then her strange position sitting at the bottom of the ladder. "What are you doing down here?" he shouts over the din to Sissy, and then shrugs as if he doesn't actually care. "Come on. He's here. It's time." There's a light in his eyes, an eagerness that's unsettling. He grabs a bottle of champagne from a nearby shelf, and Jane has half a mind to grab one herself and knock him over the head with it, but she doesn't know what good that would do. It's not like she can get the cellar doors open, and if even she could, she's not convinced she could force Sissy out of them. The glass bottles begin to vibrate and clink together from the deafening power of the blades, and they all look up to the ceiling as if waiting for the helicopter to burst through at any second. Dust rains down on their faces, and then, silence. Jane's eyes dart from Isaac to Sissy and then back to Isaac, who wears a sly grin.

Otto has arrived.

ONE HOUR AND THIRTY-SIX MINUTES UNTIL THE END

CHAPTER
18

"IS THAT A HELICOPTER?" SANDY ASKS, COCKING her left ear toward the sky.

"Huh," Kip says. "I wonder if that's the VIP."

Sandy stands, hands on her hips, brow creased. The perimeter around the van has been set, the Los Angeles bomb squad and SWAT teams are en route, and Groebner (alive and well) has been carried down the hill by one of the ambulances to the closest medical center for treatment.

"Tell us again? Exactly what he said."

Kip takes a deep breath, preparing to relay the phone call for the second time—the first to Zimmerman right when he hung up, and now to Sandy, who Kip can tell is trying as hard as he is to put his finger on the piece of the puzzle that doesn't quite fit.

Kip starts at the beginning: He called the restaurant over and over and then someone picked up. "Hello?" Kip straightened his spine in the back of the ambulance, slightly caught off guard that someone had actually answered and then equally taken aback at the informality; he expected a *Thank you for calling La Fin du Monde, this is so-and-so speaking, how may I help you?* He wondered if perhaps he'd been dialing the wrong number.

"Is this . . . Have I reached La Fin du Monde?"

"Yeah—are you the one who keeps calling here? What do you want?"

Kip hesitated. This was the Michelin-star restaurant people paid thousands of dollars to eat at? He expected a little more . . . decorum. "Yes, hello, this is Deputy Kip Grayson with the Coastal Bureau police force. We had a report of a gunshot wound in the establishment—can you confirm? And do you need a medevac?"

"Hold on. I'll get Brick."

"Who's Brick—the manager?" Kip asked, but in return there was only silence. The person who answered had already gone. Kip waited what seemed like an interminably long time—so long, he thought he had surely been forgotten; the person who answered had gotten distracted or maybe swept up in the emergency of the gunshot, and Kip was seconds from hanging up and calling for a medevac regardless when another, deeper, accented voice repeated the informal greeting. "Hello?"

"Yes, this is Officer Kip Grayson with the Coastal Bureau police force. With whom am I speaking?"

"I'm the manager here," the voice said. "Sorry for your wait, dinner service is always quite hectic, and we're tragically understaffed. How can I help you?"

Kip squinted, staring into the dark forest but not really seeing it. This didn't sound like a man in the midst of an emergency. "Do you need a medevac?"

"A who?"

"A medevac, ah . . . emergency services? We received a call about a gunshot wound."

"Here?" the man said. "At La Fin du Monde?"

Kip blinks. "Yes. Are you saying no one has been injured on the premises?"

"God dammit. I knew those kids were eventually going to get to us."

"Excuse me?"

"It's one of those TikTok challenges—they call 9-1-1, trying to get police to swarm high-end establishments and ruin the dining experience. Just happened at Matsuhisa in L.A. Called swatting, I think? Surely you see it all the time in your line of work."

"Right, yes," Kip said; though he'd never been called to a swatting case, per se, he was all too familiar with false alarms from kids. He made a mental note to look up the Matsuhisa incident later. "Of course."

"God, remember when crank calls used to be asking a stranger if their refrigerator was running? Anyway, thank you for checking. Is there anything else I can do for you, Officer? We've got a major VIP inbound and I need to make sure all my i's are dotted, you know what I mean?"

Kip hesitated, unsure if he should mention the van, the bomb. He thought back to the videos and couldn't remember protocol. He was already in hot water and didn't want to make the wrong call again. He looked around for Sandy and McLeod, but they were still setting up the perimeter. The two EMTs were near, but deep in a conversation about the Oakland A's pitching lineup, and likely wouldn't be able to advise regardless. "Did you happen to hear a loud noise thirty minutes ago?"

"A noise?"

"Yes, a loud bang."

"No, but to be honest, during dinner rush, I can hardly hear myself think." The man laughed jovially.

Kip frowned. Surely the blast could have been heard at the top of the hill. It couldn't be more than half a mile to the restaurant. "Who's the VIP?" he asked, stalling for time.

"I'm sorry, I'm not at liberty to say," the man said, and his voice did sound apologetic, deferent. "Main part of the job at a place like this is discretion, you know? That's what keeps them coming back."

"Right, right," Kip said, still unable to spot Sandy in the hazy night. He was going to have to make a call and hope this time it was the right one. "Listen, we're going to need everyone in the restaurant to shelter in place for the time being."

"What do you mean—as in, not leave? Is everything OK?"

"Yes, just while we investigate this . . . swatting incident," Kip said. He figured there was no need to cause alarm or panic by mentioning the bomb.

"Sure thing, you're the boss."

Kip couldn't help it; his chest swelled.

"We have at least two more hours of dinner service and, like I said, the VIP inbound, so shouldn't be a problem. You'll let me know if you need more time than that?"

"Yes," Kip said, the word imbued with a newfound confidence. "Make sure to stay near the line; answer when we call back."

"Absolutely. You know, this is a landline, and like I said, it's a busy night, so let me give you a cell that I'll keep on me to make sure I answer right away if you need anything else."

When Kip hung up, he found himself impressed with the professionalism of the establishment, a full 180-degree turn from his first misgivings, and he was reminded how dead wrong first impressions could often be.

Sandy nods thoughtfully now and says: "And you told Zimmerman about the VIP?"

"Yes," Kip says. "I remember because he said"—Kip puts on an affected gravelly voice to mimic Zimmerman—"*Well, he won't be getting his two-thousand-dollar meal tonight. When he gets there, turn him away. Good work on the shelter in place. Call me with any other developments.*" And Kip puffed up for the second time in as many minutes.

He frowns, realizing in retrospect they had both thought the VIP would be coming in a car—not a helicopter.

Sandy and McLeod and Kip stare at one another in the now-silent night air, the nearby helicopter having reached its destination. "I think this is a develop—" McLeod begins, but his word is cut off by the chirping of the radio on Kip's shoulder. Kip grabs hold of it with his right hand and presses the button with his thumb.

"This is 92 Grayson. Go ahead."

"Grayson, this is dispatch, we've had another comm from La Fin du Monde, a text message."

Grayson's eyes meet Sandy's and McLeod's as the dispatch relays the latest 9-1-1 transmission, the words of which cause Kip's mouth to go dry, his stomach to turn over, and the hairs on the back of his neck to stand straight up. When the radio chirps and falls silent, Kip continues to stare at Sandy and McLeod as if in a trance. Sandy gently takes the cell phone from Kip's hand, dials a number, and puts it up to Kip's ear.

He grabs on to it, holding it tight like a ring buoy thrown to him by a lifeguard. When Zimmerman's gravelly voice says into Kip's ear, "What've you got?" Kip relays the 9-1-1 text message word for word from dispatch.

"Hostage," Zimmerman repeats, more to himself than Kip. "Explains the van." He pauses for a beat, thinking, and then says, louder: "I'll get HRT en route. We need eyes up there—your department got drones, by chance?"

"We do!" Kip says. They'd only ever used them for fun, as they'd never had anything important to surveil, and Kip's eager to deploy the machines.

"Get 'em airborne and report back. We need as much intel as we can get."

Kip agrees. He has so many questions. Who's being held hostage? Who's holding them hostage? Why are they being held hostage? And why was the manager of the restaurant so calm on the phone? It occurs to him—too late, perhaps—that it likely wasn't the manager he spoke to.

But it's Zimmerman who gives voice to a question Kip hasn't even considered, muttering right before he ends the call: "Who—in *tarnation*—is Jane Brooks?"

THE IMAGE BURNED IN DAN'S BRAIN FROM HIS VISIT
to the Sistine Chapel isn't the frescoes on the ceiling (though
they were stunning, better than any picture in any book, to the
chef's earlier point); it's the view he had when he first walked
in: the bent-necked tourists, all gawking at the sky like a group
of baby sparrows waiting for their mother to drop bits of re-
gurgitated worms in their mouths. It's how Dan imagines he—
and everyone else in the restaurant—looks now, staring at the
blank restaurant ceiling, the air thick with a buzz, an energy,
the same restlessness that emanates from a crowd at a concert
in the seconds leading up to the band taking the stage.

A noise jerks everyone's attention (also like a flock of birds,
Dan thinks) to the hallway entrance, and then a sense of disappointment permeates the air when they realize it's only Isaac
and Jane and Sissy, though no one could be as disappointed as
Dan. It's a relief to see them for sure, as he spent the entire ten
minutes they were gone frantically worried about what they

were doing, but he somehow managed to entirely convince himself Jane would find a way to get Sissy out, away from this mess. That she would fix it. And it occurs to Dan that for all Jane's infuriating lack of constraint and bullheaded nature, he still counts on (and often admires) her ability to get shit done.

Brick holds his fist up to Isaac, in an approximation of a military sign for them to stop, stand still, and Isaac does, putting his hand in front of Sissy and Jane so they can't walk into the room.

Frustrated, Dan catches Jane's eye and raises his eyebrows exaggeratively in the universal expression: *Well?* and Jane sighs and shakes her head, as if she doesn't know where to begin. Or maybe it means nothing new came to light? Or perhaps she's so mad at Sissy, she can't see straight. It's anybody's guess, really.

A thud from the roof wrenches all the bird heads again, up and to the right. Then a clomping—Otto coming down the stairs, perhaps?

Brick locks eyes with Caden and Lyle, whom he stationed on either side of the entrance, and nods, which Dan interprets as an encouragement to be ready to pounce the second Otto walks through the doors.

And they do. In a span of what couldn't be more than two seconds, the door opens, Otto takes a step into the restaurant, and Caden and Lyle spring to either side of him, each grabbing one of his arms, causing Otto to let out a half-strangled noise somewhere between a gasp and a whoop. His eyebrows climb halfway up his forehead. He's known for them, his eyebrows. Einstein-like, they're bushy, unmanicured, unruly: as recognizable in the pop culture zeitgeist as Cindy Crawford's mole or Will Smith's ears. Hundreds of memes, TikToks, and an entire Twitter handle are devoted to them. And—like most celebrities—they're not nearly as impressive in person.

"What the—" he says, moving to yank his arm out of Caden's grasp, but Brick steps forward, holding his gun level with Otto's face. "I wouldn't do that if I were you."

Otto's eyebrows fall. "Who are you?" he demands. "What is happening?" And Dan feels a flash of sympathy for the man—Dan's had two hours to get used to the circumstances, but this is all brand-new to Otto. Like someone who's coming in halfway through a movie and is trying to parse out the plot. And then, as if Otto suddenly remembers why he's there, he drags his gaze from Brick's gun and frantically searches the room for his wife and daughter. When he lands on them, sitting at a table near the window, he says: "Vaughn, what's the meaning of this?"

"I believe we're being held hostage," she responds dryly, and it's clear to Dan the two have likely been married for some time.

"What do you want from me?" Otto turns back to Brick, his voice betraying no fear, and Dan can't tell if he's an excellent actor or is truly unafraid, likely thanks to years of feeling impenetrable when you have loads of power and money.

"Oh," Brick breathes, an exhale of air more than a word. He's looking at the man with thunderous murder in his eyes. Pure hatred. Dan's not sure he's ever been on the receiving end of a look like that in his life. Except maybe when he leaves the toilet seat down in the middle of the night and Jane returns to bed from using the bathroom. "It's simple, really," Brick says. "But we'll get to all of that. Have a seat."

As Caden and Lyle escort Otto to a lone chair against the wall across the room, Isaac brings Jane back to Dan's table. When she sits, Isaac kneels beside her, pulls out a zip tie, and binds Jane's ankles together as Jane mumbles: "Geez. How many of these things do you guys have?"

When Isaac finally walks off, Dan whispers to Jane: "What happened with Sissy?" at the same time Jane hisses: "I think they're *stealing* from Otto St. Clair."

"*What?*" Somehow this revelation is even more disquieting than the initial realization that she was part of this . . . gang. Or maybe it was the additional fact of it, on top of her bursting into a restaurant carrying a weapon. And he realizes he didn't allow himself to theorize the possibilities for why she might be there, as if his brain could comprehend only one horrific fact at a time. The idea that Sissy would break the law at all is preposterous, but to steal? He tries to think back over the whole of her childhood, looking for signs he was raising a bona fide criminal, and he gasps in horror when he recalls the Snickers incident. He hasn't thought of it in years—the time when he took Josh and Sissy on Sunday errands and, on the way home, saw Josh in the rearview chomping the full-size candy bar he had asked for, but Dan had refused to purchase.

"Where'd you get that?" he asked.

"Sithy," Josh said in his three-year-old lisp.

Dan pulled the car over into the nearest parking lot and turned to look at his six-year-old daughter in the back seat. "Sissy, did you take that candy bar from the store?"

"No, Daddy," she said, her brown eyes wide and brimming with innocence. "Josh did it."

"I did not!" Josh said, the melted chocolate evidence smeared all over his face and fingers. The two argued the entire ride back to the store—their voices escalating, both framing the other—where Dan made Josh come clean to the manager, which took a very dramatic and embarrassing ten-minute scene of snotty, deep-heaving sobs and lispy denials. It was so dramatic, Dan more than once doubted himself. Had Sissy taken the candy bar? She looked so innocent! She'd never done anything wrong in her life! Whereas Josh, even at the tender age of three, already had signs of rebellion written all over him.

Now he hears Jane's earlier accusation ring in his ears: *You're so permissive! Always trying to be her best friend, never giving her consequences for* anything. And he wonders if Jane (as she so infuriatingly often is) was right: Was he too lenient with Sissy? The truth was, Dan couldn't stand to see Sissy upset. Worse, he couldn't stand to be the cause of her sadness. Josh as well, to a point, but it was something about his daughter's eyes, the way she could just level him with one forlorn look. He knew it made him weak on her, but Jane could be so tough, so stubborn and unrelenting in her parenting, he convinced himself it all balanced out in the end. And anyway, is it a crime to want your own children to like you? He doesn't think so.

Unless, of course, it inadvertently turned them into criminals.

"We can't let it happen," Jane whispers. "What she's done is bad enough, but *armed robbery?*"

217

Oh God. Is that the inevitable track he set Sissy on, years ago when he let her get away with stealing a candy bar? Dan swallows. "Right." He nods. They can't let her do it. But he has no idea what Sissy is stealing and therefore no idea how to stop it. He opens his mouth to ask.

"Why is the chef still here?" Jane whispers. "I thought they were letting him go."

Dan thought so, too, but in the middle of the neurosurgeon offering his professional thoughts to Brick on how to get the chef safely out of the dining room and into a (hopefully) waiting ambulance, the faint chop-chop-chop of helicopter blades permeated the air and Brick's attention turned elsewhere.

"Ow," Otto says, irritated, as Lyle finishes binding Otto's ankles to the chair legs. "Careful."

"Get his cell phone," Brick instructs. "And his wallet." As Lyle pats Otto down, finding first the cell phone in his suit jacket pocket and then the billfold in the back of his pants, Otto looks up with a quirked eyebrow. "All this to steal my wallet?"

Brick ignores the question, taking the cell phone and wallet from Lyle and pocketing both. "The helicopter you flew here—is it one of your self-flying inventions?"

"Is *that* what this is about?"

Dan wonders this, too. Obviously they're not stealing his wallet—anyone with half a brain knows you wouldn't get far trying to use Otto St. Clair's credit cards—but the helicopter on the other hand . . . Is Brick stealing the prototype and then selling it to an international espionage organization? Dan feels a quick kick in his heart at the thought that he could be witness to something so exciting, like something out of an action movie. Then he frowns, remembering his daughter's involvement and the very real danger facing his family. He looks at Sissy with new eyes. Is she some kind of James Bond supervillain? He and Jane always used to joke that Sissy was so preternaturally intelligent she'd either be president of the United States or end up in jail. But it was a joke!

The more likely (but less interesting) explanation is this is Brick's backup escape plan. The more Dan turns that theory over, the more sense it makes. The police are likely crawling all over the hillside by now, and the only chance Brick has to thwart them is by air.

"Answer the question," Brick says.

"Yes, of course."

"Is it easy to fly?"

Otto scoffs, the sound thick with arrogance. "A child could do it. You just set the destination and then the AI CloudPilot handles everything else, including interfacing with ground control and other aircraft and getting permission to land. It's going to revolutionize cities, the way people travel. Traffic on the 605 will be a thing of the past."

"Great," Brick says, and claps once, a sharp THWACK. "We're moving the chef. Jeremy, Lyle—you'll carry him the way Rahul detailed earlier, using a chair for stability and going slow so as not to jostle him."

Otto looks at the chef on the floor by the wall, as if only just noticing him. "Is he bleeding?" His eyes go wide in horror. "No, absolutely not. It's, uh . . . the helicopter isn't equipped for medical transport."

And Dan remembers the other piece of latent trivia he

knows about Otto, a rumored character trait that defines him as much as his eyebrows in the collective social conscience— that Otto has severe OCD and cannot stand germs and bodily fluids. Apparently, he couldn't even be in the hospital room when his daughter was born. He remembers Jane at a dinner party years ago deriding, along with the other women, Otto's seemingly old-fashioned, definitely sexist, and perhaps—they'd go so far as to say—even heartless and inhumane decision. What kind of monster didn't want to be present at the birth of his own daughter?

Dan would certainly never have said it out loud, but he thought Otto might have been onto something there. The things he witnessed when Jane gave birth were images he could never scrub from his mental data bank, and he would have been just fine to go back to the days of cigars in the waiting room and being brought in when everything was clean and tidy and stitched back in place.

But to not want to save a man's life because you don't want blood in your vehicle? Well, that is inhumane.

"You"—Brick points at Rahul—"you'll go with him."

Rahul nods, as if he thought as much, but his wife looks stricken. "We're not riding in that thing. Didn't one just crash in the San Fernando valley? We'll all be killed."

It's an opening—an opportunity for Otto to agree it's unsafe and not sully his helicopter—but apparently his ego won't let the insult stand. "That was an unfortunate human error— one! Out of hundreds of test runs. A mistake in code. No one was injured and it's since been fixed."

"You don't have to go," Brick says pointedly to the wife. "He does. Let's move. We don't have all night."

Lyle and Jeremy spring into action, cutting Rahul's ankle ties and then—with the neurosurgeon's help—carefully moving the chef onto a horizontal chair, using the back for stability. The three of them lift the chair, keeping the back of it parallel to the ground and carrying the supine chef like they're handling a palanquin carrying a queen.

"Wait!" Ayanna shouts as they get to the door. "I'm coming."

Brick nods at Caden to cut her ankle ties, and she runs to the door, holding it open for the transport. Dan watches with a stab of jealousy that the couple gets to leave, going scot-free out into the night, even if it is in a slightly dangerous helicopter. And he's simultaneously grateful it's not him and Jane in the contraption. Jane's so terrified of heights, she'd never survive it—and Dan would never hear the end of it.

When the door closes behind them, Brick turns to Otto, tugging the confiscated wallet from his back pocket. Dan feels the heat of someone's gaze and turns to find Jane boring holes in his face with her eyes. This time her brow is raised, and she nods deeply, purposefully toward Otto and then lowers and raises her brow again at Dan. Does she think this is the theft? Surely she understands there's got to be more to it than simply stealing a wallet. And even if there wasn't, what does Jane want him to do—tackle Brick to the ground?

As Brick flips through the wallet, Otto stares at him, studying what little he can see of Brick's face. "Wait—you look . . . Do I *know* you?"

Brick freezes, and it's his reaction that causes the air to shift in the room and Dan's eyes to narrow.

"Oh my God . . ." Otto squints at him and tilts his head. A flicker of recognition lights in his eyes. "Theodore—is that you?"

Brick narrows his eyes. "*Who?*"

"Oh. I guess not."

"Who's Theodore?"

"I don't know. Some kid that used to be my assistant. Years ago. I'm grasping at straws here—there aren't a lot of Black guys in Silicon Valley, OK?"

Dan's eyebrows fly skyward. Otto's statement may be true on the surface, but who says that *out loud*? Brick scoffs, echoing Dan's disgust. "You are literally the *worst* person."

"The worst?" Otto shrugs. "Nah. I'm not even the worst tech CEO. BuzzFeed named me second behind Elon Musk."

The deafening sound of helicopter blades starting up on the roof fills the room, causing all the bird necks to crane up to the ceiling again. Thirty seconds later, Lyle and Jeremy reenter through the front door and the harsh chop-chop-chop slowly starts to fade as the helicopter leaves the roof and flies farther away from the restaurant.

Brick pinches a black credit card from the wallet. "Here we are," he says. Dan knows of the Hyperion no-limit card, of course, but he didn't know anyone who had one—not even the plastic surgeons who made six times his salary.

"What are you doing with that?" Otto says lightly. His tone is curious, amused, and Dan is once again awestruck by the man's seeming inability to be rattled.

"It's what you're going to do with it that matters."

222

"What am I doing with it?"

"You're going to make a purchase."

"What am I buying?"

"Dessert."

Otto narrows his eyes. "I doubt you came all the way out here to have me pay for cake and ice cream."

Brick makes a tutting sound with his tongue and the top of his mouth. "Aren't you clever? You're right. It's not just any dessert you'll be buying. It's the Semlor Guld, Chef Lars's specialty."

"Ah! The eight-million-dollar delicacy." Otto grins, as if he's not only intrigued, but downright enjoying being held hostage and robbed at gunpoint.

Brick nods and Dan blinks. Otto's strange manner notwithstanding, something about this exchange feels oddly familiar—as if he's seen it in a movie or dreamt about it.

"It comes with a Harry Winston diamond bracelet, correct?"

Brick nods deeply again.

"What are you going to do, steal the bracelet?" Otto stares at Brick, studying him, and Dan can almost see the wheels turning in the eccentric genius's brain. "No, because you would have already done so. The bracelet would ostensibly be in the kitchen and you wouldn't have needed me here." Otto cocks his head. "What's your plan?"

Dan watches the exchange, equally intrigued and also bewildered that he somehow knows the answer to Otto's question. Brick is going to run the credit card for the cost of the dessert and then hack into the restaurant account and move the money to untraceable offshore accounts, which is why he has the computer set up that Tink is sitting at. How does Dan know this? *Was* it a movie plot? Dan racks his brain, and all at once it comes to him: Jane's book! That's how the terrorists in the teahouse stole from the billionaire, by having him "purchase" the $36.3 million Ming dynasty teacup on display in the London tearoom. His mouth drops open, and he swivels his head toward his wife, who is staring at Brick and Otto and not at him.

But Dan has a thousand more questions. Or namely, just two: *How?* And *Why?* He knows Jane thinks he didn't, but Dan *did* read her book all those years ago. And though he'd never say it out loud, that Goodreads reviewer Stephen (Dan knows his name only because Jane keeps his printed-out review on a dartboard in her office) wasn't entirely wrong in his assessment of the book, even if he was unnecessarily mean about it. It *was* implausible. Terrorists taking over a teahouse in the middle of the day in the middle of London just to steal money *online*—not gold bars or bags of cash—didn't really make sense. The whole point of being a hacker is to commit crimes and theft covertly, without notice, and without resorting to violence. Their hacking skills *are* their weapons. Dan doesn't know much about hacking, but he does know there has to be an easier way for a skilled hacker to steal money from Otto St. Clair. And if *he* knows that, surely Brick knows that, too. Why would he attempt such a risky and ridiculous plan in real life? And how could he expect to get away with it?

And most important—how is Dan supposed to stop it?

"Monica, correct?" Brick says, turning to the young woman sitting against the wall next to Dan's waiter, Javier, at the end of the line of hostages. Dan blinks when he sees them. It seems so long ago that they were welcoming Dan and Jane to the restaurant, and he nearly forgot they were there.

"Yes?" she says in a small voice.

"I believe it's your responsibility to run payment at the end of the night, correct?"

She clears her throat. "Y-yes. Yes, sir."

"Wonderful. Mr. St. Clair is done with his meal here and I'd like you to close out his tab."

Lyle walks over to Monica, snips her ankle and wrist zip ties in a now practiced motion, and helps her up.

"Where do you run credit cards?"

"Up front."

Brick makes an *After you* gesture and then follows Lyle and Monica to the hostess stand. With a trembling hand, Monica takes the credit card from Brick and asks: "How much?"

Brick stares at Otto and grins as he says: "Eight-point-four million dollars. Heck, let's round it up to nine."

"Nine million!" Otto exclaims, grinning as if he's enjoying the show. "Oh-ho! That's quite a purchase."

"It is indeed," Brick says. "You're quite the generous husband."

Otto nods, as if to say, *Carry on.*

"Why are you smiling?" Brick asks.

Otto doesn't respond.

"Oh, I know why," Brick says, and he walks slowly toward the man. "Because nine million is nothing to you. A pittance."

Otto doesn't respond.

"Or maybe it's because you think the purchase won't go through."

"Well, surely you know as well as I do, it will be flagged."

"That's true," Brick says. "Fortunately for us, you're no stranger to multimillion-dollar, self-aggrandizing spontaneous purchases. Remember Leonardo da Vinci's journal? What was that—twenty-four million dollars?"

"Self-aggrandizing? It's an artifact. I was preserving history."

"What about your fourteen-karat-gold toilet seats? Were *they* historical artifacts, too?"

Otto doesn't respond, and Dan has to wonder what it is with billionaires and their obsession with sitting on gold when they take a shit.

"And who could forget the seven million you spent on a thirteen-foot tiger shark preserved in a glass container of formaldehyde?"

"That was Steve Cohen! I don't know how my name got mixed up in that story. You can't believe everything you read."

"And the island? Did the newspapers make that up?"

"Real estate is a smart investment. Look at Richard Branson! And I didn't use the credit card for that."

Brick waves a hand. "Regardless, there's a track record. I don't think your credit card company is going to bat an eye."

"They're going to call me."

"They will. And you're going to approve the purchase."

"And if I don't?"

Brick raises his gun level with Otto's face, but Otto doesn't flinch. "What, you're going to kill me?"

"No, of course not," Brick says. "I'm going to shoot you in the kneecap."

Before Otto can respond, Brick moves the gun slightly down and to the right and squeezes the trigger.

POP!

Shrieks fill the air. "No!" Dan shouts—or maybe he just thinks it. A strangled scream from Paisley reaches Dan's ears from across the room, but he barely registers it as he tries to comprehend what just happened.

"What the fuck?" Spittle comes flying out of Otto's mouth. "You are absolutely *insane*, you know that?"

CHAPTER
20

WATCHING SOMEONE GET SHOT WAS NOTHING LIKE
Jane thought it would be. Or nothing like in the movies, which
were Jane's only point of reference. (Then again, having sex
for the first time was disappointingly nothing like *Dirty Dancing* had led her to believe it would be, so she's not sure why
she's surprised.) For one, Otto didn't scream right away. In
fact, his face didn't change at all, for so long that Jane wasn't
sure he *had* been shot.

"Calm down," Brick says. "It's not like I shot you."

Oh, thank God, Jane thinks, a wave of relief washing over
her—though the information does nothing to calm her heart
rate, which took off like a sprinter from the starting blocks at
the sound of the gunshot.

"You could have!" Otto shrieks.

"I could have," Brick agrees, and Jane wonders if that's
true. Sissy said all the guns had blanks—except for Isaac's,
obviously—but maybe Brick was lying about that, too. Maybe
none of the guns had blanks. She strains her neck to try to see

the wall behind Otto—is there a bullet hole in it?—but there's a table in her line of sight and she can't tell. "Which is why you will confirm your purchase to the credit card company when they call."

Jane blinks, dumbfounded, as the entire money scheme she wrote plays out in front of her eyes. She got the idea for *Tea Is for Terror* after reading a newspaper article about some billionaire purchasing the $36.3 million Ming dynasty teacup from a Sotheby's auction on a whim with his credit card. After getting over the shock that anyone anywhere would spend $36.3 million on a piece of porcelain, she focused on the fact that the man's credit limit was clearly nonexistent—and then, as novelists do, she wondered how a thief could take advantage of that. She interviewed cybercrime experts and learned about IP spoofing, malware viruses, keylogging, wire transfers, and money mules. She learned how smart hackers bounce the money, once stolen, through multiple accounts with different owners, across jurisdictions, making it nearly impossible to trace, or at least allowing time for a thief to be long gone while all foreign state departments and investigators are figuring out how to communicate with each other and get through the legal red tape. And with just enough knowledge to be dangerous, Jane concocted a simple yet clever money heist and added the terrorist takeover of a teahouse for maximum dramatic effect.

But, of course, it's also a plan that she knows would never work in real life. Not only would real-life hackers figure out a much less dramatic way to steal someone's money, but, as writers are wont to do, Jane fudged a key element to make her plan work for the sake of her book. Artistic license and all.

(Something else that odious Stephen with a *ph* clearly knows nothing about. Nobody nitpicks the *Mission: Impossible* movies or the James Bond franchise or every movie Jason Statham has ever been in for their implausible schemes. Why? Oh, don't get Jane started.)

Jane studies Brick, scrutinizing him. There was so much setup he had to do to make this work—gaining access to the restaurant's bank account, making sure Otto would be here (which he managed through Isaac falsely befriending Paisley, though that clearly wasn't foolproof), planting the van and the bomb—and while Jane is impressed and even flattered Brick found her heist clever enough to emulate, he surely is smart enough to have done his own basic research and realize the major flaw in the plan?

Or does he know something Jane doesn't?

"Monica? Go ahead and run it," Brick says, and Jane closes her mouth and swallows, refocusing on the most pressing matter—on the off chance Jane is wrong, if this purchase goes through, her daughter is one step closer to adding armed robbery to her rap sheet, and Jane will be damned if she's going to let that happen. And that's when she notices the outlet on the wall just to the left of Dan's chair legs. And the cord running from the outlet to the hostess stand. Sometimes having the worst table in the house pays off.

"Dan," she hisses, kicking him under the table for good measure, as Monica punches in numbers on the keypad at the hostess stand. When Dan looks at her, she shifts her eyes dramatically toward the plug. He follows her gaze, and then looks back at her blankly. *Ohforthelove.* "Un. Plug. It," she says through clenched teeth.

And Dan—lo and behold—comprehends what she's saying and manages to yank the plug out of the wall the second before Monica swipes the credit card.

Monica frowns.

"What?" Brick says.

"I don't know. The machine just died."

Brick strides past Jane and Dan's table to the hostess stand, where he peers over Monica's shoulder. Then his gaze follows the cord down, along the wall to where the plug rests a foot away from Dan's chair leg. Brick's boots strike the wood floor with heavy thuds as he closes the gap between the hostess stand and Dan. He bends over, picks up the plug, and examines it, then looks up at Dan, causing Jane's heart to stop completely. What has she done?

"Did you unplug this?"

Dan's Adam's apple bobs so dramatically it looks like he's swallowed a Ping-Pong ball. "No," he says, and if his tomato-red face weren't enough to betray the lie, the high-pitched crack in his voice certainly is. God, he's always been the worst liar. Jane's amazed he got away with his affair for as long as he did.

Brick lifts his left brow while his right brow dips—an inverted seesaw. "Really," he says, firmly sticking the plug back in the outlet. Dan smartly doesn't respond and Brick stands, crossing his arms and creating a barrier with his body between Dan and the wall. He cuts his eyes to Monica. "Try it again."

Monica swipes the card once more, stares at the machine, and then nods at Brick when the charge ostensibly has gone through.

Shit, shit, shit. Now, as Jane learned from interviewing an account manager at a credit card company—and as Otto rightly predicted—a representative from the company is going to call Otto's cell phone to confirm the charges, and what can Jane do to stop that? The booster is across the room next to Tink, so there's no unplugging it (not that *that* brilliant plan did anything but delay the inevitable). Jane breaks out in a cold sweat as she glances around the room. Her eyes light on the red rectangle fire alarm, next to the door of the kitchen, close to their table, but out of arm's reach even if Dan stood.

Like clockwork, Brick's pocket starts buzzing. He nods at Lyle—silently instructing him to put Monica back on the wall—and then Brick pulls Otto's phone out, walking around Jane and Dan's table toward the billionaire. "I'm putting it on speaker. No funny business," he says, but he glances back pointedly at Dan and Jane when he says it, and Jane knows he has given them one pass and likely won't give them another. "You ready?"

"Fine," Otto says.

Brick swipes the phone screen with his thumb and holds it up close to Otto's chin.

"Hello," Otto says calmly.

A reedy voice on the other end that Jane has to strain to hear says: "Mr. St. Clair, this is Daniel Okonyo with Hyperion Credit. How are you, sir?"

"Doing good, thank you, and yourself?"

"Fine, sir. I'm obligated to tell you we're recording this call and using our voice-recognition software. Can you please repeat your security phrase in order to confirm your identity?"

"Yes," Otto says, and clears his throat. "One-One was a racehorse. Two-Two was one, too. When One-One won one race, Two-Two won one, too."

"Wonderful," Daniel says. "It appears you're having a lovely dinner at La Fin du Monde, is this correct?"

"Yes," Otto pauses. "Just lovely."

"That's good to hear. I'm calling to confirm a charge from the restaurant for nine million, six hundred and fifty-two thousand, five hundred dollars. Is this correct?"

Otto's eyes widen slightly and he says, "One moment, please." Brick covers the receiver, waiting. "I thought it was nine million even."

"Plus seven and a quarter percent sales tax," Monica squeaks from where she's once again sitting next to Javier.

"Ah. Of course." Otto glares at Brick and gives him a curt nod, and Brick removes his hand from the mouthpiece. "Yes, that's the correct figure."

"Wonderful. If you could please give me your four-digit security code, we'll get that processed for you right away."

"Certainly." Otto clears his throat. "Two-zero-one-four."

The man on the other end doesn't respond right away, and Brick's bicep twitches as he clenches the phone tighter in his grip.

"Thank you, sir," the voice says. "Thank you for being a valued Hyperion customer, and enjoy the rest of your evening."

Otto nods curtly once more and stares at Brick as he swipes

to end the call. Then Brick walks over to the wall of windows and stands in front of the far-left panel, a pane of glass the size of a door that Jane hadn't noticed before but is separated from the huge picture window by a strip of wood. Brick unlatches it, and the glass opens outward on a hinge. Jane can't tell if it's her imagination or the wind—or if the sound she hears is actually the roar of the ocean, crashing onto the rocks miles below the restaurant. While Jane knows the back of the restaurant must be at least ten feet from the edge of the cliff, looking out into the vast darkness, it's hard not to imagine the drop is right there, directly below the window. Brick winds back his arm and pitches Otto's cell phone out into the black night.

"Are you fucking kidding?" Otto shouts. "My entire *life* is on there." But Brick ignores him and pulls the window shut, latching it with a flick of his thumb and a satisfying click. The room is silent for a minute and then a *whoop* comes from the corner where Lyle is sitting. He pops up, a grin plastered on his face. "Is that it? We did it?"

Brick holds up a hand. "Almost. Tink has to work her magic once the charge goes through."

"I'm pulling up the account now," she says.

The only sound is the click-clack of the keys as Tink furiously types on her laptop, but the energy of the room has shifted. It feels lighter, more buoyant. Less like a hostage situation and more like a group of kids at Coachella. Even Sissy's eyes are crinkled in a smile.

Jane holds her breath, staring daggers at Tink. There's no way this works. *There's no way, there's no way, there's no way.*

"You're not going to get away with this," Otto says, breaking the silence. "No one steals money from me and gets away with it."

POP!

Terror rips through Jane, causing her to duck on instinct, until she realizes the sound wasn't another gunshot or a bomb exploding, but Isaac opening the champagne he brought up from the cellar.

"What the hell, Isaac?" Tink says, glowering at him, and then training her gaze back on the screen.

"What? I'm celebrating," he says, taking a swig from the bottle, then holding it out to Tink.

"We're not done," she replies. The click-clacking of her keys has fallen silent. "We're waiting for the money."

"It could take up to fifteen minutes," Brick says. "Refresh every thirty seconds or so."

Fifteen *minutes*? Jane nearly laughs out loud.

Tink merely nods. A buzzing emanates from the table she's working on. She looks back up at Brick. "It's the police again. Second time they've called."

"Ignore it," Brick says. "We're almost done."

After a minute or so of semi-silence—the only sound in the room is Isaac taking sulky pulls from his bottle in the corner—Otto speaks up: "I have a question."

Brick continues ignoring him, keeping his eyes trained on Tink's screen. He puts his thumb up to his mouth and starts chewing on the nail.

"Why did you need me?" Otto says. "Surely you know—since you know everything else—that my wife has a no-limit Hyperion card as well."

Brick stops chewing, but still doesn't respond.

"Brick?" Jeremy says. "Is that true? Did you know about Vaughn's card?"

"Of course not."

"Hm." Otto grunts and continues as if Brick hasn't spoken. "No, this is personal. You wanted to take the money from *me*, didn't you? You wanted the satisfaction of it."

"You." Brick points at him. "Shut it."

Otto ignores the directive. "I *do* know you. I must. Or you know me. But the question is *how*."

Brick stares at him thunderously, and it suddenly becomes clear to Jane and everyone in the room that Otto must be telling the truth. He does know Brick.

"Brick? What's he talking about?" Jeremy tries again.

"Brick?" Lyle echoes.

"Jesus Christ," Brick mutters, and then says, louder, "The SierraX Competition. Two thousand thirteen. Does that ring a bell?"

"Oh!" Otto says, and Jane can see that it does. And then another look of confusion settles on Otto's face: "You won, right? You got your money—what exactly are you mad about?"

A fury envelops Brick so completely that it makes his earlier countenance, when Jane *thought* he looked murderous, pale in comparison. He grips the body of his gun so tight the dark knuckles turn white as the bone beneath the skin. His teeth clench, causing his strong jawline to become even more pronounced. Finally, he opens his lips just wide enough to say: "You stole my idea." He says it so low, Jane isn't even sure she heard him correctly.

"What?" Otto says.

"You. Stole. My. Idea."

Otto lets out a puff of laughter. "I didn't steal a thing. You signed away the rights to your invention. It's not my fault you were too stupid to see the financial opportunity right in front of your nose."

Jane's not sure if it's the name-calling or if Otto saying the word *nose* gave Brick a fit of inspiration, but it's all the provocation Brick needs. He clenches the knuckles on his right hand, cocks his fist back, and slams it into Otto's face with all his might.

"My nose!" Otto screams in a garbled sound.

Jane stares as blood gushes out of Otto's nostrils; she can hear Paisley crying so hard from two tables over, you'd think she was the one who got punched.

"Paisley, he's OK. He's going to be OK," Vaughn repeats over and over.

"Brick! Jesus," Tink says. She stands and grabs a napkin from the nearest table and holds it to Otto's face.

"He deserved it," Brick says, his eyes so dark they're black. Then, as if he slightly regrets his impetuousness, he sighs. "Isaac. Get a glass of water for Mr. St. Clair, please."

"Sure, boss," Isaac says, and Jane can't put her finger on what irks her about his response, until she realizes Isaac called Brick *boss* without an ounce of sarcasm. She stares at him as he takes off to the kitchen, and notes a glimmer of an evil grin on the kid's face.

Jane freezes. A glass of water. In the hullabaloo of Brick and Otto knowing each other, and the idea of Sissy going to prison for the rest of her natural life, Jane had all but forgotten a key plot point in her book, after the theft but before the bomb. The cup of tea! They offer it to the CEO they're stealing from after they steal from him. But it's spiked with strychnine, a clear, odorless poison that in a large enough dose is fatal instantly. It's obvious Brick hates Otto, but surely he doesn't plan to kill the man right in front of everyone. She stares, wide-eyed, as Isaac returns from the kitchen with a crystal goblet full of water—when there were plenty of glasses on the tables, and a water pitcher at the hostess stand.

Her heartbeat revs as Isaac closes the gap to Otto. What if it is poison? Otto may be kind of a pompous asshole, but he doesn't deserve to *die*.

Isaac holds the glass to Otto's lips and Jane screams: "No!"

"Jane!" Dan shouts, the word infused with fear.

But Jane ignores him. "Don't drink it! It's poison!"

21

EVERY HEAD IN THE ROOM TURNS TO JANE ONCE more, Sissy included, all wide-eyed and disbelieving that her mother is embarrassingly interfering. It's a look Jane is all too familiar with.

Brick's countenance is more annoyed, as if he can't believe he's dealing with yet *another* outburst from Jane. He studies her for a beat and then, cocking his head like a parrot, he finally says: "Who *are* you?"

Indignant, Jane stiffens her back, and, still staring at Sissy, she opens her mouth to announce: "I'm her—" but stops herself before saying *mother*.

She remembers the point Dan made earlier—if she reveals Sissy's identity, she's revealing it to all the other people in the room. *Witnesses*. Who could then reveal it to the police—who are, apparently, halfway down the hill, having been stopped by the detonated bomb. But how else to respond to Brick's question?

Tears prick her eyes as she realizes, despite her initial fumblings and resentment of the title, over the years motherhood wormed itself so deeply into the core of her identity, the fabric of her very being, that though her children are far too old and too big to be held, Jane catches herself swaying when she holds something in her arms—a watermelon in the grocery store, the neighbor's cat.

And yet, as hard as she worked and worried and strived to succeed in the position, Jane has still failed at the most basic tenet of the job: to keep Sissy safe from harm.

"Well?" Brick says.

Jane blinks. "I'm . . . I'm Jane."

"Yes, I gathered that from your husband shouting it at you. But you're not . . ." He tilts his head and squints at her. "Are you . . . are you Jane *Brooks*?"

Jane swallows. "Yes."

"The author."

Jane can't help it. Despite the self-flagellating despair of her failure, a buzz of pride wells up in her chest. She's dreamt of this moment—a stranger recognizing her in public—but somehow she never pictured it exactly this way. "I am."

"What are you *doing* here?" he says.

"I was hoping to eat dinner," she says dryly.

But he keeps muttering, mostly to himself. "There's coincidence and then there's . . . this." His eyes dart around the room. "Well, no matter." He shrugs and offers a sardonic grin. "I enjoyed your book."

She tries to shoot him an annoyed look but is still too chuffed to make it believable. She knew it! She knew it. She wants so badly to turn to Dan and say *SEE? I told you so,* but instead she fixes her face and says measuredly to Brick: "I've

240

noticed." Then—it can't be helped—she cuts her eyes to Dan with an *I told you so* look for good measure.

"Let's just say it was inspiring," he says. "But, as I'm sure you know, strychnine is very bitter. If I had any interest in poisoning Mr. St. Clair, I certainly wouldn't put it in water."

It's true, which is why Jane concealed hers in tea in the book, but she's not entirely convinced. "I don't know anything about what you would or wouldn't do."

"Well, then I'll tell you. This is a glass of water because Mr. St. Clair appears to have some blood on his face, and I thought he could use a rinse out."

Isaac offers the glass to the billionaire once more. Otto eyes it warily, then purses his lips together and gives his head a quick shake.

Brick sighs. "Suit yourself." He looks back at Jane with a quirked brow. "I never did understand why you bothered poisoning the CEO, instead of just letting him perish in the explosion. Don't you think that was a bit of . . . overkill?"

Jane glares at him. It's a fair criticism, but he's just so smug about it and she wants to slap the look off his face. "No, I don't. But I do know you're not getting that money."

It works. Brick's eyes narrow. "What do you mean?"

"If you had done even the most basic research, you would know it takes up to three business days for credit card companies to transfer money into a merchant account, not fifteen minutes. Or did you plan to be here that long?"

Brick smiles, and it's so disarming Jane thinks she imagined the brief flash of anger she saw in him. "Jane, Jane, Jane," he says, slowly shaking his head. "If *you* had done your research, you would know Hyperion guarantees next-day funding to their A-list clients, so the transfer will take place at midnight."

Jane frowns. Is that true? And even if it is, it's not yet nine p.m. "That's still three hours—"

"Eastern time. Hyperion is headquartered in New York."

Jane's jaw drops slightly. Her heist was actually *completely* plausible. Take that, Stephen with a *ph*! And then her heart stops. The payment is going to go through. Tink is going to bounce it around the multiple accounts in various jurisdictions, and Sissy is going to be on the hook for collaborating to steal *nine million dollars.*

"You have certainly been a thorn in my side this evening," Brick says, his face growing serious as he moves toward her. "What am I going to do with you?" Jane tenses, disliking how the playful tone of his voice belies the menace in his eyes. "Though I suppose it won't be much longer now. You could stay for the ending. You did write it, after all."

Jane shivers. The bomb. God, she hates being right all the time.

"No," a voice says from across the room.

"No?" Brick and Jane turn to see who's spoken up.

"She's a liability and we can't have any more . . . interruptions," Lyle says. "Enough has gone wrong this evening."

Jane stares at him, feeling betrayed and surprised she ever thought of him as innocent and kind.

Brick pauses, considering. "What do you suggest?"

"I don't know—put them somewhere."

"I'm not going *anywhere*," Jane says, mostly because it's instinctual to go against the directives of the person holding you hostage, but also because she is a mother and she will absolutely not leave her daughter.

"Isaac," Brick says, ignoring Jane.

Isaac jumps down from his perch on one of the tables where he's been watching the entire exchange. "Where do you want 'em? The deep freeze?" His eagerness is unnerving to Jane. Like it would be pure joy to put humans in a freezer.

"What about the van?" Lyle says. "That way you can lock them in."

"No! Absolutely not," Jane shrieks as Isaac walks menacingly toward her. "I'm not leaving." She glances past Isaac to her daughter. Surely she'll say something. *Do* something. But she just drops her gaze to the floor.

Isaac reaches down to pull Jane to her feet, but she makes her body go limp, so that she's 155 pounds of deadweight. "Lady, if you don't cooperate," Isaac growls, "I'll be forced to make you."

"What are you going to do, *shoot* me?" Jane says, echoing Otto. She knows she's making a scene, but she doesn't care. She's not leaving her daughter.

"No," he says, and takes a few steps to the left, lifting his gun straight up and out, the barrel pointed directly at Dan's head. "I'm going to shoot him."

Dan's eyes go wide, and Jane remembers Isaac definitely has bullets in his gun—and thinks he's just crazy enough to do it.

"OK! OK," she says. "I'll go."

Isaac nods. "Someone cut his ankle ties?" he says, while Isaac snips Jane's.

"Lyle, go with them," Brick says, and in no time, Jane and Dan are marched single file through the dining room with Isaac and Lyle close behind, their path taking them right past Sissy.

She wants so badly to grab the girl, hold her tightly in her arms—or violently shake her within an inch of her life to knock some sense into her, Jane's not quite sure which. She doesn't trust herself to find out, so she keeps her arms down next to her sides and keeps walking through the swinging door to the kitchen.

They shuffle into the eerily quiet room, the counters a disarray of pots and pans and food detritus—indications that the chefs were stopped midcooking. A red-rust color on the floor and a swipe of it on the stainless steel fridge catch Jane's eye. She's never seen a crime scene in real life, and she shudders.

But something else grabs her attention—the huge pressure cooker sitting on the counter. Its metal sides gleam in the overhead fluorescent lights of the kitchen.

Then they're through the kitchen and walking out the back door into the cool night air. Jane freezes, staring at the white van parked near the cliff, glowing in the moonlight, and she panics as she realizes they'll be stuffed in there for who knows how long. A touch claustrophobic, she's never been good with cramped spaces. Isaac pushes her in the back with the muzzle of his gun. "Move it," he says, and she takes a step forward gingerly, her stockinged feet bracing for the sharp points of the gravel. She wishes she'd put her heels back on. She stumbles across the gravel, and as they get closer to the cliff and the black nothingness beyond, Jane's heart feels like a bird about to take flight. She's never been good with heights either. She doesn't know how far it is to the bottom—a mile? More?—but she's now positive she can hear the crashing of the surf below. And while that used to be a soothing sound, the susurration of waves methodically beating the rocky shoreline, now it reminds her only that if she fell, if *anyone* fell—she shudders; she doesn't want to think about that. Her legs go weak and she stumbles backward into Lyle, who grabs her by the shoulders and steadies her.

"Please," she says, turning her head up to him. "Don't do this."

But it's Isaac who answers with a devilish grin. "Don't worry. It will all be over soon enough."

She ignores him and continues directing her words at Lyle. "Does your mother know you're here?" Lyle blanches, and Jane knows she's struck a chord. "Please," she says, a dog with a bone. "Let us go. This isn't going to end well."

"Lady, I've had about enough of you," Isaac says, and he pulls something out of one of the pockets in his cargo pants. The silver skin of duct tape flashes in the moonlight.

Jane shakes her head as he rips off a long piece and manages to stick it directly over her mouth, even as she moves her chin every which way to try to evade him. He does the same to Dan. Dan, resigned, doesn't even make it hard for him.

"Get in," Isaac says, opening the van doors. Given that she's about six feet from the cliff and, if she listens carefully, can hear the surf crashing on what she imagines to be very sharp rocks below, Jane doesn't have to be asked twice. She and Dan both turn, sit on their bottoms, and scoot into the van, their legs stretched out in front of them, their feet hanging off the edge. "Do their ankles," Isaac says to Lyle.

Lyle grabs a zip tie from his bag and binds up Dan's ankles. Then he goes back in his book bag and digs around it. He comes up empty. He pats his pockets down on his army pants.

"Shit," he says. "I'm out of zip ties."

Finally, Jane thinks. She thought they had a never-ending source of them. He looks at Isaac, who also pats down his pockets. "I don't have any!"

"Go back in and find some," Lyle says, and Jane is as surprised as Isaac appears to be at Lyle's demand. For the evening, Lyle's been on the receiving end of orders, not giving them. "Go!" Lyle says sharply. "I've got this."

Isaac, looking slightly dazed, nods and takes off back into the restaurant. Lyle watches him go, and when the door is fully closed behind Isaac, he looks directly at Jane, pulls down his gaiter, and grins a weirdly friendly and boyish full-tooth forty-watt smile, as if they're at a cocktail party and have not been in a hostage/terrorist situation for the past two hours. "Oh, thank God," he says. "I thought he'd never leave."

Jane's eyebrows go skyward. She can't say anything because her mouth is taped, but she doesn't know what she'd say if it wasn't.

Lyle stares at her a beat, still grinning, and then says: "Jane! It's *me*!"

FIFTY-EIGHT
MINUTES UNTIL
THE END

CHAPTER

22

"HE'S STILL NOT ANSWERING," KIP SAYS, PULLING the cell away from his ear.

"Shoot," Sandy says. "What do we do?"

After they remembered that the two department drones were out of commission—they were still being repaired from last month's family picnic, when the kids were playing chicken with them—Kip called Zimmerman, who advised him to keep trying to make contact with Brick (if that was his real name).

"What do I say?" Kip asked, having never been involved in anything near a hostage negotiation, unless you counted the time his ex-wife refused to hand over his dog Harold in the divorce, even though she always complained about his snoring and drooling and the way he licked his privates (the dog, not Kip, though she had plenty of complaints about Kip as well). Anyway, she still owned the dog, so Kip wasn't confident in his mediation skills.

"Try to build a rapport, gain his trust. And see what information you can glean—how many hostages are being held, what he might want."

"OK," Kip said. "What do I do if he asks for something?"

"Say you'll pass it up the chain of command and call me. We won't give him anything for free. We'll be there in less than an hour and my crisis negotiator will take over. We want to give him as much information as possible so he has a head start."

"Got it," Kip said.

Now he stares at Sandy and repeats Zimmerman's instructions in his mind: *Pass it up the chain of command. As much information as possible.* He makes an executive decision. "If he's not going to answer the phone, we have to get eyes up there," Kip says. He knows he fucked up with the van bomb and he's determined to make up for it. But he also wants to impress Zimmerman with his investigation skills; he wants to have so much intel when Zimmerman arrives that Zimmerman wonders why he's working in such a small precinct and asks him to come work for the LAPD! Kip flashes on a reverie, sometime in the future, Zimmerman—no, the *president!*—awarding him the Medal of Freedom for his heroic efforts in containing what could have been a disastrous hostile hostage situation. And then a lightbulb. "The robot dog! We'll strap a GoPro on his back and send it in." Even though he didn't think it was the wisest way to spend taxpayer money, Kip had been dying to use the canine android since it arrived a month earlier, for more than programming it to deliver a different random dog joke in its robotic monotone every day. (Kip's favorite: *A three-legged dog walks into a bar and says, "I'm looking for the man who shot my paw."*)

"We'd have to send it up the hill," McLeod says. "What if it steps on a second incendiary?"

It's a valid concern. Guillermo would be pissed if their $150,000 android got destroyed—especially if it didn't capture any intel beforehand.

"What about the chopper?" McLeod says.

"Yes!" Sandy says, her face brightening. "Brewster can fly it."

Kip frowns. The MD 500 Defender they bought three years ago had never been flown before because no one on their nine-person team had a pilot's license. Brewster took two lessons six months ago, threw up from motion sickness both times, and quit. "I don't think—"

"It's an emergency," Sandy says. "And it's the fastest way to get eyes on the restaurant."

Kip chews his lip, weighing the option. If Brewster could get close enough before getting sick, he may be able to see through that infamous picture window—get a visual on the hostage taker, the number of people in the restaurant. Even the number of cars in the parking lot would be helpful, to give them some kind of idea of what they're dealing with.

He nods resolutely. "Call Brewster," he says. "I want him wheels up in five."

23

JANE STARES AT LYLE'S ENTIRE FACE FOR THE first time that evening. He's even younger than she thought—his cheeks are baby smooth; his eyes barely even crinkle when he smiles; but more surprisingly, he doesn't look even the slightest bit familiar. Is he a friend of Sissy's that she can't remember meeting? Or maybe even Josh's? She racks her brain trying to place him.

"It's so nice to finally meet you!"

Oh. Since Jane's mouth is taped, she merely cocks her head like a parrot. So she hasn't met him before? How does he know her?

"It's me! Kyle!" he says, jutting his chin forward, as though he expects she'll recognize him at any second.

Jane has a number of thoughts, the first one being that changing one letter in your name, from Kyle to Lyle, for a covert nickname doesn't seem like too much of a stretch, or too bright, to be honest, if you're trying to go undercover. The second: she still has no idea who this person is. She tries to say

Who? but the duct tape muffles her word, transforming it into a grunt.

"Kyle Conner! The new publicist at Jar House! We've been emailing," he says, as if this explains it all.

Jane continues to stare at Lyle's face while piecing this news together. She vaguely remembers a new name on the author email updates she was getting from her publishing team, but under duress (ha!) she never would have been able to produce the name Kyle. She barely even skims the few emails she receives from Jar House every year, because what's the point? They didn't want her latest manuscript, and *Tea Is for Terror* is so old no one cares about it anymore (if they ever did in the first place). But none of that explains what the new publicist from her old publishing company is doing here. Or the fact that he's apparently part of—what did Sissy call them?—an *underground environmental activist group.* She waits for him to say more words, to explain, but he's staring at her expectantly as though she is going to say something. Then, as if it's just occurred to him why Jane's not talking, he reaches up and rips the tape off her mouth in one swift motion.

"OUCH!" Jane yells, the skin around her lips smarting from the sting.

"Sorry about that."

Jane has a thousand questions, but the first one that comes out of her newly released mouth is: "How *old* are you?"

"Twenty-three. I know, I have a baby face. I started Botox at twenty and I probably overmoisturize, but the best wrinkle is the one you never get, amirite?" He winks.

Jane has no idea how to respond, so she doesn't.

"Anyway, like I said in my email, your book—it's brilliant! Completely lends itself to this kind of guerrilla marketing."

"What . . . what are you talking about?"

"This was all my idea! I mean, your idea. *Our* idea. Once you're on the news, having survived a terrorist attack, *just like in your book*, it'll go viral." He shrugs. "Or it won't. There are no guarantees with that kind of thing, but I have an excellent track record. That's why Jar House hired me. Kind of a last-ditch effort to save the company. If I can make just one book a bestseller, they won't have to shut their doors."

Jane goes a bit lightheaded as she absorbs this information, processing it in slow motion, like she's had too much to drink and her brain isn't firing on all cylinders. She hears all the words coming out of Lyle's—er, Kyle's—mouth, but she's having trouble sorting them. Guerrilla marketing. Going viral. A track record? He's *twenty-three*. "I don't . . . understand," she says, even though she's beginning to.

"How do you think Brick got your book, silly?"

"*You* gave it to him?"

He nods triumphantly.

"You coordinated . . . all of this?"

"Well, no. Brick really ran with it once I planted the seed. You know how some men are—you have to let them think it's their idea."

"Wait, is *he* with Jar House?"

"What? No, of course not."

"I'm sorry . . ." She closes her eyes for a beat, the way she does when she feels a monster of a headache coming on. "I'm not sure I'm following. So this is all for . . . publicity? None of it is real?"

"Oh, no," Kyle says, frowning. "This is definitely real. Force of Nature is aptly named. Whew. I didn't know how serious they were when I joined. I thought it was a peaceful protest group—you know, chain yourself to bulldozers at new pipeline construction sites, that sort of thing."

"Wait, did you join just for this? Because of my book?"

"No! No, I joined about a year ago. I have serious climate anxiety—I actually don't know how anyone doesn't. The world is literally on fire and I couldn't just sit around and do nothing, you know? But." He says the word in a singsongy voice, like he's a character on a children's educational program. "I also have to make a living, and turns out I have a knack for marketing. Anyway, Brick's been trying to plan something for months, and when I found your book, the idea hit me and BAM! Two birds, one stone, you know?"

"So . . . this was all your idea," Jane repeats. She feels like she's playing that cup game where the person is moving the cups really quickly, and she can't quite keep up with where the ball is.

"Oh, stop, it's your idea, too!" He waves at her modestly, as though he doesn't want to take all the credit.

Jane is horrified. "People have been shot! That chef could have *died*. He could still die!"

Kyle makes a sucking sound with his teeth. "Right. Yeah. That was . . . unfortunate. Who knew Isaac was such a wild card? Wouldn't be surprised if he had a pile of dead bodies somewhere. Oh, and the bomb, too! None of that was supposed to happen." He frowns and pulls his lips back in an exaggerated cringe. "Yikes. And Brick really has it out for Otto—didn't realize it was so personal. That's a plot twist, huh? Anyway, so glad I was able to get you out of there."

"Why? What are they going to do?"

"Who knows? Who cares? Not my problem anymore."

"But the end of my book! Is that what they're planning?"

Kyle looks at Jane blankly. "What do you mean?"

"What do you mean what do I mean? If they're following my book, are they following the entire thing?"

"What happens at the end?"

"You have got to be kidding me! I thought you said you read it!"

"Oh! No, you misunderstood. That's not actually my job. I just have to find a way to market it. I skimmed the important bits."

"But you said it was brilliant! If you haven't read it, how do you know it's good enough to market it?"

He laughs as if Jane has told a clever joke. "Oh, you're adorable. Books don't have to be good to sell. They just need a catchy hook, a good cover, and the most important part—visibility. Once you and your book cover are *everywhere*, people will buy it. And it's my job to make sure it's everywhere."

He glances back at the door. "We don't have much time. Isaac's going to figure out there are no more zip ties and will eventually realize he can use duct tape." He puts a hand up to the side of his face in an exaggerated stage whisper. "Between you and me, I don't think he's the brightest bulb, which worked to our advantage in this instance." He reaches for the piece of tape hanging off the side of Jane's face. "I've gotta put this back on you. Sorry."

"Wait!" Jane yells, and Kyle freezes. "Why aren't you letting us go?"

"You can't leave, silly. If you leave, this will all be for nothing. The police have to find you in the van. That's why I called them."

"*You* called the police?"

"Of course! Cops equal news vans, and news vans equal—" He looks at Jane to supply the word.

Jane stares at him blankly.

"Visibility!" He grins. "Anyway, I've got to run before that Isaac gets back. Boy, he's got a few screws loose."

"Wait!" Jane screeches. "My daughter's in there!"

Kyle looks stricken. "She is? But the gift card was a reservation for two."

"*You* sent the gift card?!" Jane turns to Dan. "I thought you said you won it in a charity raffle."

Dan raises his eyebrows and grunts.

"Clever, right?" Kyle says. "God, I'm good at my job. So how'd you get your daughter in, too?"

"We didn't! She's one of you . . . a Force of Nature!"

"Oh. Then she'll likely be fine," he says, and pulls the tape taut over Jane's mouth once again.

"Likely?" Jane shouts, but it comes out like *Mmmph-mmph?*

"Not long now and all this will be over." Jane makes another grunting noise and Kyle boops her on the nose like she's a toy poodle. "Don't worry! You two will be perfectly safe in this van."

The squeak of the back door to the restaurant opening draws Kyle's attention and his eyes widen as he throws a glance over his shoulder at Isaac. "Shit. Gotta run!" And then he does literally that—he grabs both straps of his book bag, as if holding them taut, and then turns and runs at a full sprint toward the cliff. Jane gasps as he leaps into the darkness, his body completely disappearing like a magic trick right before her eyes.

Jane screams, though the noise doesn't carry very far thanks to the duct tape. She looks at Dan, whose wide eyes mirror hers. Then he says something, but Jane can't understand.

"What?" she asks, but it comes out *Mmph?*

He says it again.

"I think he's telling you to run," Isaac says, appearing at their side and startling Jane even though she knew he was coming. What with having the most bizarre conversation with Kyle and then watching him jump to his sure death off a cliff, her nerves are a bit on edge. Isaac grins. "Too late!" Then he scratches his head and looks toward the cliff behind him. "Guess Kyle was ready to leave the party, huh? Doesn't surprise me—not everyone has the balls for this kind of thing. Anyway, we're out of zip ties, but lucky for you guys, we've got plenty of duct tape."

Jane knows she should kick and scream and do whatever she can to get away from Isaac, but her hands are tied behind her, her mouth is taped, and honestly, she's exhausted from the shock and fear of the evening. Isaac winds the tape around her ankles three times, and when he's done, he rips it from the roll, pats it down, and then makes a shooing motion at them with his hands. "Scoot back," he says. "I've got to close the doors."

Jane does as instructed, if for no other reason than to be as far away from the cliff—and unstable Isaac—as possible. Dan inches his way back as well, pulling his knees to his chest, and then the door shuts and the two of them sit staring dumbly at each other, bound and duct-taped, as Jane tries to make sense of what just happened.

"OWWWW!" JANE SHRIEKS FOR THE SECOND TIME that evening. "GOD DAMMIT, that hurts."

"Sorry," Dan says, looking at her over his shoulder, but his duct tape is still in place, so it sounds more like *mahr-we*. Since their hands are literally tied behind their backs, Dan spent the first few minutes in the van trying to wriggle his arms down below his butt and then pull his legs through so that he could get his hands in front of him—but it was something that looked much easier than it ended up being in real life. With the cramped space in the back of the van and their advanced years making their limbs not quite as limber as they once were, neither was able to accomplish the task. He thought Jane was trying to do the same, but after a few minutes of sitting and struggling, he looked at her to see how she was progressing and she was just staring at him, waiting.

"What?" he said, but it came out as an unintelligible grunt and then she said something in return that was also an unintelligible grunt, so he shrugged his shoulders, and they would have sat there in a complete standoff for much longer if she hadn't bent at the waist and put her face behind him and directly in his hands. It took him a minute to grasp the edge of the duct tape on her mouth and a little more maneuvering from both of them to get the leverage with which to rip the tape from her mouth, but then finally she was free.

"What the hell were you doing for the first five minutes?" she asks. Dan simply raises his eyebrows.

"Right. Your turn," she says, and turns around so her hands can reach Dan's face. Dan turns, too, bends at the waist, and ducks his head down. If anyone were to look in the windows of the van, they'd likely have trouble understanding exactly what was happening inside, but would definitely think—on first glance—that it was something untoward.

"Unh," Dan bellows once his mouth is free. He wishes he could rub the skin around his mouth to stop the sting. He shakes his face like a wet dog, hoping it will help lessen the throbbing, and then says: "I was trying to bring my arms down and step through them. I saw it on *Cops* once, a guy slipped right out of his handcuffs, but it's a lot harder than it looks." And then the episode comes more clearly back to him. "Actually, I think he dislocated his shoulder doing it, but he was high on meth at the time and didn't feel it."

"Dan, focus. What are we going to do?"

"Let's try the doors," he says. He inches his way to the back doors and tries both handles, which is awkward in itself considering his wrists are tied behind him, but the handles won't budge. "Shit, the child locks must be on."

"It's a utility van. Surely children aren't riding in the back of it?"

Dan clears his throat, puts on his best salesman voice. *"Are you in the market for your next kidnapping vehicle? This one is not only white and creepy-looking but now equipped with child locks, so your victims absolutely do not have a chance at escape!"*

Jane doesn't laugh.

He steps back and then hurls his body at the door, throwing his shoulder into it. The door still doesn't budge, and Dan bounces off it and falls clumsily to the floor. He glances to the front seat longingly, where the two sole windows that actually roll down are located—and impossible to get to thanks to a fixed metal grate separating the driver and passenger seats from the rest of the van.

The only two other windows in the van are the back windows. Sitting on the floor, Dan lies back and lifts his legs, and then hits one of the windows with his heels. They land with a soft thud. He can't get enough leverage to even come close to breaking the glass.

"God, it's hot," Jane says, and though Dan is sweating from his exertion and it's a bit stuffy in the cramped space, Dan knows Jane is overheated not from the actual temperature (it can't be more than sixty-five degrees outside, and falling), but from her anxiety, and possibly a hormonal hot flash, something that's been happening with more frequency lately.

He maneuvers and wriggles his body until his back is against the metal van wall, right next to Jane, their arms awkwardly behind them, their knees bent and their legs bound at the ankles.

"What are we going to do?" she whimpers again, and Dan

knows this time it's rhetorical, so he just sits in the silence staring off at the other wall.

"Dan!" Maybe it wasn't rhetorical.

"What?"

"What are we going to do?"

"I don't know! I don't see a way out."

"We have to get Sissy out of there. All of them! Did you hear Brick? They're going to blow up the restaurant, Dan. Kill *everyone*."

Dan chews his lip. "I'm sorry I didn't believe you. That they were using your book."

Jane sighs. "That's OK. I wouldn't have believed me either." She hangs her head and closes her eyes. "I cannot believe this is happening. It's all my fault."

"*Your* fault? I'm pretty sure it's that lunatic Kyle's fault."

"Do you think he's OK?"

"Only if he sprouted wings and can fly."

Jane's face falls in worry and Dan wishes he had said something more reassuring, but he also doesn't know how one can survive a thousand-plus-foot fall off a cliff.

They sit in silence, the floor hard under Dan's butt, while he tries to think of something to lighten the mood.

"You remember when we were going to buy one of these things?"

Jane turns her head slightly to the left and side-eyes him. "What?"

"On our third date, I think it was. We were lying on the beach. We had just got done surfing, and that group of kids— they were probably our age at the time—pulled up in one of these vans and it was clear they were living in it, and instead of being horrified, we thought it was the greatest idea. And we talked all night about how we were going to get one of these vans and fix it up and live in it. Just travel the world and hike, and you would write and I would . . . What was I going to do?" Dan trails off, both because he realizes he's rambling about something inconsequential to fill the space and because he's unable to remember the rest of the harebrained scheme.

"Give drum lessons," Jane supplies.

Dan looks at her, momentarily surprised. "That's right! Oh my God. I had just started to play. I completely forgot that."

"You were awful," Jane says.

"I was," Dan agrees. "What happened to those kids?"

"We got pregnant."

"Oh. Right." Dan studies Jane. He wasn't exactly thrilled when Jane shared the news three months into their relationship. *Stunned* would be a better adjective. He had four years of podiatry school in front of him! He wasn't even close to being ready to start a family. But he was also surprised because of what her announcement instantly threw into sharp relief— Jane was it for him. Forever, which had until that moment seemed such a ridiculous, abstract concept. He wanted to get married and have kids and buy a house and save for retirement—he wanted all the things he never was quite sure he wanted, and he wanted it all *with* her. All the pregnancy did was speed up his timeline.

For Jane, though, it really seemed to rock her world. "I don't know if I'm ready to be a mother," she said, more than once. And Dan always wondered if it was more than that. If she wasn't sure about Dan. He always wondered, if Jane hadn't gotten pregnant—would she have still married him?

They sit in silence for a few beats more, both lost in their own thoughts.

"It's not too late for us to buy a van," Dan says.

"It is," Jane says. "We're middle-aged and this is wildly uncomfortable."

"Well, I think the bondage has something to do with that," he says, lifting his ankles an inch off the floor of the van in front of him as if to illustrate his point. "I can't believe some people are into this. I think it's cutting off my circulation."

"What do you mean *some* people? Aren't you the *some* person who brought those fuzzy handcuffs to Cabo that time? As I recall, you were quite into it."

"Hey!" he says, mock-mad. "What happens in Cabo . . ."

She's grinning at him, and despite their insane circumstances, Dan feels a tiny buzz—a thrill that his wife, who lately has been so disengaged from him at best, cutting at worst—is displaying a genuine warmth toward him. But then abruptly, like the sun being eclipsed by the moon, her expression morphs into a frown. She clears her throat. "Yes, well. Maybe *Becca* will be interested in the van life."

Though he knows Jane saw the text messages, Dan is still caught off guard that she knows the specific name from a part of his life he's kept so separate from her. Jane mistakes his expression as one of guilt, and to be fair, he does feel guilty, but not for the reason she thinks he does. She smirks. "You really thought I didn't know."

He knows it's time to come clean. Past time, really. It's

ridiculous that he's been keeping it secret for as long as he has, which is partly why he's been keeping it secret, because then the fact that he'd been keeping something so benign a secret became the bigger quandary—too difficult to explain.

He takes a deep breath. "It's ultimate frisbee," he announces, his voice loud in the enclosed space.

Jane turns to him, confused by the outburst and the seemingly bizarre fork in conversation. "Huh?"

"Where I've been going. What I've been doing. I'm not cheating on you. I joined an ultimate frisbee team."

Jane stares at him, mouth agape, and Dan can't tell if her expression is incredulous in a you-expect-me-to-believe-that? kind of way or a you've-allowed-our-entire-marriage-to-crumble-over-*ultimate-frisbee*? kind of way. He thinks it's likely a mix of both, and he can't blame her. "You *hate* sports. Your dad always makes that lame joke at Christmas that you have to shop at Walmart because you can't find the Target."

Dan inwardly cringes at the reminder that he's always been a little disappointing to his father. "I don't hate sports. I've just never been very good at any of them. Turns out I kind of have a knack for frisbee."

She lets out a small puff of air that's a half chuckle and then frowns again, her brows knitting together the way they do when she's trying to work those spelling puzzles in the *New York Times* app. "You're telling me that for the past six months, when you leave the house and say you're going for a run or to a meeting or drinks with friends, you've actually been going to . . . play ultimate frisbee."

"Yes," he says. "Well, sometimes I do actually go for runs.

If ultimate frisbee has taught me anything, it's that my stamina is shit, and I've been trying to get in better shape."

"You're joking."

"I'm not."

Jane blinks. "I suppose next you're going to tell me *Becca* is someone on the team?"

"She is."

Jane continues studying him, obviously trying to find the lie, and when she's satisfied it's the truth, she leans her head back and lets out a real laugh that's part relief, part incredulity. "Jesus Christ, Dan," she breathes. "Why didn't you just tell me?"

"I did. Well, I mentioned I was thinking about it at that dinner at Tyson and Gina's house last year, and you laughed like it was the most ridiculous thing you ever heard."

"I did not!"

"You did. And you said something about grown men desperately trying to hold on to their adolescence."

"Oh. That does sound like me. But who cares what I think? You still could have told me."

"I know," Dan says. He tries to find the words to explain himself. "Have you ever wanted something . . . I don't know"— he leans his head back until the crown of it finds the metal wall right next to Jane, their cheeks only inches apart—"that's just *yours*?" It sounds stupid when he says it out loud. A terrible excuse for having lied to his wife for so long, for having wreaked such havoc. Though to be honest, he stupidly believed he *wasn't* wreaking havoc, that Jane was none the wiser and he did have this activity, this hobby, this *secret*, that was his alone and he enjoyed it. These past six months, he was happier than he'd been in years, until Jane announced at dinner that she wanted a divorce because he was cheating, and the reality of his utter obtuseness hit him squarely in the gut.

"Oh my God," Jane says, and he closes his eyes and braces for the tongue-lashing he deserves for his immaturity, his selfishness, his thoughtlessness. But when he opens his eyes and looks at her, Jane is just staring at him—for the first time in a long time—as though she really *sees* him. "All the time," she says.

Warmth radiates from his core into his limbs, and he grins at his wife, feeling more connected to her in this moment than he has in months. "Sometimes I want my own bed to sleep in, especially when you snore," she adds.

He laughs.

"And I want to go on vacation. All by myself. And wake up when I want and drink coffee in silence and read books and walk the beach and be *alone*." She's on a roll now and Dan just watches her, listening like he hasn't listened to her in years. Maybe ever.

"Sometimes when I'm driving, after dropping Josh off at lacrosse or going to the dry cleaner's or home from the grocery for the fifty billionth time that week, I think, what if I just kept driving? What if I passed the exit to our house and pushed the gas and just *drove*? Where would I end up? Who would I be?"

The smile slowly seeps from his face like a deflating balloon. "You want to run away—from *us*?"

Jane stops short, clearly startled by his question. "What? No. Of course not," she sighs, and stares at the opposite side of the wall, as if searching for the words. Then she says: "Sometimes." She takes a deep breath. "I mean, I love the kids, of course I do. They're my *lungs*. I couldn't breathe if anything ever happened to them, and I worry about it all the time, you know? What if something happens to them?"

Dan understands. The kids are his lungs, too, but so is Jane. And it doesn't go without notice that she didn't include him.

"But I don't know," Jane continues. "Sometimes it feels like I love my family, but I hate my life."

"You *hate* it?" Dan says, alarmed. "What do you mean?"

"The monotony of it—it's exhausting. For eighteen years, I've been keeping up with all the things, the schedules and the doctor's appointments and the practices and the field trips and the permission slips and the friends and grocery shopping and the music lessons and the meals—"

"Hey, I cook some," Dan interjects.

If she hears him, she ignores it. "It's all so overwhelming. Literally overwhelming; it overwhelms me to the point that I feel like I've lost myself. I am Sissy and Josh's mother and I'm your wife, but who was I before I was those things? Does it even matter? Who would I be *without* being those things? Who would I have been if I hadn't gotten pregnant? And I don't wish I hadn't, that's not what I'm saying. I don't want to be without the kids. I'm actually scared—terrified, really—for Sissy to go to college. Before you know it, Josh is going to be gone, too, and then who am I? Who will I be? I always thought I would be . . . I don't know . . . successful. I don't even know what that means, though. A bestselling novelist, maybe? I just thought I would do something that mattered. Something important. Do you know what I mean? But it feels like nothing I do matters."

Silence overtakes them once again, and Dan feasts on Jane's words, rolling them over in his mind. How did he not know she felt this way? How does she not know how important she is to them? To him.

"Is she pretty?" Jane says, interrupting his thoughts.

"Who?"

"Becca."

He almost laughs, but stops himself just in time. Becca is a total smoking-hot sexpot, with her pouty lips and svelte body with its hourglass curves—big curves—but through forty-three years of living, Dan has learned the art of tactful restraint. "I mean, I guess."

"Are you attracted to her?"

"No." He's also learned when it's imperative to lie. "God, Jane, she's like, twenty-six. A child. I don't look at her that way." Of course he had looked at Becca *that* way. A blind man would look at Becca that way. But he's not stupid enough to say that out loud. Right or wrong, he understands the societal hypocrisy that means his wife can ogle Harry Styles or Tom Holland, who are both nearly twenty years her junior, or any of those boys in that high school vampire show that she religiously watches reruns of solely because she finds them so attractive, but if he so much as glances at a woman in her twenties, he's a creepy old man.

And the truth is, Becca doesn't hold a candle to Jane. Not because Jane is so objectively beautiful, but because she's Jane. His Jane. The Jane who once wanted to run away in a van and the Jane who would never live in a van all at once. He's seen every side of Jane, every part—and while some people think it's the air of mystery, the unknown, that is alluring in a partner, for Dan it's always been the knowing. The seeing of Jane, warts and all, and loving her anyway. He'd never lie and say he loved her *for* her flaws, like some of those poets who are much better linguists and romantics than he is claim—because in all honesty, some of her flaws are downright obnoxious and maddening. But he knows her flaws, and there is a comfort in that that people don't often talk about. It's beautiful to Dan, therefore Jane is beautiful. He'd never say that either, though, because Jane would brush it off as a line while simultaneously twisting his words, somehow deciding that he didn't find her objectively beautiful (a prime example of one of her many maddening traits, the way she can turn anything Dan says into an insult).

"Oh, Dan," Jane breathes, slowly tilting her head until they're temple to temple. "How did we get here?"

"Like, abstractly—how did we get to this point in our marriage and our life? Or specifically, how did we get locked in a van when we're supposed to be enjoying our twentieth anniversary dinner?"

"Nineteenth," Jane says. "And both?"

Dan isn't sure if it's the heat of Jane's breath or the fact that he has nearly died twice, but he is suddenly, wildly, and inappropriately aware of his half erection. He feels like he remembers reading somewhere about the release of adrenaline from high-risk activities like jumping out of an airplane (which he has never done and would never do), or walking across hot coals correlating with sexual arousal or something, but he's never experienced it before now. Or maybe it's just that he thinks he's going to die, and, like a last meal, Dan's body wants to have sex one last time before he goes; either way, before he can stop himself, he turns his head one inch to the right to close the gap between his and Jane's lips. Jane pulls back her head and stares at him in surprise.

Embarrassed at the inappropriateness of his action, Dan opens his mouth to apologize—the saying *It's neither the time nor the place* has never been more true—but before he can get the word out, Jane has slammed her face back into his, hungrily thrusting her tongue into his mouth, sucking and exploring and, frankly, kissing him like she's a dying woman in the middle of a vast, sandy desert and his mouth is the Bellagio fountain.

It's not like they haven't kissed in a long time—they kiss nearly every day, Dan thinks. Or maybe they don't kiss every day, but they've kissed so often in their lives that it feels like they've kissed every day. But it's been a long time since they've kissed like *this*, Dan thinks. And then he stops thinking altogether.

He lets the weight of Jane falling toward him topple them both to the floor, where they continue—albeit awkwardly—kissing like their life depends on it. Jane pushes her body up against his, and when she feels his erection on her thigh through his pants, she whispers: "I *knew* you were into bondage," and then laughs into his mouth. He laughs and then covers her lips with his once again, kissing her more deeply this time, not only because her quick wit is so attractive, but because he's always adored how funny she finds herself.

They keep kissing, struggling to get closer, but with their

hands and feet bound it's wildly frustrating and ridiculously hot at the same time—and Dan thinks maybe he really *is* into bondage after all—until a sudden loud thump at the back of the van turns both their bodies to stone and stops Dan's heart altogether.

Isaac, he thinks. Back to shoot them both, maybe? Throw their bodies over the cliff? There's no telling. He breaks away from his wife and sees the fear in her eyes before they both turn toward the window to see the face pressed up against it.

Their daughter, Sissy, who couldn't look more disgusted if you put an entire platter of smoked salmon in front of her.

"Ewwww, gross. What is *wrong* with you guys?"

CHAPTER
25

"SISSY!" JANE SAYS, STRUGGLING TO SIT UP WHILE hoping Dan's erection isn't pitching a tent in his pants. Even in a hostage situation, she doesn't want to traumatize her daughter by reminding her that her parents are sexual beings. Though, to be honest, Jane herself nearly forgot. What *was* that? She hasn't been that turned on by Dan in years. Breathing heavily, she rolls onto her knees and awkwardly shifts forward toward the back of the van door. "What are you doing?"

With a butter knife in her right hand, Sissy bangs on the glass again, panic in her eyes. "I think you're right! I think Brick's going to bomb the restaurant," she says. "I came to get you out." Her voice is a bit muffled by the glass, and Jane fills with relief, not because Sissy is rescuing them as much as because Sissy *wants* to rescue them. Her sweet, kind daughter isn't completely gone.

"With a butter knife?" Dan says.

"Yeah, to pick the lock."

"Honey, I don't think that's going to work," Jane shouts at

Sissy through the glass, wondering again how a girl who can calculate quadratic equations and write binary code in her sleep can lack so much common sense. As if reading her mind, Dan lowers his voice to Jane. "You were right. We should have sent her to private school."

They can hear the clank-clunks as Sissy is already fumbling with the knife and the latch, cursing a blue streak. Jane and Dan both manage to scoot to the back of the van and maneuver to their knees, pressing their faces against the windows to try and gauge Sissy's progress.

Sissy looks up at them, helpless.

"Have you tried the front door?"

"What?"

"The front door."

Sissy gets a bright look in her eyes and then rushes off. Seconds later, she's back. "Locked!" she says, her face crumpling in distress.

"Get a rock," Dan says.

"What?"

"A rock," Dan yells. "Bust out the window."

Sissy looks around and, not seeing anything in the near vicinity, disappears from view. Seconds later, she reappears, her hands empty. "There's nothing! Just tiny pieces of gravel."

"Shit," Dan mutters. Jane can tell he's thinking but coming up as empty as Sissy's hands.

"Where's your gun?" Jane asks, and Sissy stares at her for a beat before reaching into the back of her waistband and brandishing her pistol. "Shoot out the front door window," Jane says.

"I can't."

"Yes, you can." Jane's only about 10 percent confident it will be fine, but what choice do they have?

"No, I mean I *can't*. I don't have any bullets."

"I know, but you said you have blanks, right?"

"Yeah."

"That will still work!"

"It will?"

"Yes! Blanks are shell casings loaded with gunpowder, they just don't have the bullet. At close range, they can shatter glass easily."

"What?" Sissy asks, leaning closer to the window, and Jane realizes she couldn't hear her.

"Hold it up close to the glass and shoot the window!" she shouts.

Dan is staring at her, mouth agape. "How do you know that, about blanks?"

"Book research," Jane says. "Let's hope it works better than that *Cops* handcuff trick." Sissy disappears once again.

"What's the plan here?" Dan asks.

"We get out of this van, get into our car, and get the hell out of here."

"But the police!"

"We'll tell them we escaped, which is true."

"And Sissy?"

"We'll say she was eating with us. A family dinner. To celebrate Stanford or something."

"Look at what she's wearing."

"All teenagers dress weird. They won't even notice." Jane

isn't sure if she's trying to convince Dan or herself, but really, what other choice do they have?

Dan nods once emphatically, and then startles as the *BANG* of the gun is followed by shattering glass. Jane closes her eyes and hopes that no one, namely Isaac, heard a gun blast and comes outside to play detective. The door locks click and Sissy reappears at the back window. "Hurry!" she says, opening the door. "We have to get those zip ties off you."

Jane offers her bound hands to Sissy, who manages to snap through them with the pressure of the blade. As Jane rips the duct tape off her ankles, Sissy cuts through Dan's ties, and then they're free, Jane and Dan jumping to their feet out of the van.

"Let's go!" Dan says, shoving his hand in his pocket and, finding nothing, pulling it out and starting to pat his other pocket and his chest. "Dang it," he says.

"What?" Jane asks, but she already knows.

"I can't find my keys."

Jane stares at him a beat, a jumble of emotions running through her at once. Rage wins. "GOD DAMMIT, DAN!"

"Sorry!" he shouts back. "They're in my jacket pocket. I think."

The wheels in Jane's brain turn faster. "We'll just run for it. Hide in the woods or something until this is all over." It's not a great plan, admittedly, but Jane unwittingly planned the entire fiasco that has unfolded this evening and she's all out of great plans for the moment. "Come on." She starts off in the direction of the woods, but Sissy doesn't move.

"I'm not coming with you," she says.

"Not this again, Sissy. We don't have time. Let's go."

"No. I know them, Mom. I *know* them. I can fix this. You have to trust me."

"*Trust* you? Oh, I think that ship has sailed, Sissy."

"Mom—"

"Sissy, ENOUGH!" Jane roars. "He lied to you. Brick lied. This has nothing to do with climate change or *saving* the world or whatever you thought you were doing. It's clearly some personal vendetta. He used you. He used all of you to get to Otto. And it's OK! You made a mistake. You didn't know. But now you do. And you owe him nothing."

Sissy drops her gaze to the ground.

"Sissy." Jane studies her. "Sissy, you didn't know, did you?"

"Mom, if you knew what Otto did to Brick . . ."

"What?"

"He stole his invention! *Years* of grad school research in nanotechnology to create the most efficient surfactant to clean up oil spills. It was ingenious, truly. World-changing. It could have made environmental disasters like the *Exxon Valdez* if not a thing of the past, at least exponentially less harmful when they happened. Brick entered it in Otto's environmental competition, knowing someone like Otto had the capability to manufacture it and get it to where it was needed most all over the world. As it turns out, the technology that works so well to clean up oil spills also works like a charm to more efficiently *extract* oil from the ground. Otto patented the invention, renamed it the Ottomatic Oilpump, and sold it to all the huge oil corporations, becoming a billionaire in the process— and thanks to an NDA he made Brick sign, Brick's never been able to tell the truth about what happened. Not that anyone would care."

Jane frowns. Then tilts her head and listens. She can't tell if she's imagining it or if she can hear a faint chop-chop-chop in the air.

"Mom, did you hear me? He's destroying the environment with the very thing Brick invented to help restore it."

"Yes, I heard you," Jane says. She heard words, anyway. Surfactants. Nanotechnology. This is how Jane often feels when Sissy talks—about binary code or cryptocurrency or anything else that flies just above Jane's breadth of knowledge. But regardless of Brick and Otto's beef, this has *nothing* to do with Sissy, and she somehow needs to make her daughter understand the severity of the consequences. "If you stay here and the police catch you—and they *will* catch you—you can kiss Stanford goodbye."

"I'm not going to Stanford," Sissy says.

"What?"

"I'm not going to Stanford." Her eyes are hard. Defiant. Full of fire.

Jane looks from Sissy to Dan. "Are you hearing this?"

"Yeah. It sounds like a helicopter," Dan says. He peers out into the night.

Jane groans and turns her attention back on her daughter. "Yes. You are."

"No. I never wanted to go there!"

Jane can feel Dan's eyes on her, but this time won't meet his gaze. She won't give him the satisfaction of being right. "Don't be ridiculous. Everyone wants to go to Stanford!"

"No, Mom. *You* want me to go to Stanford."

"Why would *I* care if you go to Stanford?"

"Guys, I think—" Dan interjects, but they both ignore him.

"I don't know—so you can brag about it to your friends? So you can feel accomplished in your duty as a mother? So you can live vicariously through me, since your life is so boring?"

Jane closes her eyes, stung as though she's been slapped. Her life is boring, yes, but that's not what wounds her. Jane did view helping Sissy get into Stanford as her motherly duty. Not to brag about it (although she has to admit, she does wear it as a badge of honor), but because what else is her job as a mother if not to make sure Sissy has more opportunities than Jane had, to *be* more? Sissy is so smart, so much smarter than Jane ever was. By the time she was seven, she was reading at least five books a week—on a high school level. At nine, she was patiently explaining to Jane how binary code worked, something Jane didn't understand in college, much less when Sissy tried to explain it to her. That kind of intelligence needed to be harnessed, developed, given direction in the way a college like Stanford could do, so Sissy could reach her full potential. But Jane doesn't know how to explain all of that to Sissy.

"It's not for me, Sissy!" she says lamely. "It's for you. You have to go to Stanford so you can *make* something of yourself."

At that, the fire in Sissy's eyes blazes to a full inferno, and she roars: "I ALREADY AM SOMETHING."

Jane and Sissy stare at each other like boxers squared off in the ring, the now-loud staccato filling the air and impossible to ignore. All three of them look up at the night sky to see the lights of a large helicopter approaching the cliff, the beam of its spotlight focused on the restaurant, leaving them in the shadows.

"What is that?" Jane asks.

"I think it's a helicopter," Dan says.

"I know it's a helicopter, Dan. I mean *who* do you think it is?"

Suddenly, the spotlight from the helicopter swings over and shines directly on them, as though they're center stage at a Broadway performance.

Jane holds up her hand against the glare, looking into the bright light, and gets a terrible feeling in the pit of her stomach. "Let's go," she says, at the same time that a voice on a loudspeaker shouts at them from the helicopter, but she can't see anything or make out what they're saying.

"Did you understand that?" she says to Sissy and Dan.

The voice warbles loudly—and nonsensically—again.

"Something about a gun?" Dan says.

They all look at Sissy's hand. "Oh my God! Sissy, drop the gun!" The words are no sooner out of Jane's mouth when the unmistakable sound of a machine gun firing rips into the night air around them.

"Run!" Dan says. Jane takes off around the van, not even feeling the gravel pinch her soles. She dives behind the front bumper, the ping of bullets ricocheting off the metal sides of it, causing her to flinch every second. Dan, right behind her, throws his arm around her, and they slide down to sitting, both hoping they'll be safe from the barrage. It takes Jane only a second to realize Sissy is not with them.

"Where's Sissy?" Jane yells. "I thought she was right beside you!"

"She ran back into the restaurant."

"NO!" Jane shouts. "Is she OK?"

"I don't know. I think so." Dan tries to peer around the edge of the front bumper and a bullet goes whizzing past his head. "Jesus!" he says, jerking back.

"Why are they shooting at *us*?" Jane yells. "Is that more Force of Nature people?"

"I'm pretty sure it's the police. I think they think Sissy's one of the bad guys."

"SHE IS ONE OF THE BAD GUYS!" Jane covers her face with her hands. "What do we do, Dan? What do we *do*?"

She remembers hearing once—maybe a friend said it to her, or maybe she just saw it on Instagram—an adage about parenting, and it lights in her mind now, unbidden: Little kids, little problems; big kids, big problems. She thinks now perhaps she underestimated how big the "big" problems were going to be.

The barrage of bullets suddenly stops, and Dan goes to peer around the van—more cautiously this time.

"Is it still there?" Jane asks, which is a dumb question because she can clearly hear the loud staccato of helicopter blades, but it's almost as if her question prompts it to leave—slowly the din starts to fade.

"They're leaving!" Dan says. "I think they're leaving."

Sure enough, the chop-chop-chop grows dimmer and dimmer until it's just silence ringing in Jane's ears.

"Let's go!" Jane says, jumping to her feet. "We have to go

back in. We have to get her. And all those people! Oh God, they're all going to die!"

"No," Dan says.

"What do you mean *no*? Yes, they are, Dan!"

"JANE," Dan roars, grabbing her wrist and yanking it hard. "Sit. Down."

Jane freezes, staring at Dan. Her levelheaded husband who—though he gets irritated and annoyed and sometimes even says mean things—rarely raises his voice.

Jane sits.

"Thank you," Dan says. "Now. Can we *please* just think about this for a minute?"

Jane turns to him, half-incredulous and half-furious. "Are you joking? All I've been doing all night long is thinking about what to do."

"No—you've been *acting*. It's what you always do. You just go off half-cocked with no plan, consequences be damned."

"At least I *do* something!"

"You haven't given me a chance!"

Jane glares at him, fire in her eyes, but then relents. "OK, fine. What do you suggest?"

Dan sticks his tongue in his cheek, thinking, and Jane has to resist throwing her arms in the air in impatience. Finally, Dan says, "Tell me exactly what they do in your book. Where's the bomb?"

"They use a pressure cooker. And I saw one—in the kitchen."

"OK, good. And then how do they escape?"

"I don't know! In my book, the terrorists put the bomb on a

timer, then used the network of sewers beneath the London teahouse to escape. But up here?"

"No underground tunnels," says Dan. "That we know of."

"Right."

"OK, well, maybe it doesn't matter. We get rid of the pressure cooker, so no hostages die. Then all we have to do is get Sissy out and let the police handle the rest."

"How are we going to do that?"

"I have a plan. Just trust me! You run down to the police."

"The police that just opened fire on us? *Those* police?"

"Yes—and tell them she was having dinner with us."

Jane frowns. "OK, but what about the people who have seen her? Who *know* she was one of *them*?"

"I don't know. It's our word against theirs?"

"We can't take that chance." Jane shakes her head. "I'm going in. I can't *not* be with her."

"No! Absolutely not," Dan says. And as if to underline his sentiment, he abruptly stands up and runs to the door. She stares after him, open-mouthed. If she were given a multiple-choice question about what methodical, stick-to-the-plan Dan would do in this scenario, the last option she'd pick would be "jump up and run back into the restaurant, without so much as a backward glance."

She's felt this way before, of course. No matter how long you've lived with someone, how well you think you know them, there are always times when you look at them and think *Who are you?* Sometimes due to little revelations, like when she learned he kept a toothbrush and floss at work and brushed his teeth every day after lunch like a Boy Scout. Or like when she discovered Becca's text messages. Or when she learned that his clandestine affair was merely an affair with ultimate frisbee.

But it was other times, too—a vague feeling when lying beside him at night, watching the slow rise and fall of his chest as he slept. How well can you really know anybody? Even the person you've lived with—slept beside each night—for nearly half your life.

"Dan!" Jane hisses, even though the door has shut behind him and he is securely in the restaurant. "Shit." She clenches her teeth and stares at the closed back door of the restaurant.

And that's when she feels it: the weight of an elephant on her chest; the sudden loss of blood in her hands, making her fingers go numb; a dizziness so acute, her vision blurs. A full-blown panic attack. She's only had one once before—in the middle of the Pacific Ocean when she was snorkeling on a family vacation in Maui. Her goggles fogged up and Jane couldn't see a thing—and without the advantage of sight, her thoughts turned on her. She was out in the middle of the ocean! Where there were sharks! And jellyfish! And *where were her children*? Every blob she could barely make out was some deadly being hunting her loved ones. Jane broke the surface of the water frantically flailing her arms in horror, unable to breathe or think—aside from the acute memory that flailing in water attracted sharks, which only amped her panic. And while having a panic attack on land is certainly preferable to one in the middle of the ocean, she still feels like she's going to die. Worse, she's afraid Sissy and Dan are going to die, too—and just like her panic attack, there's nothing she can do to stop it.

TWENTY-NINE
MINUTES UNTIL
THE END

26

"BREWSTER! *BREWSTER!*" KIP IS SCREAMING INTO his CB. He's been trying to get ahold of him for three minutes, ever since they heard the gunfire.

Everything had been fine. Brewster relayed what he could see: a large picture window on the west end of the restaurant facing the cliff, revealing a few diners at their tables, but when Zimmerman asked him for a visual count of hostages and hostage takers, he answered in the negative. "I can't get a good angle to see."

"OK," Kip replied. "Hold tight. Await further—"

"Wait!" Brewster said. "There are three people outside the restaurant, standing next to a van."

"A white utility van?" Kip asked, eyeing the one in front of him that had been burned to a crisp.

"Yes. One of them is holding a gun!"

"Advise the person to drop their weapon."

A few tense moments passed. "She didn't do it. Do I have permission to engage?"

She? Kip thought.

No sooner had he replied "No! Hold your fire" than they heard a barrage of gunfire over the radio. "I said HOLD YOUR FIRE, not GO FIRE," Kip shouted, and then they lost him, the line nothing but static for the next three minutes as Sandy and McLeod and Kip stared at one another, Kip's heart pounding in his throat.

Now they hear what sounds like someone vomiting profusely over the crackle of the connection. Brewster moans.

"What happened? I told you not to engage!" Kip says.

"It was an accident! I panicked and pressed the wrong button."

Kip squeezes his temples with his stretched-out right hand. "Did you hit anybody?"

"No, I don't think so."

"Retreat. That's an order. Go back to the station."

"I already left," he says. He moans again. "Unnh. I hate this stupid bird."

"So much for intel," Kip says, kicking the tire of his police car.

Kip's cell phone buzzes in his pocket and he recognizes the number as the one he's been redialing for the past hour. He waits a beat to collect himself before answering. "Hello?"

"Are you *insane?*" the deep, accented voice of Brick not-the-restaurant-manager booms. "Opening fire from a helicopter! You could have killed someone."

Kip closes his eyes. This is likely not the best way to build rapport or gain Brick's trust *or* impress Zimmerman. He swallows past the lump in his throat. "Yes, that was an unfortunate accident. Is everyone OK?"

Brick ignores the question. "No more helicopters, drones, flying machines," he says. "If I see so much as a kite in the air, I swear to God, the only thing left of this restaurant will be online reviews. Understood?"

Kip nearly chokes on his own saliva. It's not a request or a demand so much as a . . . "Is that a bomb threat?" he asks.

"Yes, it is a bomb threat!" Brick roars.

"So am I to understand you want the airspace clear?"

"YES!"

Kip nods, even though Brick can't see him, and he hears Zimmerman's words on loop in his mind: *We won't give him anything for free.* "I will run that up the chain of command and get back to you," he says weakly while he tries to pinpoint when exactly everything started to go so poorly.

And then—as if in answer to his unspoken prayers—he finally, *finally* hears the roar of engines racing up the hill toward him, and he puts his hand up to the glare of the headlights and breathes a great sigh of relief that he is no longer in charge.

The cavalry has arrived.

THE THING IS, DAN ABSOLUTELY DOES NOT HAVE A plan. He doesn't know why he told Jane he did, except maybe the carnal activity in the van triggered some latent part of his caveman brain and, like some twenty-two-year-old lothario, he wanted to impress her. Now he stands in the empty kitchen, his eyes darting to all the corners and tables, half hoping Sissy's hiding behind one, will materialize, and they can run out together, join up with Jane, and go straight to the police.

And then *home*. As someone who is naturally a homebody anyway, Dan has never wanted to be safely in his own house with his family more than he does right now. Why did he think this was a good idea? A stupid, overpriced restaurant an hour and a half away from home. If they had just gone to Macaroni Grill, they'd be in bed by now, Jane reading by the light of her Kindle, Dan drifting off to sleep beside her, receiving a sharp elbow in the back every now and then when his deep breathing bordered too closely on snoring.

Loud shouting from the dining room startles him. He leans

forward, straining to hear. It's Brick's deep voice, but the only two words that come through crystal clear are *bomb threat*. And then a clatter as if Brick has thrown the cell or something else—a fork or spoon maybe—onto the ground, where it skidded across the floor.

The mention of the bomb reminds Dan of the one—and only—part of the plan he was sure of. He scans all the pots and pans in the kitchen, looking for the pressure cooker—and suddenly realizes he has no idea what one looks like.

Shit. Don't they have buttons or something? A timer? As quietly as he can, he tiptoes around one of the metal tables and into the main space of the kitchen, where he spies his sports coat on the floor in front of the refrigerator. He picks it up, causing his keys to jangle, and he freezes, holding his breath, his heart tap dancing as he waits for someone to burst in and catch him. When no one does, he slowly digs out his keys to the Subaru from the inside pocket, and then, holding all the keys tightly together so they can't clink, transfers them to his pants pocket, feeling at least a small sense of accomplishment or relief to have them once again in his possession.

Then he turns to the large range with its multiple burners that have long been shut off, pots half-full of congealed food, and he tries to determine which of the many stainless steel cooking vessels is the pressure cooker. He nearly resorts to *Eeny meeny miny moe*, when out of the corner of his eye he sees a large stainless steel pot on the counter that looks slightly different from the rest because its lid has brackets. Yes! The lid would need to be secured to the pot for the pressure to build up. That must be it. Excitedly, he picks it up, but it's much lighter than he anticipated, and he realizes too late—the top isn't firmly fastened. It slides off and Dan doesn't have a free hand to catch it. In what feels like slow motion, he watches help-lessly as the pot lid falls, then hits the ground in a cacophony of clanging, whirring round and round like a spinning top un-til it finally comes to a stop, the sound echoing through the still kitchen like a cymbal hit by a drumstick.

He feels rather than hears the dining room door swing open behind him, and, standing with his shoulders so tense they're nearly up to his ears, eyes closed, he waits for the inevitable.

"What the hell?" Great. Dan recognizes Isaac's voice. "Pot down, man."

Dan slowly lowers the pot to the counter and turns to find, as expected, Isaac's gun pointed squarely at him. "Hands where I can see them."

Dan sighs a deep, world-weary sigh, cursing himself for his ridiculous mistake, and then, on Isaac's order, raises his hands to the ceiling and walks back through the dining room door toward his table and his plate of cold barnacles. Heads swivel toward him, and Dan briefly meets Sissy's eyes, where he glimpses a mix of surprise and concern before she drops her gaze. He slides into his seat in silence, shoulders drooped, until Brick finally says: "What are *you* doing here?"

"I . . . uh, came back," he says, slightly embarrassed.

"I caught him messing with the pans," Isaac says.

Brick tilts his head, digesting this information. "I thought you locked them in the van."

"I did."

Brick turns back to Dan. "Where's your wife?"

Dan sees no reason to lie. "Probably halfway down the hill on her way to talk to the police."

"Huh," Brick says, and whether he's taken aback at Dan's honesty or Jane's actions, Dan's not sure.

"Want me to go after her?" Isaac says, a little too eagerly for Dan's liking.

"No. We won't be here much longer." Dan wonders if it sounds as ominous to anyone else, or if it's just because he knows what Brick plans to do. "It's done?" he asks Tink.

"Done." She nods, shutting the laptop with a click.

So that's it, then, Dan thinks. His daughter has officially aided and abetted in the stealing of nine million dollars. The police are waiting just down the hill, and he has no idea how he's going to get Sissy out of here, much less convince the police she was dining with them when every other hostage knows—and will likely attest to the fact—that Jane and Dan were alone.

An ear-piercing scream from one of the hostages, though Dan can't tell which one, fills the air, and Dan looks in time to see Brick carefully pull something the size of a toaster out of one of the book bags and set it on a table.

"What is that?" Vaughn asks, panic in her voice. Dan strains his neck to see around Brick's body, but fails. The cacophony of voices from the hostages sitting against the wall grows, and Dan looks at the fear on their faces, trying, like Vaughn, to determine what has them so on edge. And then his ear picks out three words that rise above the din: "It's a bomb!"

Dan's head jerks back to the table, and Brick, who has kindly stepped out of the way so Dan can see that what look to be two tan-colored bricks strapped together with duct tape, wires, and a digital wristwatch are now perfectly visible. Dan blinks and then nearly laughs at how it looks exactly like something Wile E. Coyote would use to ensnare the Road Runner.

"Brick?" Dan looks over at Sissy, the fear in her voice apparent. "Is that real?"

"Yep," he says, pushing a few buttons on the watch. "Fifteen minutes ought to do it."

"You said no one would get hurt," she says.

"No one is going to get hurt." He claps his hands together once. "We have fifteen minutes to get everyone out of this restaurant. Goldie, Caden, and Isaac, please cut the zip ties. When your zip ties have been cut, please line up at the front door. When Jeremy opens it, please run as far away from the restaurant as you can."

Dan stares at Brick.

"You're letting us go?" one of the elderly women at a table says.

"I'm letting you go."

A murmur of voices fills the air, and Dan senses the disbelief he, too, feels. Is this really the plan? What's the catch? And more important, how is Sissy going to get out without being caught?

"Please! Move. We only have fourteen and a half minutes."

Tink shuts her laptop with a clack and stands up to stuff it back in her book bag, which sets off a chain reaction—Sissy, Caden, and Jeremy grab their book bags from the pile, and then Sissy and Caden fan out to a table to cut ankle zip ties while Jeremy goes toward his station at the front door.

The elderly women are the first to stand and walk to the door, with the four-top following, and then Vaughn and Paisley, but when Vaughn tries to usher her forward, Paisley stands rooted to the ground. "Dad?" she says.

"Yes, he's coming, too," Brick says.

Dan, who could stand at any time and move to the door, finds he's as rooted to his spot as Paisley is, unable to leave his daughter behind. And he finally gives voice to his most pressing concern. "How are you getting out?"

He means to ask Sissy, but he's staring at Brick, who tilts his head and grins. "Through the front door like everyone else."

Dan stares at him. *That's* the escape plan? Nothing about this evening has made any sense to Dan, but this makes the least sense of all. "But the police!"

"Will have no idea what's going on in the chaos of people sprinting from the front door and then the subsequent explosion of two bricks of C-4. Should be plenty of cover for most of us to get away."

Most? Dan's eyes find Sissy, but she's staring at the explosives. The timer reads 13:46, 13:45, 13:44 . . .

"Jeremy, go ahead and let the first wave out."

"No!" Isaac screeches, and that's when Dan notices he hasn't joined the others. Everyone looks in his direction, and Isaac, standing in front of the door to the kitchen, waves his gun wildly in an arc. "Nobody. Is going. Anywhere."

"Isaac," Brick says calmly, his voice low. "What are you doing, mate?"

Though Isaac's hard, cold eyes are on Brick, Dan feels the

297

chill in the air. His stomach hollows in fear as Isaac enunciates each word: "Finishing what we started."

"Isaac, we got the money," Brick says. "Put the gun down."

"No! You think this was about the stupid money? That money isn't going to do anything. Not enough, anyway. The world is *dying*." His face alternates between stone-cold steel and pain, like someone is sticking him with a hot poker. Dan's never seen anyone have a mental break with reality, but he thinks it likely looks a lot like this. "In fifteen, twenty years, it's not going to be recognizable. There will be mass famine, wars over resources, flooding, displacement, death, and destruction. And no one cares! You know why? Because it's mostly the poor who will suffer. The people who no one cares about anyway. Well, maybe they'll start to care if a bunch of rich yahoos die in a huge explosion in a rich restaurant in a rich California town."

"Someone *do* something," Vaughn hisses. "He's not the only one with a gun!"

"No." Isaac smirks. "But I'm the only one who has bullets." He swings his gun, pointing it directly at Vaughn, who flinches.

"Is that *true*?" She looks at Brick. "What kind of criminals are you?"

"Isaac, put the gun down," Tink says. "The world is a mess, I agree. But killing a bunch of people? What's that going to fix?"

"What does gluing your hands to famous works of art do? Or that man who set himself on fire on the Supreme Court steps. Sometimes you have to do something extreme to wake people up."

298

"But those things don't work. They didn't actually change anything."

"Because no one cares. But killing the wealthiest man on the planet? It will be the headline of every newspaper the world over. Bonus points that he's enemy number one." Isaac points his gun at Otto. "Killing the earth and making billions in the process."

Dan stares in bewilderment at Isaac. He's even more cracked than he thought. The hostages start to murmur and then one of them shouts: "Keep him, then! Let us go!"

Otto looks wildly around, trying to figure out who said it. "Oh, you think you all are so innocent?" he spits, looking almost as crazed as Isaac with his wild eyebrows and now-dried, crusted blood on his upper lip and chin. "Eating your two-thousand-dollar meals at La Fin du Monde. How'd you get here? You can't *all* have electric cars. Did you walk? Ride a bike? And what are you doing to save the world? Taking cloth grocery bags to the store? Driving an electric car? Buying organic meat? All while you're taking planes to see the Grand Canyon and the Eiffel Tower. And buying clothes for a season that you'll throw away the next. And the plastic! Good Lord, the plastic. You can point fingers all you want, but you don't want your lives to change. Not really."

Brick scoffs. "Yes, yes. Climate change is definitely the fault of individual Americans who simply don't recycle enough and has nothing to do with the corporations who continue to make the plastic and the fast fashion and the airplanes. You must blame all the sea turtle deaths on third graders who aren't cutting up the six-pack rings fast enough with their little fingers."

"You joke, but it's true! Look at your stock options," Otto says, and he looks straight at Dan when he says it. "I bet all of you have SierraX and Exxon and Shell and every other company responsible for carbon emissions in your BlackRock portfolios."

Dan blinks. Does he?

"Why? Because you want to get rich, too! You can make me the scapegoat all you want. But at the end of the day, you all want to *be* me. Or at least want to have the kind of money I have. Isn't that what everyone wants? To be rich?"

"No," Brick says. "Not everyone does want to be rich. Some of us just want to leave the earth a little better than we found it."

Otto laughs. "Which is why you stole nine million dollars from me. Because you *don't* want to be rich. Got it."

"I'm just getting even," Brick growls.

"Well, I guess it doesn't matter now. Looks like we'll both be dead in"—Otto glances at the timer on the C-4—"ten minutes and six seconds."

Dan's forehead pricks with sweat. Why isn't Brick, anyone, *doing* anything? They need to tackle Isaac to the ground. Yes, someone may get shot in the process, but at least everyone else would be able to escape. His eyes dart around the room, hoping someone is going to step up, be the hero, but it becomes apparent that, like Dan, everyone is waiting for someone else to do it.

"Isaac, please!" Sissy shouts plaintively. "This isn't what we planned. No one is supposed to get hurt."

Isaac swings his gun to Sissy. "Everyone gets hurt, Goldie. That's life."

And that's when Dan realizes the hero is going to have to be him. He doesn't want to die. But he wants Sissy to die even less. Never mind the fact that he'd never forgive himself—he'd never be able to face Jane again.

He takes a deep breath.

And then he sees the swinging door fly open.

And that's when he grabs a plate.

JANE CLAWS AT HER THROAT AS IT CLOSES UP, THE hard rubber of the van's tire digging into her back, her chest so tight, she can't breathe. *It's just a panic attack*, she tells herself. *You're not dying.* But it feels like she is. She squeezes her eyes shut and thinks again of snorkeling in the Pacific, the blind terror she felt, and then the hand on her arm—which at first she was 100 percent positive was the tentacle of a giant octopus (the Kraken! Risen from the depths!) clamping on to her limb to drag her to the bottom of the ocean. But of course, it wasn't.

It was Dan.

"Breathe, Jane!" he demanded. She tore at her life vest. It was too constrictive, the reason she couldn't inhale. "Look. At. Me." Jane stilled her hands and opened her eyes, but through her foggy goggles she could see only the suggestion of Dan's face, like a Gerhard Richter painting. She gasped for air, creating a strangled, squeaking goose honk. And then Dan ripped off her goggles and grabbed her face in between his hands, and she stared at his now-distinct greige-blue eyes while following his calm instructions to *breathe in for one-two-three-four-five* and then *breathe out for one-two-three-four-five.*

And she does it now. She pictures Dan's face, his tranquil, soothing eyes, and she breathes in and out for the next five minutes, maybe ten, until her rigid fists uncurl, her muscles relax, her heartbeat slows to normal.

Then she stares at the door to the kitchen where Dan disappeared. She turns and looks down the gravel driveway, where it ends before the forest. Where she is supposed to be running for the police, because Dan has a plan. Dan said to trust him. And she does! She always has trusted Dan, to be honest. Even when she saw the text messages, she knew in her gut he wasn't cheating. She just wanted an excuse to leave. To shake up her boring life. To do something different. To *be* someone different.

But she's not someone different. She's Jane. She's a failed author. She's the mother of Sissy and Josh. And she's been the wife of Dan for the past nineteen years—which is how she knows he didn't really have a plan. And he needs her now.

She stands up and runs back across the sharp gravel in her bare feet and through the back door of the kitchen, easing it closed behind her. She spies the pressure cooker first and sighs—Dan had one job! Well, two. But getting rid of the pressure cooker was the easiest and he failed to do it. She tiptoes over to grab the pot, thinking the best thing to do is take it out the back and throw it over the cliff, when she hears the high-pitched shrieks.

Her heartbeat revs as she quickly moves to the swinging door and puts her ear to it. Though the kitchen is eerily still, she can hear only every third word or so espoused by that maniac Isaac, but what's clear is Brick is no longer in charge. She stands, listening, unsure what to do, until she hears her daughter's voice—and it awakens something primal in her.

She pushes the swinging door open with all her might in time to see Isaac training his gun directly on her Sissy. She growls and charges him. At the noise, he turns, swinging the gun in her direction, and Jane stops short and flinches, realizing too late the error of her rash action. She braces herself for the bullet she's sure will hit her at any second, but suddenly a plate comes whistling through the air, hitting Isaac's temple with a sickening thud. He crumples to the ground. No one moves. "Oh my God," Jane breathes. She looks over to Dan, who's standing with his hand out, as though he's a still portrait caught in the middle of throwing a frisbee. "Did you do that?"

Dan nods.

Jane squints, still not believing. "You did?"

Dan nods again. And Jane looks back at Isaac's body, prostrate on the floor. "Oh God," she repeats. "Did you kill him?"

"No," Brick says, already at Isaac's side, picking up the gun. The boy groans, putting his hand up to his head. "He'll be OK."

"Jane," Dan says levelly. "Don't move."

"What?"

"You're right next to the bomb."

"What?" Jane repeats, confused. "No, the pressure cooker is in the kitchen."

"Yes, but the C-4 is on the table next to you."

Jane glances down to see two bricks with wires coming out

of them, connected to a timer that reads 6:27. She lets out a strangled scream and then looks at Brick. "Please don't do this," she begs. "I know sometimes it seems like blowing everything up is the only solution, that it will fix everything, but it won't. It never does." She stares at Dan as she keeps talking. "It's the easy way out. You can't run away from your problems, from real life. Life is about staying. Putting in the work. Even when it's hard."

"Lady, I have no idea what you're talking about," Brick says. "But we've got about five minutes to get everyone out of here."

Jane blinks and looks back at Brick. "You're letting everyone go?"

"Yes."

"Oh," Jane says.

"I really did like your book. Such a brilliant metaphor for the evils of capitalism and how the powerful and wealthy and corrupt can act solely in their best interest with impunity from consequence." He cuts his gaze to Otto.

"Yes," Jane says. "Yes! That's exactly . . . that's exactly . . ." She stammers again, her ability to form words suddenly failing. Earlier she might have said there was nothing more attractive than a rebel with bulging biceps—but a rebel with bulging biceps who *understands what she was trying to achieve with her work*? She thinks of Patty Hearst and swallows.

"I hope you don't mind that I changed the ending a bit." He grins and Jane feels woozy. Have her knees always been this weak?

"I don't mind," she says.

"Simply because I don't think I'm the bad guy here."

"You're not."

Dan clears his throat, and Jane slowly turns to him. When greeted with his hard stare, she snaps out of her reverie.

"Jeremy?" Brick says. At the prompt, Jeremy opens the front door, the hostages rushing toward it like horses out of the starting gate at the Kentucky Derby, while Tink and Caden snip the zip ties of the sous chefs and Javier and Monica, who pop up and follow the crowd.

Brick saunters over to Otto, the final hostage, and stands in front of him while Otto shifts his gaze back and forth between the timer (5:13) and Brick.

"I really should leave you here."

"But you won't. You're not like that boy," Otto says, trying to stare defiantly at Brick, but the quaver of his voice belies his fear. "For all your faults, you're not a killer."

Brick beckons Caden with a wiggle of his forefinger, and Caden steps forward to cut Otto's wrist and ankle ties. Otto stands on wobbly legs, looking up at Brick. "I look forward to seeing you in court the day they put you away for this."

Brick tenses his muscles and fake-jumps at Otto, who lets out a small screech and runs to the door without a backward glance.

"Jane," Dan hisses.

"What?"

"The bomb."

Jane glances at it warily (4:06). "I see the bomb, Dan!"

"Well, fix it!"

"What? How?"

"Cut a wire!"

"What wire?

"Like they do in the movies! The blue one or the green one or the red one!"

"How do *I* know which one it is?"

"Like you knew everything else! Book research!"

"I don't know how to disarm a bomb, Dan. I'm not Mac-Gyver!"

Brick steps directly between them and reaches out to push a button on the digital watch, and the clock stops.

"Oh, thank God." Jane exhales. She had no idea it was just that easy—the movies always made it look so hard.

"What are you two still doing here?" Brick asks.

Jane glances at Sissy. "We can't leave yet."

Sissy steps forward. "They're my parents," she says, lowering her gaiter now that the hostages are all gone.

And Brick's jaw drops an inch, befuddled for maybe the first time that evening. "Huh," he says, gaping at her and then Jane. "I can see the resemblance. Wait, did you know they were going to be here?"

"No! I couldn't believe it! Did you really use her book?"

"Yeah, Kyle gave it to me."

"Apparently he's the one that invited us here," Dan says.

"And then he jumped off the cliff!" Jane screeches.

Brick doesn't bat an eye. "Speaking of, it's time for us to go."

"You can't!" Jane says, remembering all the sirens. "The police are here! They've probably got us surrounded by now."

"Not completely surrounded." He winks.

They all turn and look at the expansive window just steps from the cliff's edge.

"Let's go, let's go, let's go!" Brick says, striding to the large panel he tossed the cell phone out of and pushing it open. Caden's the first to step through it, followed by Tink and then Jeremy. Brick walks over to Isaac. "You good, man? We gotta roll."

Isaac nods and stands, stumbling a bit, and Brick puts an arm out to steady him.

"You did great, by the way. You may have a future in Hollywood after all."

Isaac grins, and Jane can see he's just a boy after all. Not evil, not menacing. His mom probably thinks he's at a friend's house watching a show.

"Wait," Jane says. "None of that was real? What is happening?"

Brick grins. "All part of the plan. Granted, I was supposed to tackle him and take him out, but your husband's frisbee trick worked just as well."

"But why?"

"As a novelist, don't you know?" He grins. "Every great heist has a wild card. Ours was Isaac."

Confused, Jane watches as Isaac follows the others out the window. "Where are they going?"

"Over the cliff. We're BASE jumping." Sissy smiles. "We practiced it. I told you Brick had a plan."

"What?" Jane breathes as horror wraps itself like a vine around her lungs, her stomach.

"Come on, Goldie, not much time left."

"What?" Jane repeats, grabbing her daughter's arm. "No. No! You are absolutely not going over that cliff."

It reminds her of the platitude she repeated ad nauseam to Sissy and Josh over the years when they wanted the name-brand shoes or the brand-new edition of the video game console they already had or to be on WhatsApp in the fourth grade and whined *All my friends are doing it.* Jane inevitably replied: *If all your friends were jumping off a cliff, would you do that, too?* She was parroting what her own mother had said to her and likely what Jane's mother's mother had said to her. It was part of the canon of parenting, along with *There are children starving in third-world countries!* and *Because I said so!* Jane never in a million years thought her child would *actually* be in the position to decide whether or not to follow her friends off a literal cliff.

Yet here they were.

"Mom, I have to! Otherwise I'll get caught."

"She's right, Jane. Everyone that was here knows she was one of them," Dan says.

"No! It's too high up. It's not safe!" Jane's brain buzzes as she tries to think of alternatives. "Change clothes with me."

"What?"

"Change clothes with me. I'll go over the cliff. You can say you were at the restaurant with Dad."

"It won't work! Besides"—her face screws up in disgust—"I would never wear that."

"It doesn't matter!"

"Mom, c'mon, you're terrified of heights. You would die midair of a heart attack."

That's probably true, but doesn't Sissy understand by now? Jane would do *anything* for her daughter.

They say when you're about to die, your life flashes before your eyes, but Jane wonders if, when you're viscerally afraid your child is going to die, *their* life flashes before you. All at once she sees Sissy the infant, her baby face squawking, her mouth a cavernous hole of noise and pain. Sissy at two, wobbly on her chubby legs, giggling at the ridiculous faces Jane made to entertain her.

At six, Sissy went through a phase (though Jane didn't know it was a phase, because when you're a first-time parent, every new behavior feels like it's a defining character trait and that *this* is who your child now is and will be in perpetuity) where she couldn't go into any room of their house alone. If she needed shoes from the mudroom, Jane would follow. If she wanted a snack from the pantry, Jane would follow. Jane became a shadow more than a mother and she was sure it was her fault—she had passed her anxiety on to her daughter, which was her biggest fear. Her greatest parental failure.

And that's when she realizes what she wants for her daughter—more than going to Stanford or happiness or any of the other clichés that parents want for their children—she wants her to not be terrified of every goddamn thing, the way Jane has been ever since she became a mother. Maybe even before then, too.

She wants Sissy to march out into the world and grab her life with both hands. To experience it all—heartbreak and pain and anger and the raw, throbbing joy of loving someone so much your skin is on fire. She wants Sissy to *live*. She doesn't want Sissy to jump off a cliff, not knowing if she's going to make it to the bottom. But deep down, Jane knows that living is sometimes jumping off a cliff, not knowing if you're going to make it to the bottom.

It's time to let Sissy go.

It's time to let Sissy live.

"OK, OK," she says, her voice shaking. "You're right."

"I am?" Sissy asks.

"She is?" Dan echoes, bewildered. "What? No."

Jane looks at Dan, wild-eyed. "*You* said I had to let her go."

"Yes, but only because I didn't think you were *actually going* to let her go! It's a cliff, Jane."

"Jesus Christ," Jane mutters. She stares at her daughter's eyes. "You can do this?"

"I can do it."

"How do you know?"

"I learned from the best—you."

"How to *BASE jump*?"

"No." She cocks her head. "How to believe in myself."

"What?" Jane breathes. She shakes her head no. "No. I've never believed in myself a day in my life." When Jane says it out loud, she realizes it's true. She's questioned everything as a mother: *Did she breastfeed long enough? Are there BPAs in that sippy cup? Did I read to her enough? Feed her enough organic foods? Is her car seat secure? Is she getting enough fresh air? Too much screen time? Is she sitting alone at recess? Does she have enough friends? Did she turn in her science project? Did I help too much? Was I too easy on her? Too hard? Did I yell too loud? Does she know how much she's loved? Does she know she's the goddamn air that I breathe?*

"Yes, Mom," Sissy says. "I believe in myself because you always believed in me."

"Oh," Jane breathes. "I have. I have always believed in you. I do believe in you."

"I know."

Jane nods once. "And you're sure? You've practiced."

Sissy nods back.

"OK," Jane says. "Go do it."

Sissy turns and Jane reaches out for her. "Wait!" She pulls Sissy to her and wraps her arms around her as if it's the last time she may hold her daughter. The world is harsh and desolate and brutal, but Jane can't protect her from it any more than this Force of Nature group can stop corporate America from continuing to make billions of dollars on oil and plastic and destroying the earth. She can't hold Sissy's flame in her hands anymore. It doesn't belong to her any more than the stars belong to the moon.

She grabs Sissy's face in both her hands. Jane's nose is nearly touching Sissy's nose, and she stares into Sissy's dark brown eyes and thinks of the first time she stared into them, before she loved Sissy with all her heart, before she was a real mother. And she wishes she could go back to that time and say all the things she feels now. She would say:

Welcome to the world, my girl.

It's a cruel, horrible place and I'm so terrified for you to be here.

It's a wonderful, beautiful place and I'm so glad you're here.

What Jane says: "You *are* already something." Tears are flowing down her cheeks in earnest now.

"I know," Sissy says. She smiles then—a sight as rare and beautiful as seeing the sunset when dining at La Fin du Monde—and she's nine and two and four and thirteen all at once. And then she squeezes her mom's hand once, turns, and steps through the open window, and it feels like Jane's heart has exploded from her chest and is now running away from her and there's nothing Jane can do to stop it or protect it or get it back.

It feels like her skin is on fire.

It feels like motherhood.

She stares at Sissy's back, her ponytail swishing as she runs at full speed toward the edge, and then Sissy is gone, off the cliff, like an offering to the wind, to the world.

"Dan!" Jane says, turning and throwing herself in his arms. He holds her. "Oh, Dan. I think . . . I think we were really good parents," she wails.

"We were. We are," he says, gently smoothing her hair.

A beep drags their attention to Brick, who's standing next to the bomb, the numbers once again rolling down: 2:59, 2:58, 2:57 . . .

Jane's blood runs cold. "What are you doing?"

"I've gotta run. And I suggest you do, too."

"You're still blowing up the restaurant?"

"Yeah." He makes a clicking noise with his cheek. "A necessary distraction for our getaway, I'm afraid. That's the most important part of any heist, don't you think?" He grins. "Misdirection. Anyway, nice meeting you, Jane. Again, I'm a big fan," he says, and then he turns to take off out the window.

"Wait!" Jane yells, and he stills, looks at her. "Can I have my cell phone back?"

"Sorry." He grins. "I don't have it."

Jane frowns, confused, and then Brick jumps out the window, straightens his backpack, and is gone, leaving Jane and Dan the sole two people left standing in La Fin du Monde, minutes before it explodes.

THREE MINUTES UNTIL THE END

CHAPTER
29

KIP PEERS THROUGH THE DARK NIGHT AT THE RES-
taurant on the top of the hill. Though the air is cool, his forehead pricks with sweat, his hand shaking as he tries to keep his
service pistol—a Glock 22 that he's only ever fired at a practice
gun range—trained on the front door.

The last fifteen minutes unfolded so quickly. Zimmerman
arrived with every acronym force on the LAPD: SWAT, the
HRT, and the EOD—and, upon hearing it was Otto St. Clair
likely being held hostage, immediately ordered the EOD to
sweep the hill and clear a path to get SWAT in position as close
to the restaurant as possible.

As they crested the hill, a swarm of civilians (including Otto
St. Clair! Kip recognized him immediately on account of his
eyebrows and got almost as big a thrill as when he met Emilio
Estevez) came flying toward them as if their hair was on fire.

"Whoa!" Zimmerman said, trying to stem the chaos. His
men managed to corral everyone into a circle a hundred feet
from the restaurant door and peppered them with questions to

try to determine as quickly as possible what was happening—to which he got a variety of responses.

It was unclear if this was everyone or if other civilians were still in the restaurant—it could be two or five or none. Same with the number of hostage takers: Ten? Six? Some said they planned to come right out the front door, which Kip thought was unlikely. Not just because it was a bold move, but since eyewitnesses are notoriously unreliable.

The only thing they all agree on? The bomb.

That there is one, inside the restaurant, and it is absolutely going to detonate.

They don't agree on when. Ten minutes? Two? Or not at all, according to Otto, who thought it was fake—a scare tactic. Kip frowns, disliking the man almost instantly. At least Emilio had been humble; kind, even. Otto has an air of superiority about him, demanding the police immediately charge the restaurant. "He stole nine million dollars from me and he's right there! Inside the door. Go arrest him!"

But the truth is, all they can do is wait. (Behind the perimeter set by the bomb squad—which, though it's a full football field, still feels uncomfortably too close to Kip.) For Brick to answer the phone. For the restaurant to explode. For more people to be released. Hopefully not in that order. Or for the hostage takers to actually come out the front door (which seems doubtful to Kip).

The front door opens and Kip's heart jumps to his throat.

"Hold!" Zimmerman, the incident commander, directs his fellow officers.

Two figures—a man in a white button-up that looks stained

with blood and a woman in a dark dress—step out the front door, and they're off like a shot, running from the restaurant like they're being chased by a wild pack of dogs. Hand to God, Kip would swear they were faster than Usain Bolt running the hundred-yard dash. Briefly, it occurs to him how much faster Olympians could be were they running from an explosive device. Running for their *lives*. The Olympics would certainly be more entertaining, anyway.

Abruptly the man stops, but the woman doesn't notice right away.

He puts his hand in his pocket, causing Zimmerman to shout through his bullhorn: "Hands up where we can see them!"

The woman throws her hands in the air and swivels her head to the right. Realizing she's alone, she stops and turns all the way to look at the man she unwittingly left behind. She yells something to him.

Kip can't quite make out what she's saying, but he hears the screech and the panic of her voice—a tone Kip, though only with his ex-wife for a total of seventeen months, is all too familiar with. It's the unmistakable sound of a woman confounded by her husband's actions. And that's when Kip realizes they're married.

The man shouts a reply and then cuts right, toward the cars in the small gravel parking lot.

Where is he going? What could be more important than getting away from the restaurant?

The woman stares at the man in disbelief, as if she is wondering the same question.

319

Zimmerman is shouting into the bullhorn, but they're ignoring him, and Kip can't just stand there and watch. They're in danger! Kip takes a step forward to add his own voice to the cacophony, to tell them to run, to move *faster*—he even briefly thinks he might dash out and grab the woman. He could be a hero!—but before his foot can connect to the ground, before his voice enters the night air, he's thrown as though someone has swept both his legs, and then the *CRACK-BOOM* of the explosion reaches his ears.

30

WHETHER SECONDS HAVE PASSED OR MINUTES,
Jane doesn't know, but she is somehow on her back, looking at
the cold, dark sky full of blinking stars. She thinks of Sissy
first. Always. Is she OK? Did she make it over the cliff, floating
gently like a feather to the water below, or did she plummet
like a stone? She rolls onto her side and expels her anxiety onto
the ground in the form of bile and vomit.

That's when she sees him. Dan. The small balding pate of
his head gleaming in the moonlight and staring at her like a
third eye. Is *he* OK? Is he hurt?

"Dan," she says, but it comes out low, hoarse. She clears her
throat and tries again. "Dan!"

He doesn't move.

Jane's brain flashes on the few but fervent times in their
married life that she fantasized about Dan dying—after one
particularly tense blowup over breastfeeding, of all things
(Jane was hormonal!), when she found the text messages with
Becca (being a widow would be infinitely easier than being a

divorcée; so much less hate involved), and every time she sat on the cold hard top of the toilet seat in the middle of the night (her rage at his inability to leave the seat up was nothing short of murderous)—and she now knows that's all it was: a fantasy. Fiction.

She slowly sits up, mentally checking for injuries. When nothing apparent jumps out at her, she puts one foot on the ground and pushes herself to standing. The wind shifts and smoke and debris billow into the air between her and Dan, stinging her eyes, making it hard to breathe. She drops to her knees again, coughing. And then, though she can no longer see him, she starts crawling toward where she thinks he is. The gravel digs into her knees and palms, but she barely feels it, her determination to get to him making every other sensation pale in comparison.

Finally, she reaches him. "Dan," she says again, and presses her palm to his chest. Is he breathing? Please let him be breathing. Is that a heartbeat? She can't tell. And then her eyes travel down the length of him and she sees the blood on his pants. Was that there already? From before? But as she looks closer she sees it's a huge gash.

Tears roll down her face, and not just from the smoke. "Dan!" she wails. "Ohmygod, Dan." She scoots closer on her knees and presses the hem of her skirt to his leg to stem the blood.

Suddenly Dan coughs, and Jane's eyes fly up to his face. "Dan?"

He blinks, looks at her. "Yeah?"

"Are you OK?"

"I think so," he says. "My leg hurts like the dickens, but I think I'll live."

Instantly her anxiety morphs into full-body relief that he is alive, and then just as quickly into complete irritation, and she swats him on the shoulder with her open palm. Hard. "What the hell were you doing? I thought you were right behind me. You could have died!"

"Ow!" he says, grabbing his shoulder. "I told you—I was getting the car!"

"The *Subaru*?" It's official. She is married to the cheapest man on the planet. "Dan, that thing isn't even worth a thousand dollars." Jane knows because she looks it up on Kelley Blue Book every couple of months hoping she can convince Dan it's time to sell it, but he never budges.

"I know," he says. "But I've had it for twenty years."

"Exactly! It's time to move on."

Dan stares at her. "I don't want to move on," he says, and Jane wonders if he's still talking about the car. "Remember when the alternator died at that red light on Sullivan and you were so mad you just left it in the middle of the road and walked home?"

Oh. Apparently he is still talking about the car. "Yes. I was furious," Jane says.

"And that time we were driving to Colorado and the kids had been watching that god-awful Peppa Pig DVD over and over and over until you finally took the DVD and threw it out the window. On I-70! And the kids' faces! Like you had thrown out the family dog!"

Jane frowns. She does remember. It wasn't her finest moment of parenting.

"And that fight! When the kids were in bed asleep that time and we were having that terrible argument and you made us go out to the car so we wouldn't wake them up and we were just screaming at each other. I have no idea what in the hell we were fighting about. Something about snacks, I think." Dan's body is shaking now, and it takes Jane a beat to realize he's laughing. She wonders if he's suffering from a head injury from the blast. She leans closer, looking for wounds. He's laughing so hard now, tears are streaming down his cheeks.

"Oh God, and remember . . . remember when Josh threw up that entire cherry milkshake?"

"It was an Icee."

"It went everywhere! And you tried to catch it in your hands. Your hands!"

"Dan!" Jane says. "These are awful, terrible memories."

"I know," he says through guffaws. "Oh, they're awful. But they're *our* awful, terrible memories."

Jane stares at her husband. She had forgotten so many of these incidents—for good reason. And he had, too, apparently. That huge argument in the car was about McDonald's, of all things. Well, it started out about McDonald's, and then, as married arguments tend to do, it ballooned into the built-up resentments they'd each been holding in for weeks or months. But just now, she can't quite remember what any of those resentments were.

"That's why you've never wanted to get rid of it? I thought it was because *cars depreciate the minute you drive them off the lot* and *this one gets us from point A to point B just fine, doesn't it?"*

"Well," Dan says. "That, too."

She starts chuckling and then it grows, thinking about the Peppa Pig DVD and the kids' faces, and Josh vomiting like something out of *The Exorcist*, until she's laughing as hard as Dan was moments earlier.

"Anyway, they're not *all* bad memories," Dan says, grinning at her. "We made up in that car, too, after the snacks fight, if I recall."

Jane doesn't remember, but the way Dan's smiling, she thinks it best for his ego to let him believe she does.

"And I proposed to you in that car!"

At this, Jane rounds on him. "You did not! You never proposed to me."

"I know." His face grows serious. "But only because I was afraid you wouldn't say yes."

"Oh, Dan," she breathes.

"Did I push you into it?" he says. "Did you really never want to get married?"

"What?"

"The first night we met, you told me you never wanted to get married."

"I did?"

"You did."

"Oh Lord. That was something I said back then to everyone, so guys would think I was breezy and casual."

The truth is, Jane had been twenty-six. A child! What did she know what she wanted out of life? What does anybody really know about life—about *marriage*—until they live it? She loved Dan when she married him, of course, but it was all a crapshoot, wasn't it? How do you know what you'll need out of a partner? Who you'll be ten years, twenty years down the road? You just hitch your wagon to someone and hope you both keep heading in the same direction, through all the bumps and detours and peaks and valleys. And for better or for worse, Dan had proven a formidable and dependable partner. Unwavering. Steadfast. Even while Jane was off looking for something else.

She groans. *Never let the things you want make you forget the things you have.* God dammit, maybe those influencers were right after all. Jane has so much.

"I've been wrong. I've been so wrong, Dan. I don't want anything else, anything more . . . exciting. I don't even know what that is! I want to be home with you. In our boring house. In our boring life."

Dan frowns. He tries to take a deep breath and wheezes on the exhale.

"Dan?"

"I'm OK . . . it's . . . hard to breathe . . . with all this smoke."

"Don't talk. Just rest."

He shakes his head. "No, you were . . . right. I've been stuck in a rut. You've tried to tell me so . . . many times. I should have listened. I could have . . . done more. I could do more! We can try . . . We should try the . . . honey."

"The honey?" Jane asks.

"Yeah, the sex thing. I should have . . ."

Jane laughs. Her sweet Dan. She shakes her head. How can she make him understand? "You're not my arm."

"I'm on your arm?" He tries to move.

"No, no. Don't move. You're *not* my arm."

"What? Jane, are you—"

"You're my lungs, too."

Dan stares at his wife. To anyone else, it would be gibber-ish, nonsense, what Jane is saying. But he's not anyone else. He's Jane's husband. He's her lungs. And she knows he under-stands.

"I'm so happy . . ." Dan says, and then falters.

Jane smiles at him, her eyes filling with water once again from the smoke in the air and from the heady emotions of the night. "Oh, Dan." Jane's happy, too. That Sissy got away and is hopefully OK, and she's happy to go back to their boring life. Why did she ever think she wanted exciting? Let the young people have their cliff jumping and honeyed sex and sticky sheets. Jane likes boring! She likes safe. She likes Dan, which she realizes is more important than loving him. To love the man you've been married to for nearly half your life is easy, but to *like* him? Jane thinks it's a rare thing indeed.

"I'm so happy . . ." he tries again, and Jane can see his chest rising with the difficulty of his breathing, and she stares in his greige-blue eyes, and her tears threaten to spill down her cheeks as she waits with bated breath to bask in her husband's reciprocal declarations of love.

"I'm so happy . . . we didn't have to pay for that meal," he says, and then he closes his eyes, a small grin of contentment on his face.

FOUR HOURS
AFTER THE END

CHAPTER
31

JANE'S MOUTH IS DRY AS COTTON AS SHE WAITS FOR the older policeman's response.

His gaze hardens and she has no idea what to expect next. Should she have asked for a specific lawyer? She goes through the mental Rolodex of lawyers she and Dan know and can think of only one—their friend Nicole Waller, who works as one of the corporate attorneys for In-N-Out Burger. She frowns. Though Nicole started her career as a prosecutor, the last time she was in a courtroom must have been fifteen years earlier, and Jane isn't sure she'd be the best person to represent her. Though it surely would be a step up from a random public defender. She pictures some harried man in an ill-fitting suit with a greasy comb-over. It's not a flattering image, but aren't public defenders notoriously overworked and underpaid?

"OK, well," the older policeman, Zimmerman, says in his gravelly voice. "You can leave."

"What?" Jane stares at him, open-mouthed. Is this some kind of trick? A test? "I'm not getting a lawyer?"

"Whether you get one is up to you, but we're not detaining you, so you may go."

"We're not?" asks Kip, whose own look of surprise mirrors Jane's.

"No."

"But we're onto something here!" Kip says. "This is important."

The older police officer shrugs. "She's not our suspect."

"She wrote this book!"

"Yes, and we'll continue to investigate the matter. But she also texted 9-1-1 to alert us of the hostage situation, and it's been a very long night. If she wants to lawyer up, she can, but right now, I think we could all stand to get some sleep. We can continue this line of questioning another day, if need be."

Another knock on the door interrupts them.

"Come in," Zimmerman says.

A third man pokes his head in. "We have a situation."

"Another one?"

Jane tenses. Did they find Sissy? Has she been arrested? The cop lowers his voice to address Zimmerman directly, but the room is so small Jane can hear plain as day.

"It seems the nine million dollars Mr. St. Clair claims was stolen wasn't actually stolen."

"What do you mean?"

"I mean, the charge went through, but the credit card company hasn't even paid it out yet. They've been alerted to the fraud and will not be completing the transaction."

Jane's forehead wrinkles deepen in confusion even as she fills with relief. Sissy isn't in the clear yet, but at least she's not a thief!

"I'm free to go?"

"You're free to go. Please don't leave the state, as this is an ongoing investigation and we'll be in touch—with your lawyer, I suppose, when you employ one—with any further questions."

Jane nods and stands on shaky legs. She walks through the quiet precinct, running over the events of the evening, something niggling at the edges of her mind. Why did Brick say Hyperion had a different policy and would deposit the money by nine if it wasn't true? He clearly wanted Otto to believe he was stealing the money, but to what end? He obviously has a personal vendetta against the guy, but it seems like an awful lot of trouble to go to just to make Otto *think* Brick got the best of him.

Then Jane stops midstride, her eyes going wide as the words Brick said echo in her mind: *That's the most important part of any heist, don't you think? Misdirection.*

Jane resumes walking, wheels spinning, as she tries to piece together what Brick was actually after. And then she reaches the front door, opens it, and is surprised to find it's still dark when she steps out into the night. The sun has yet to rise on a new day.

"Mom!" A body suddenly flings itself at her, and with a mother's instinct she wraps her arms around the form before she fully realizes it's Josh, with his musty boy scent. And right behind him is Sissy, fresh-faced and hesitant. "Are you OK?" Josh says into her neck. "What happened?"

Jane had asked to call her kids when she finally arrived at the police station to let them know where she was, that their dad was in the hospital but OK, and that she would be home soon. But Josh insisted on coming straight to her. He's always had a penchant for drama.

"Sissy," Jane says, reaching out to cup her daughter's face with her hand. "You didn't have to come, too."

"She almost didn't," Josh says with a sneer. "She wasn't even home when you called. She missed curfew!" Josh waits, almost gleefully, to see what punishment might befall his sister, but Jane just ruffles his hair and then grasps Josh's palm with one hand and Sissy's with her other.

"She's an adult," Jane says. "I guess she's capable of making her own decisions now."

"What?" Josh protests.

"C'mon," Jane sighs, thrilled to be out of that restaurant, for her daughter to be safe, for her family to be out of harm's way. "Let's go get your father."

ONE HOUR
AFTER THE END

32

SISSY STARES IN THE MIRROR, HER LEGS STILL SHA-king from the adrenaline pumping through her veins. *Holy shit!* She just jumped off a cliff. And she didn't die! She definitely thought she was going to. BASE jumping at night off a cliff was nothing like the practice they had done in broad daylight. That was more on the exhilarating side of terrifying. This had been far more terrifying-terrifying.

"You ready?" For the fourth time in as many minutes, Brick's voice floats through the thin wooden door separating Sissy from the $89-per-night motel room somewhere in the middle of the coast of California. Sissy, having changed into a dry tank top and sweatpants, rubs a cheap threadbare towel through her hair and opens the door. "Geez. Keep your shirt on," she says. "I told you to go ahead and start without me."

Brick is flipping the tiny square metal disk over and over with his thumb as easily as he often flips quarters—which, Sissy now recognizes from knowing him for the past six months, is a nervous tic. He probably doesn't even realize he's doing it. He stops when he sees her and grins. "Crazy night, huh?"

"You could say that," Sissy laughs. And then affixes a mock frown on her face. "You could have told me about the bombs."

"No, I couldn't have—you wouldn't have gone along with it."

"And Isaac? You knew he was going to do that?"

"Of course. I didn't know your *dad* was going to knock him out with a plate, though. I was supposed to tackle him with about two minutes to go and let everyone rush out the front, so the police would think we perished in the explosion."

"I cannot believe my parents were there."

"I cannot believe your mom is Jane Brooks!"

Sissy rolls her eyes.

"You're a lot like her, you know."

"What? Gross."

"You are," Brick says. "Fearless, almost to the point of being reckless." He raises a brow, giving her a hard stare, and then once he thinks he's gotten his point across, his face relaxes. "I can tell your mom's good people. Just like you."

Sissy concentrates on keeping her face stone-still, but inside she's positively melting. Her knees go weak again. She'd never admit it to anyone—least of all her mom—but she is slightly in love with Brick. Or in lust. Is there a difference? Sissy doesn't care. He's gorgeous.

"Anyway, I feel bad I had to throw your mom's cell phone out the window, but how perfectly did that work out? I couldn't have planned that if I tried. And my sleight-of-hand switch to make Otto think it was his?"

Sissy rolls her eyes again. "OK, David Blaine. What's next—you're going to make the Empire State Building disappear?"

"Maybe." He grins and then claps once. "Now. Let's finish what we started." He turns to Tink. "You ready?"

Tink looks up from the rickety chair in front of the wooden desk that has been carved with expected graffiti by pen tips and markers. "I was born ready." She laces her fingers together and stretches her arms out, cracking her knuckles, then flips open her laptop, types in her password, navigates to the screen she needs, and looks at Brick. "You're on."

Sissy sits primly on the bed, the adrenaline she thought had worked its way out of her system starting to pump through her veins again, causing her teeth to chatter a bit. What if it doesn't work? What if all of this was for nothing?

Brick grabs the burner phone he purchased yesterday off the nightstand, pushing the numbers he had memorized for this exact occasion. He puts the audio on speaker mode and holds the phone out, so Sissy and Tink can hear. The line rings twice and then a voice says: "Thank you for being a Signal Mobile's preferred customer. You've reached our twenty-four-hour concierge help line. This is Samantha. With whom do I have the pleasure of speaking?"

Sissy knows Brick is barely suppressing an eye roll. He can't stand the trappings of wealth, the privileges it buys. Everyone else has to abide by the nine-to-five, Monday-through-Friday customer service hours—unless you have money. Though he can't be too irritated, Sissy reasons. In this case, it's working out in his favor. Brick takes a deep breath, and Sissy does, too. This is the moment of truth.

"Yes, this is Devon Wang," Brick says in a voice an octave higher than his regular tone. He speaks in a rush to signify urgency, which isn't hard. "I'm the assistant to Otto St. Clair, and his phone was destroyed this evening in an . . . *incident*." He waits a beat for his implication—that it was somehow the fault of Otto's temper and he is kindly covering for his erratic boss—to sink in. "Fortunately, the SIM card is undamaged and Mr. St. Clair would like it transferred into a new device yesterday, if you get my meaning. I'm sure you're aware business never sleeps at SierraX." Brick offers a nervous laugh and Sissy raises an amused eyebrow at him.

"Yes, I'm sure that's true," Samantha says solemnly. "First, let me say I'm so sorry for the inconvenience of the phone being damaged, and we can absolutely get Mr. St. Clair's SIM card set up in a new device. I assume you have the new device with you?"

"I do."

"Great. And for security purposes, do you happen to know Mr. St. Clair's birthdate and email address?"

"Sure. Birthdate is four fourteen seventy-one, and his email is Otto Saint—that's just *S T*, no periods—Clair at Sierra X dot com."

"Perfect. Now, I see here on his account we have a two-factor security authentication, so I am going to need to speak with Mr. St. Clair directly. Is he available?"

"Of course. Please hold one moment."

Brick hands the phone to Tink and mouths, *Ready?*

She nods, and with one hand deftly navigates her mouse on the screen to the digitized and transcribed recording, and with the other she holds the phone up to the laptop's speaker. She clicks that mouse and Otto St. Clair's voice rings out clear as a bell.

"Hello?"

"Mr. St. Clair? This is Samantha at Signal Mobile. How are you?"

Tink clicks another phrase on the screen. "Just lovely. And you?"

"Wonderful. I understand your cell phone has sustained some damage and you'd like to transfer the SIM card and activate it in a new device?"

Tink clicks: "That is correct."

"For security purposes, can you please give me your voice authentication phrase?"

Sissy holds her breath. This is it. The moment that could make or break the months of planning—and for Brick, the culmination of years of dreaming about his revenge, about resetting the scales of justice. Tink clicks the mouse.

"One-One was a racehorse. Two-Two was one, too. When One-One won one race, Two-Two won one, too."

Silence. Sissy and Brick lock eyes and the seconds tick by. Sissy's shoulders begin to drop, and she thinks maybe their luck has run out. It's possible—even likely—Otto chose a different phrase for his voice authentication. Finally, Samantha speaks.

"Thank you so much, Mr. St. Clair. We can proceed with the SIM card activation in your new device."

Sissy's eyebrows go skyward, her mouth opening in a silent scream, while Brick thrusts a silent punch into the air with his

341

right hand. Tink just grins, handing the phone back to Brick. He leans into the mouthpiece. "This is Devon again. Did you get everything you needed?"

"Yes. If you have the new device on hand, please remove the back and read me the serial number and we'll get Mr. St. Clair's new phone set up right away."

"Wonderful," Brick says.

Five minutes later, he's off the phone with Samantha and Signal Mobile and the new cell phone screen glows in the dimly lit room, lighting up his face like gold in a treasure chest.

Sissy smiles and collapses, throwing her back onto the mattress. It's all downhill from here. She doesn't have to watch Brick to know he's navigating to the Ottobyte app, where he will click "Forgot Password" on the login page and seconds later his—well, *Otto's*—text message notification will ding (there it is!) with a new security code to reset the password. Brick will input the code and suddenly be in Otto St. Clair's crypto app as easily as a fox in the henhouse. She knows exactly what he's doing, because the plan was her idea.

"How much?" Sissy asks. Brick doesn't answer right away. He stares at the phone in a moment of reverence.

"How much?" Sissy prods.

"Two thousand seven hundred and fifty Ottobytes," Brick says slowly.

It's the largest-held jackpot of the most popular—and now hottest—cryptocurrency on the market, having just overtaken Bitcoin yesterday. Sissy quickly does the calculation in her head—at $38,000 per Ottobyte—$100 million, give or take.

And then Brick promptly drains all of it, transferring it to the account Tink set up a few weeks earlier. "You're up," he says to Tink, who nods and begins navigating to their account, where she will transfer the Ottobytes to another anonymous crypto wallet, using a VPN to hide the IP—and continue to do so, bolstering its untraceability with each transaction. And then they'll sell it off a few coins at a time to the many eagerly waiting buyers until Brick has one hundred million real dollars. Sissy listens with great satisfaction to the click-clack of Tink's keystrokes for the next ten minutes until she finally turns around and says: "Done."

Sissy slowly sits up, a little stunned that her plan worked out so well.

"Well, Goldie," Brick says. "You definitely earned your nickname."

"I guess I did," she says, a little grin playing on her lips. And then, as quickly as it came, it disappears, as she knows this is the last time she'll see Brick.

"Do you have all your documents?" she asks.

"Yeah," he says.

"Where will you go?"

"I don't know yet. Maybe somewhere tropical."

"Be careful," she says.

"Aw, you don't have to worry about me. What about you? What are you going to do with that big brain of yours?"

"I don't know," she says.

"Sarah," he says, and the way he says her real name takes her breath for a second. "You should go to Stanford. You could do so much good in the world."

"I already have."

"I know." He grins. "But legally."

She grins back. If nothing else, it would make her mother happy. And maybe that's not the worst thing in the world. "Maybe I will."

FIVE MONTHS
AFTER THE END

EPILOGUE

JANE SWIPES THE TUBE OF RED ACROSS HER MOUTH and stares in the mirror at her reflection, pulling at the skin on her forehead. She frowns and watches the lines grow deeper.

Dan enters the small hotel bathroom, checks his bald spot in the mirror, and, satisfied it hasn't grown any bigger since yesterday, puts the hand mirror down and stands behind Jane, smiling at her reflection. "You look beautiful," he says.

"It's not too much?"

"What, the red?"

She nods.

He tilts his head. "It's different," he says. "Edgy."

Jane cocks an eyebrow and then wrinkles her nose. "I don't think it's me."

She pulls a wad of toilet paper from the roll and swipes the lipstick off with one swift motion. Then she applies her un-flavored lip balm in its place.

"Still beautiful," Dan says, leaning down to kiss the top of her head.

"Gross," Sissy says as she pokes her head in the open door to the bathroom. "Get a room."

"We have a room," Dan says. "You're in it."

Sissy pulls a face. "It's not my fault nonprofit work doesn't pay." Sissy deferred Stanford for a year to intern at an environmental lobbying group in Washington, D.C. She works fourteen-hour days and does a lot of grunt work and can't wait to start college next fall. This thrills Jane, though of course she doesn't say so. But who knows? Maybe Sissy will change her mind once again between now and then. Or Stanford could rescind her application. Or the apocalypse could happen, rendering higher education null and void! She takes a deep breath and tries to rein in her rising anxiety. If La Fin du Monde taught her anything, it's that most things in life are out of her control and often entirely unanticipated. Jane still worries, of course, but she's gotten better at not spiraling.

"Hey, thanks for coming up for this," Jane says to her daughter now.

"Are you kidding? I wouldn't miss this for anything."

Jane grins. "You're a good kid. You know, when you're not being a terrorist."

Sissy groans. "Can you get new material? That joke has really worn out its welcome."

The television is blaring when Jane steps into the room with two queen beds, and Josh is propped on one of them, zoned out in his phone.

"Are you even watching this?" Jane asks. "If not, can we please turn it off?"

"*—another anonymous donation from a benefactor using*

the moniker ByteMe, funding what appear to be all eco-conscious sustainable innovations like the multimillion-dollar grant last month to EverGreen Tech, the newest start-up to shake up Silicon Valley. One of those lucky recipients is Calvin Brenou, right here in Manhattan. Calvin, you received a hundred thousand dollars to continue your work on the—"

The TV screen goes black.

"Hey! I was watching that."

"You said to turn it off!" Josh retorts.

Jane sighs.

"Is everyone ready to go?"

"Yes," Jane says.

"Yep," Josh says.

Dan looks at her and nods, and then he glances around the room while patting his back pockets. "Have you seen my wallet?"

THE BRIGHT LIGHT is blinding. Jane squints, unable to see anything, and sweat pricks her hairline and her underarms. She's never been so nervous in her life—even when she was interrogated by the police. She hopes she doesn't trip and fall flat on her face. She hopes the extra-strength deodorant she applied three times is working to prevent pit stains on her mulberry silk blouse—a gift from Vaughn, sent with a note: *Congrats on all your success! xx.*

She was surprised by the gesture, and it reminded Jane of the other thing she had promised herself she'd work on—her cynical snap judgments. The truth is, most people are doing the best they can, given their situations.

Well, not Otto. He doubled down on his dealings with Big Oil, trying to make up for the money he lost, which the FBI was still having trouble tracking down. Vaughn left him and had been making headlines ever since for donating the majority of her earnings from the divorce to charity.

Still, Jane had no intention of keeping the $740 shirt (she couldn't help it, curiosity drove her to look up the price on the Neiman Marcus website) until she made the mistake of trying it on and it felt like being cocooned in, well . . . silk.

She reaches the chair and gratefully sits down, as she isn't sure her legs will hold her weight anymore.

"Welcome back, everybody," the familiar nasal voice says. "Tonight we've got a very special guest—a real-life heroine. Jane Brooks is here, the author of our Fallon Book Club pick of the summer, *The End of the World*. Welcome to the show, Jane!"

"Thank you, Jimmy," Jane says, unable to control her smile, even if she does look like a cartoon horse.

It turns out that Kyle was wrong—Jane's book didn't see a bump in sales at all immediately following the night at La Fin du Monde.

She saw a bump two weeks later, after Jar House rereleased it under a new title and food influencer Ayanna Baskhi, with three million followers, posted about the book that was loosely based on her experience at La Fin du Monde, the famous restaurant that she was dining in the night it burned down. The next thing Jane knew, her book was the number one book not just in crime fiction, but on all of Amazon. And Barnes & Noble. And the *New York Times*.

Though Jane still feels hopeless at technology, Ayanna has

kindly given her some of her best social media tips, and Jane uses her new platform to showcase the small steps she and Dan have been taking to combat climate change (taking their stock money out of oil companies, for one) and highlight businesses and people that are doing good things in the world. She knows it's just a drop in the proverbial ocean, that she's not making big waves. She's just trying to do the best she can, given her situation.

Jimmy Fallon holds her book upright, propping it on the desk so the audience can see the cover in all its glory.

"Now, as I understand, you wrote this book six years ago about a terrorist group taking over a teahouse, but you were actually dining at La Fin du Monde—the famous restaurant—just a few months ago when a group of terrorists rushed in, taking everyone hostage."

"That's right."

"You couldn't make that up if you tried!"

Jane smiles and offers the joke she practiced in the mirror: "It's true. If I had known my life was going to imitate art, I would have written about being stranded on an island with Idris Elba."

Jimmy throws his head back and claps. The audience bursts out in raucous laughter, which Jane knows isn't because her joke was so funny, but because the warm-up comedian reminded them to laugh harder and louder for the benefit of television. Still, it feels good.

"Your book has sold nearly eight hundred thousand copies since it was rereleased. How does it feel? After all those years of failure, to finally be something, to be *somebody*. Did you ever imagine you would be such a success?"

Jane peers into the audience, and she finally lands on the bright smiles of her husband, Dan, and her children. *I already was something*, she thinks, her eyes lighting on Sissy. And then her gaze moves to the person next to Sissy—Kyle is sitting beside Ayanna, grinning his forty-watt, wrinkle-free grin. He gives Jane two overly enthusiastic thumbs up. Jane clears her throat and takes a deep breath. "No! I had no idea my book would go on to sell hundreds of thousands of copies, Jimmy. It's all been very surreal."

Then she looks back out into the audience at Dan, and her mind flashes on his plate-throwing heroics and how he didn't hesitate to help the chef and how he always patiently talks her off the ledge of her anxiety—sometimes literally, like when they went BASE jumping together for the first time two weeks ago. It was terrifying, and in the end she couldn't actually go through with it, confirming what Jane knew in her gut to be true. Much like her unflavored lip balm, she's not actually edgy and prefers to live with both feet firmly on the ground, thank you very much. It only took her forty-six years to accept who she actually is, and not some version of herself she thought she should be.

Dan smiles at her, and it reminds Jane to add the other bit she's practiced over the years: "But I couldn't have done any of it without my family, especially my husband, Dan." Because that's what people say when they're feeling very magnanimous about the state of things.

And if they're lucky, sometimes it also happens to be the truth.

ACKNOWLEDGMENTS

Such is the creative process that some books come joyfully flying out of you (or so I've been told) and some books you have to pry out of yourself with a crowbar, the Jaws of Life, and vodka. This book, for me, was the latter. And though the actual writing of a book is a solitary process, the *whining* of a book takes a village. Thank you to the following people who listened to me for hours on end during the writing of this book, when I lost all perspective and confidence—and for handing both back to me, over and over, like a gift: Stephanie Rostan; my mom, Kathy Oakley; my dad, Bill Oakley; my sister, Megan Oakley; Karma Brown; Nicole Blades; Amy Reichert; Blane Bachelor; Kirsten Palladino; and Jaime Sarrio.

Special thanks also to:

The booksellers, librarians, and book influencers who enthusiastically tell people to read my books—sometimes even physically putting copies into readers' hands. I'm ever so grateful for your support.

ACKNOWLEDGMENTS

My very patient and talented editor, Kerry Donovan, and the entire phenomenal crew at Berkley: Christine Ball, Ivan Held, Claire Zion, Craig Burke, Jeanne-Marie Hudson, Tina Joell, Danielle Keir, Chelsea Pascoe, Jin Yu, Kate Whitman, Randie Lipkin, and Genni Eccles. You are a dream team of publicity, marketing, and sales, and I am so lucky to work with you.

My agent, Stephanie Rostan (yes, I have to thank you twice). If you ever decide to bill me for all the hours of therapy you have given me on top of your incredible agenting skills, I will have to leave the country and assume a different identity.

My film agent, Anna DeRoy, for working so hard to bring Jane and Dan to life on a screen. Thank you for believing in this book. My friends, some of whom also double as the best beta readers, and all of whom kept my spirits raised and my glass filled with wine during the writing of this novel: Megan Lobe, Caley Lyles, Jessica Chamlee, Laurie Rowland, Kelly Conner, Kristy Barrett, Jen Brock, and Melinda Servick.

Fellow author friends who have all offered a listening ear and support: Elle Cosimano, Annabel Monaghan, Jo Piazza, Laura Hankin, Jeneva Rose, Mary Kay Andrews, Lynn Cullen, Patti Callahan Henry, Kristin Harmel, Kristy Woodson Harvey, Emily Giffin, Shelli Johannes, Julia Chavez, and Kimmery Martin, as well as all the authors who have blurbed or reposted or shouted out this book. There are so many of you I'm grateful to, and it's one of the things I love most about this industry—the incredible upswell of love and support from fellow authors. Thank you.

Thank you to the following people, who shared their time and wealth of knowledge in their respective fields:

Jeff Brown for his expertise on police work.

Allan McLeod with the ATF (and his wife, who also chimed in with her knowledge while we were on the phone) for his insights on federal terrorism, hostage negotiations, and bomb squad work.

Andrew Worthen for taking me through the ins and outs of nanotechnology and oil spill remediation.

Chris Tilton for answering my questions on cybercrime.

Sarah Penner for the intel on strychnine.

Dr. Brent Stephens for always helping me injure and then medically repair my characters.

Riley Yale, Andrew Yale, and Alex Yale for helping me brainstorm the crypto-theft part of Brick's heist. If I ever need to commit a financial crime and get away with it, I now know who to turn to for the planning. I'm relieved you all use your vast wealth of intelligence for good (as far as I know).

Any and all mistakes or details that push the boundaries of believability in any of these fields are very obviously mine.

The following books also helped fill in the gaps of my knowledge: *Stalling for Time* by Gary Noesner; *Radicals Chasing Utopia* by Jamie Bartlett; and *Deep Green Resistance* by Aric McBay, Lierre Kieth, and Derrick Jensen.

It should be noted that I absolutely stole the name Cloud-Pilot from the R550X, a real self-flying helicopter that was not invented by Otto St. Clair.

I've never met him, but I have to thank Rick Rubin, music producer and author of *The Creative Act*, a book that helped me remember why I write and in particular inspired me to get across the finish line with this book.

ACKNOWLEDGMENTS

To my children, Henry, Sorella, Olivia, and Everett, thank you for putting up with a mother who constantly has her head in an imaginary universe and for loving me anyway. Henry, a special thank-you for trying to teach me how cryptocurrency works using potatoes. I still don't understand it completely, but if cryptocurrency actually was potatoes, I would be more inclined to buy it.

Last but not least, Fred. I could not have written this book (or any book for that matter) without your steadfast, unwavering support. Thank you for listening compassionately and for brainstorming ideas enthusiastically and for somehow knowing the exact right time to do one or the other. When I'm writing about how terrible marriage is, I'm writing about marriage. When I'm writing about how wonderful marriage is, I'm writing about us.